Bleeding Heart Librarian

Bleeding Heart Librarian

A Texas Flower Farmer Cozy Mystery

Jackie Layton

LEVEL
BEST BOOKS

First published by Level Best Books 2025

This novel is entirely a work of fiction. The names, characters and incidents portrayed in it are the work of the author's imagination. Any resemblance to actual persons, living or dead, events or localities is entirely coincidental.

Jackie Layton asserts the moral right to be identified as the author of this work.

Author Photo Credit: Kellianne Layton

First edition

ISBN: 978-1-68512-974-3

Cover art by Level Best Designs

This book was professionally typeset on Reedsy.
Find out more at reedsy.com

This book is dedicated to my husband, Tim. He always encourages me. It's also dedicated to librarians and my readers. Thanks for reading my cozy mysteries.

Praise for Texas Flower Farmer Cozy Mystery Series

"Pretty flowers, a murder at a Farmers' Market and a long list of suspects make this a fun summer read!"—~Sarah Can't Stop Reading Books

"Bottom Line: *Clover Covered Corpse* by Jackie Layton is warmly written with lovely characters and a clever mystery." —~Reading is my Superpower

"*Clover Covered Corpse* is a fine addition to the Texas Flower Farmer Cozy Mystery Series. Ms.Layton's characters easily draw you into their lives and make you eager to follow them page by page to a very satisfying conclusion." —~Escape With Dollycas Into A Good Book

"I recommend *Clover Covered Corpse* to cozy mystery readers, especially those who enjoy flowers, herbs, plant facts and lore, and puttering around their own gardens when they don't have their nose in a book." —~Guatemala Paula Loves to Read

"This is such a fun and enjoyable book with a solid mystery that kept me immersed in the action. The author did a great job in staging this whodunit with suspects and clues for us to decipher. There were a few twists and turns and I had a good time narrowing down the list of suspects. Overall, a good read."—Dru Ann Love

"Definitely an engaging cozy mystery! ***** Author Jackie Layton knows how to write cozy mysteries which keep the reader guessing! There are many different suspects who have all sorts of motives. I enjoyed scrutinizing the suspicious folks and letting my mind swirl with the possibilities. However, I never could decide who did it. Great fun to read this intriguing mystery!"—Sherida Stewart

Chapter One

Fourth of July in Lutz, Texas, never disappointed me. My day had begun at the farmers' market before the sun rose. For most of my adult life, I'd dreamed of growing flowers and selling them here. This year, it'd finally happened, after I had dared to leave a safe career as a pharmacy technician. I'd traded stability to become a flower farmer. Despite a few challenges, it was a dream come true.

The market usually only operated on Saturdays, but people came to town for vintage and antique sales on holidays, and our community decided it'd be a good idea to open the farmers' market too. I handed the last floral arrangement to Daniel Moore, an older adult who'd recently moved to our community. "Thank you, Daniel. You made my day."

"How's that?" He wore a fishing hat, but curly, dark, and gray curls peeped out.

"For the first time since starting my business, I sold out of flowers." I fanned myself with the straw cowgirl hat I usually wore to protect my fair skin from burning.

He looked from the daisies to me. "I'm happy to be a part of your history, Emma."

"Thanks. This is your first Independence Day in Lutz. Do you have plans today? The parade is special."

He smiled. "The Nelle sisters are saving a seat for me on a shady bench in town."

"I'm glad you're making friends. Those ladies know everyone, and they'll make it easy for you to get connected here." The sisters were all in their eighties, and I believed Daniel was too. "Be sure to stay hydrated, and I hope you have a wonderful day."

"Thanks. You do the same." He walked away in a slow and steady gait.

I loaded the supplies into my truck and perspired in earnest. Not only had I sold out, but it was still early. This called for a celebration. I headed to the designated food area, specifically Anytime Coffee House's truck. It was a converted VW van, but they sold plenty of coffee and tea despite the small size. I waited in line until I reached the counter.

"Good morning, Sunshine." Jake Hunter greeted me with a smile and a wink.

My face warmed. "Good morning. Why are you working here today?"

"Coop decided to take his wife to the coast for a few days, and he gave all of us time off too." Jake had come to Lutz, hoping to work for the police department. For now, he was helping Brett at the coffee shop and working for Coop Henderson's construction company. The police gig hadn't worked out yet. "How do you have time to order a drink?"

"I sold out of flowers." I couldn't contain my happiness, and I wanted to do a backflip. Instead, I smiled.

"Atta girl, Emma. What can I get you to drink?"

"I would love an iced green tea."

"Coming right up." He turned to the prep area.

"So, I get that Coop gave you a few days off, but what's Brett doing?"

Jake added local honey to my drink, just like I preferred. "His great aunt is visiting, and he didn't want her out in the heat for long, but he also didn't want to abandon her. It only made sense for me to work here."

"That's nice of you. Where is she from?"

"She lives in a small community, but I'm not sure exactly where." He slid the tea across the counter. "This is my treat."

I'd learned not to argue with Jake unless absolutely necessary. "Thanks. I better move along so you can wait on the others." I pointed to the line behind me.

"Hold up. Do you want to go to the parade together?"

"Oh my, your first 4th of July parade in Lutz. You're in for a treat. Come to my house. We can watch from the shade of my front porch. Feel free to invite Celia, Brett, and his aunt." Jake's sister was dating his best friend, Brett. The two made a sweet couple and were fun to spend time with.

"Okay. See ya later."

I took my drink and meandered off. A glance at the empty field of clover reminded me of a murder a few months earlier, but I wouldn't let the memories steal my joy. This was a day to celebrate our freedom, not think about death.

I veered back to the vendors. One farmer was selling bundles for a vegetarian cookout. Corn on the cob, marinated asparagus, one foil-wrapped pouch contained carrots, zucchini, and pepper strips. I could just imagine how yummy it'd be. It was Monday, and my book club had decided to read a patriotic mystery and meet this evening at my house. We primarily read mysteries, and it was fun when we shared why we'd suspected different characters.

Some of the ladies didn't have families nearby to celebrate the holiday with, and they'd requested we meet. Not wanting anyone to be alone on this special day, I'd agreed.

I bought enough veggie bundles for our group, plus a few extra. The police were preparing the street for the parade, so I walked home. I'd pick up my truck after the parade.

Two hours later, my doorbell rang. I'd showered even though I'd probably start sweating again during the parade.

Cowboy barked and raced me to the door. My adopted puppy probably loved Jake more than he loved me.

"Slow down, boy."

He skidded to a halt at the door and panted.

I ran a hand down my red, white, and blue T-shirt and flowery denim skort before opening the door. "Hi, Jake."

"Hey, Sunshine. For days, I've been hearing how amazing this parade will be. I'm glad we can enjoy it together." Jake stood on my porch, wearing a patriotic polo and navy shorts.

"Come in. I fixed lemonade. Would you like a glass?"

"Sounds good."

My golden retriever mutt barked, and Jake bent down and rubbed his head. "Hey, boy. You behaving yourself?"

Cowboy wagged his tail.

Jake followed me through the gathering room and the breakfast room to the kitchen of my airplane bungalow. He'd been here often enough to feel comfortable in my home. "The others plan to meet us closer to the start of the parade."

"Okay. I hope they don't get tangled up in holiday traffic. Abby decided to watch the parade with her friends on the square, so it'll be nice to have y'all hanging with me." My daughter was home after her first semester at college. I poured Jake a glass of lemonade in an insulated glass, and then I dropped a cherry and a sprig of peppermint on top before passing it to him.

"What about Sophie?"

My best friend owned a bakery on the square. "She said the parade is good for business, and she's going to work."

"Makes sense. I want to talk to you sometime about my business plan." He took a drink of his lemonade. "Umm, perfect. Not too sweet, and not too tart."

"Thanks." His words made me ridiculously happy for a glass of lemonade. "Do you want to go to the porch? It's fun to people watch."

"I enjoy people watching, too."

I leashed Cowboy, and the three of us traipsed to the front porch. We sat in rocking chairs, and an oscillating floor fan blew on us.

Jake pointed to the porch's ceiling. "What happened to the ceiling fan?"

I shrugged. "It quit working, and it'll be a while before I can afford to fix it."

"That's one thing I wanted to discuss with you. I think it's time."

"Time? For what?"

"To start my handyman business. The police department is making no moves to hire me, and I can't keep waiting. Working for Coop has helped sharpen my construction skills, but it was a temporary solution until I decided what to do with my life. Working at the coffee shop is only temporary to help Brett out of a jam. He really doesn't need me."

"Jake, I think you're going to help a lot of people who are looking for an honest person to deal with small projects that big construction companies consider a waste of time."

"I hope you're right. You know I've done a few small jobs as a side hustle. I'm building a list of people who will recommend me. Will you allow me to fix, or replace, your fan?" He raised his hand. "You'll be doing me a favor."

He'd be doing me a bigger favor, but I'd be sure to do something special for him. "Sure, and thanks."

A red Honda Accord pulled into my driveway, and Celia exited first. She helped an elderly Black lady out of the front seat.

Brett joined them and held onto the lady's arm while she walked up the stairs to my front porch. "Emma, I'd like you to meet my great aunt. This is Maebell Franks."

"Pleased to meet ya." She reached out and shook my hand.

"Nice to meet you, too. Your hands are so soft."

"Thanks. I put thick cream on them every night and sleep in gloves." She squeezed my hand.

"Well, I may try that too." Working in the gardens took a toll on my hands.

"You might consider a lotion with capsaicin or magnesium to warm up your hands. It'll help them not be so cold. It's also good for your feet, and I imagine they're cold too."

My hands and feet were cold, yes, but my face had grown warm. "Thanks for the advice. Please have a seat, and I'll get us all some lemonade. Ms. Maebell, you should take the chair closest to the fan."

Brett met my gaze. "Thanks, Emma."

"You're welcome."

Jake reached for the leash. "I'll take care of Cowboy."

I scooted inside and prepared three more glasses of lemonade. Something more was needed. I rummaged for pretzels in the pantry and poured them into a red bowl. Patriotic napkins completed my offering. Once it was all on a sturdy tray, I rejoined the others.

The sight of Tess Carranza surprised me, but our local librarian was always welcome. "Hi, Tess."

Tess wore a blue dress with white polka dots. Her makeup and hair were perfect, no signs of perspiration on her. "I hope you don't mind me joining you."

"The more the merrier, and I'm glad you're here." I set the tray on a table and passed out drinks. "Tess, would you like something?"

"I'm drinking water, but thank you." She lifted a stainless-steel insulated blue tumbler that matched her dress.

In the distance, drums began beating.

Ms. Maebell slid forward in her chair, probably to get a better view.

Tess tapped my shoulder and pointed to a shady spot in the front yard. "Can we talk over there?"

"Sure." I followed her. "Is everything okay?"

"I'm not sure, but I'd like to talk to you about something. Today. It's important. Maybe before, or after, book club. I can help you prepare for our meeting."

"Okay." I studied her serious expression, but she gave nothing away. "Can you at least give me a hint?"

She laughed. "I knew you'd be the perfect person to talk to. Let's just say, I may have stumbled on a real-life mystery. I'd like you to help me figure it out."

* * *

Uncle Sam and Sam Houston opened the Lutz Fourth of July parade. High school flag girls carried a banner followed by the school's marching band. They played "America the Beautiful," and the high school fight song.

I stood to get a better view. Something about parades filled me with excitement and joy. It was like I reverted to being a child.

The sidewalk grew crowded, and a family with a baby asked to stand in my shady yard.

"Of course, or you can join us on the porch." Now I wish I'd made brownies or something they could snack on. My pretzels seemed like a meager offering. "Would you like a glass of lemonade?"

The mother smiled. "No, thanks. Our older children are riding on the youth baseball league float, and we want them to see us wave."

"We'll be sure to cheer extra loud when they come by."

Farmers rode horses, high school football players rode on one of the floats decorated with a goalpost, and the swim team walked and fired water guns at kids.

Jake wrapped his arm over my shoulders. "The town goes all out for the parade."

"I told you so." I leaned into him. "Wait until you see the fireworks tonight."

Paige Booker, the owner of Paige's Turn Bookstore, wore a T-shirt with the names of Texas authors. She walked beside a convertible and handed out bookmarks to children. Buddy Hewitt drove the car ever so slowly.

Celia gasped. "The kids on the other side of the street aren't getting anything. I'm going to help Paige. Brett, I'll catch up with you later."

"Sure thing. Have fun." He gave her a quick kiss before she raced away to catch up with Paige and the convertible.

Brett elbowed Jake. "Your sister sure enough loves working at the bookstore."

He ran a hand over his face. "It's more like she loves you, and the job worked out."

The owner of one of the yoga studios threw out small towels.

A familiar truck appeared. Nick Jones, a local exterminator, tossed candy to children.

Tess gasped and then stepped closer to me. "I can't believe he's in the parade."

I gave Jake an apologetic smile and moved away with Tess. "The parade committee may not have had a good reason to reject his application."

"He's got so many people snowed. It sickens me."

Her angry tone alarmed me. "Does your mystery involve Nick?"

"No, but I still believe he was to blame for his first wife's death." She inhaled a deep breath. "Rhonda didn't deserve to die like she did."

"You're right." Nick's first wife had been poisoned, but the killer had never been caught. "It's been close to twenty years. Don't you think you should let it go? The stress can't be good for your health."

"Rhonda was my friend. Until her killer is caught, I'll never drop the matter. In fact, the library pays Nick for pest control. I like to keep tabs on him, and thankfully, he gave us the best bid." Her fists clenched. "That's enough about him. There's another situation I'd like to discuss with you."

"We should have plenty of time before the day's over."

The baseball float was next, and we all cheered and waved. Jake put two fingers in his mouth and released a loud whistle. It was obvious which children belonged to the family in my yard. A dark-haired boy and a blond girl waved with exuberance.

Fire engine sirens wailed, and firefighters waved to people. Two police cars followed with a blip of their sirens, smiles, and popsicles.

I waved at Matt Young, the police chief. We'd known each other for years through our kids. This year our paths had crossed during a couple of murder investigations, and I was relieved there'd been no recent murders in our little town.

Cowboy barked, and I turned my attention to him. "It's okay, boy."

My golden retriever was around nine months old. I'd rescued him from a dark alley, and we didn't know his exact age. Before him, I hadn't been a dog owner. I looked at Jake, who had more experience with dogs. "Should I take him inside or stay here and hold him?"

"My best guess would be to sit in a rocker and hold him. It might teach him to not fear loud noises." He looked at my dog. "Whatever you decide, I don't feel like he should be alone."

"Okay." I led the puppy to a rocking chair and picked him up. At first, he settled into my lap, but it didn't last long. I continued to hold him firm but not tight. "You're okay, boy."

The firefighters handed out candy and coloring books to children.

I held Cowboy and talked to him in a soothing voice until the parade was over.

Jake came over and rubbed the dog's head. "Just wait until the fireworks tonight."

I sighed. "Oh, boy."

Brett joined us. "I'm going to take Aunt Maebell home so she can rest. Between the heat and the excitement, she's tuckered out."

Tess turned to us. "Maebell? As in Maebell Franks?"

Brett's eyes widened. "Yes, do y'all know each other?"

"It's more like I know of her. Would you give me a minute to speak to your aunt?" Tess's mixie hairstyle remained as perfect as the moment she arrived. The Texas heat and humidity hadn't damaged or frizzed her style in the least.

"She'll be visiting for a few days. What about I introduce you two, and you can arrange to meet later?"

"That will work." Tess moved to the other rocking chair, knelt, and started a conversation with the older woman.

"Weird." Brett looked at me. "First, she didn't give me time to introduce her. Second, what's that all about?"

I shrugged. "I have no idea, but something is going on with Tess. She's not as calm as usual."

"Hmm. I just hope she doesn't upset Aunt Maebell."

Cowboy wiggled, and I let him down but kept a grip on the leash.

Jake winked at me. "Can I take him for a little walk?"

"Thanks." I passed the leash to him.

The two headed to the side yard, and I gathered cups and napkins while attempting to eavesdrop on the conversation between Tess and Maebell.

Attorney. Land rights. Offer.

Those were the three words I heard before Brett ended the conversation.

"Aunt Maebell, let's get you out of this heat." Brett held a hand out to his aunt.

"Oh, dear, Tess and I just started our conversation."

Brett paused. "Tess, will you be at the library tomorrow? Can we schedule a time for you two to meet?"

Tess nodded. "I'll take my break at a time convenient for you."

Maebell said, "I like to get an early start on the day."

"That she does." Brett gripped his aunt's elbow and helped her stand.

Tess said, "Early it is. Tomorrow I'm scheduled to open at nine. You come as early as you like."

"See you tomorrow." Ms. Maebell waved and leaned on Brett as they descended the steps.

I waved. "See you later."

After they left, I turned to Tess. "It's time to let me in on your secret."

Chapter Two

Tess stepped close to me on the front porch of my bungalow. "Emma, I'm concerned somebody is trying to take advantage of Ms. Franks. Financially. Nothing physical. Unless you consider she might not be able to afford to eat if they steal all her money."

"Steal Ms. Maebell's money?" I met Tess's intense gaze. "What are you talking about?"

Jake and Cowboy returned. "Am I still manning the grill tonight?"

"If you don't mind the heat, that'll be terrific." I could've grilled our food, but Jake lived in the apartment over Paige's Turn Bookstore. Last week, when he confided he missed cooking out, I asked him to oversee my Fourth of July grill.

"I'm happy to do it." He confirmed his earlier statement.

Tess shook off her gloomy mood. "How can I help?"

"Let's go inside, and you can either pat out burgers—"

"Nope, that's my job." Jake's eyes crinkled as he grinned. "There's a specific way I like to prepare the meat before it hits the grill."

I laughed. "You're in charge. Tess, you can work on a salad, and I'll make grilled veggie packets. Um, Jake, will there be room for a few packets?"

"You bet. Be sure to use the strongest aluminum foil."

"Yes, sir." I saluted. The foil was in my secret pantry, but it wouldn't remain a secret if I allowed everyone to know about it. "Tess, first, would you mind to look at my herb garden? I should have enough mint to pick and add to iced tea later."

Her gaze met mine. "I'm not sure if I know the difference between mint

11

and other herbs."

"Oh, I'm sorry."

Jake said, "I'll show you and check on the grill at the same time. Come on. We can walk around the house and meet Emma in the kitchen."

I led Cowboy inside and refilled his bowl with cool water. He lapped it up while I retrieved the necessary items from the pantry.

Cowboy moseyed to his crate and got comfortable.

I began food prep and was surprised when Tess entered the kitchen.

She held up sprigs of green spearmint. "Jake gave me a little education on herbs. Is this enough?"

"Yes. Everything he learned about herbs, he recently learned from me. It sounds like he deserves an A." I laughed and took the mint and rinsed it under cool water, feeling pleased to know Jake had paid attention.

"You must be a good teacher then."

I patted the green leaves dry between layers of a cotton towel. "Thanks. I've washed the veggies. Would you like to cut them up and toss them in this big bowl? It'll make for a cool, crispy salad at dinner tonight."

"Now that's something I can do."

"Who's trying to take advantage of Ms. Franks?" I checked the veggie pouches I'd bought earlier. They all looked yummy, and the foil was sturdy. It turned out there was nothing for me to do but pass them on to Jake.

"I'm so glad you asked." Her gaze jumped to me.

My phone vibrated.

"Hold on. It's Sophie." I swiped. "Hey, girl. How's it going?"

"Staying open was a good move. I sold out of all the cookies, cupcakes, and brownies. There was even a rush for sandwiches."

"Yay." My friend worked so hard to make her bakery a success. It was exciting to hear about her good day.

"I wanted to tell you not to make a dessert for tonight. I'll bring over a Texas white sheet cake. It's my star-spangled banner version. A farmer brought me some pecans, and I'll make us pecan pie another day."

"Yum, and thanks." I was about to start drooling, thinking about Sophie's desserts. "Tess and Jake are already here, so come over anytime."

"Another customer just walked in, and he's wearing a suit. Seems strange when everyone else is so casual today. Oh, well. I'll see you in a bit."

I placed the phone on my charger. "Sophie will bring dessert, so I don't need to bake something like brownies or slice-and-bake cookies. I'll cut carrots, while you tell me what's going on, Tess."

She washed and dried her hands, then stood ramrod straight. "It started out innocently enough. A man was in the research area of the library. His phone rang, and he walked to the entry area where it's okay to talk on the phone. I know people use their phones in other areas, but it's a distraction. I do my best to encourage patrons to take their calls other places."

I held back a smile. I'd seen her stern librarian expression a few times, and I didn't want to get crossways with Tess. "Did you hear something?"

"Yes. Somebody called this man from a courthouse. I can't be positive it was ours, though." She tore up iceberg lettuce. "It could've been any courthouse."

I chopped enough carrots and began slicing and dicing a green pepper. "And?"

"The man in the library mentioned if they could get to three more people on his list, they'd be free and clear."

"What do you think that means?"

"I don't know, but he ended the call and returned to the research area." She found the spinach and layered it in. "The thing is, there were maps of our area. Not Lutz specifically, but land from here to Houston."

"That's a lot of land, but why would he be in our library?"

"He also had some genealogy books. One was written by a Black man who lived in Lutz before his death. What's the connection between genealogy and Texas land?"

"I honestly have no idea." I fluffed the salad. "Why are you worried?"

"There are rumors that Texas businessmen want to build more suburbs around Austin and Houston. I'm worried it'll destroy small towns." She frowned.

I didn't completely understand her frustration. "If the big cities continue to grow, and the suburbs spread out, won't the land become more valuable?"

Tess pounded the counter with her fist. "That's my point."

Maybe the heat had gotten to me, but her point wasn't clear. I sprinkled diced green pepper on the salad. "We need red too, for more color."

Tess passed a red pepper to me. "What do you think?"

Cowboy turned over and continued to sleep. This time his paws were in the air.

I smiled at my puppy. "I'm not sure what the mystery is. "

Tess washed her hands and dried them on a paper towel. "Maybe I'm bored and looking for a problem where there's nothing to worry about."

"How old are you?" I couldn't remember exactly, but she was older than me. I propped my hip against the counter.

"Forty-eight. Fifty is just around the corner. How did the years go by so fast?" Tess was coming unglued, and she was always put together.

Ten years older than me. "I know what you mean. Abby is in college now, and I'm currently pursuing my dream of being a flower farmer. I was in survival mode for eighteen years, and at last there's room to breathe."

"I would imagine money would be tighter. Is Abby on a full-ride scholarship to Baylor?"

"No. Her father left money for her college expenses in his will. Nothing else. I think Bo never imagined he'd die so young." Although he'd become addicted to drugs, and it wasn't a huge surprise.

"I'm sorry, Emma, but I get what you mean. I focused on my career and lost track of time. Then it seemed too late to date and get married. Plus, not many single men hang out at the library." She shrugged. "That could be one reason the well-dressed, handsome man caught my attention. Not many strangers appear, wearing suits and ties."

"He wore a suit?" What were the odds it was the same man who was at the bakery?

"Yes. He's quite handsome. Married, but handsome." Tess's face reddened.

"You think he's up to no good, though. Have you contacted the authorities?"

"Um, well—"

Jake entered the kitchen. "What time is everybody planning to arrive?

Celia also wants to bring Brett. His aunt prefers to relax at his place and watch the celebrations on the TV."

"If I was eighty-something, I'd probably rather watch fireworks on TV, too. Of course, Brett is more than welcome." I needed time to process Tess's comment about the man at the library.

"I know you said that earlier, but what time?"

I checked my watch. "Oh dear, the book club ladies will start arriving in about an hour."

He whistled. "I better get to work."

* * *

The meal was a success, even with a smaller than normal crowd for our book club meeting. Celia, Sophie, Tess, and Laurel Holley had been able to attend. Laurel was the new assistant library director. She was probably mid-twenties with beautiful long curly blond hair.

We ate dinner and discussed our book of the week. When the conversation wrapped up, Sophie presented our dessert. The sheet cake had a white frosting, and it was decorated with berries on top to resemble the American flag. "Ladies, I've made this cake every year since I moved to Texas. I hope you enjoy it."

Sophie had moved to Texas from Germany, and I'd helped her study for her citizenship exam. Nobody was more thrilled to be an American citizen than my best friend. Her excitement led me to be more appreciative of my freedom.

"I assure y'all that it's delicious." I refreshed everyone's drinks, and then we ate on my back patio and watched fireworks.

After the grand finale, my friends left one by one.

Tess hung back. "Emma, Ms. Franks will meet me at the library tomorrow morning. Would you like to join us? Together, we should be able to decide if my imagination has gone crazy or if there's something to be concerned about."

"What time?" The beauty of owning my business was I could tweak my working hours.

"If you can be there by eight-thirty, I'll let you in. We can prepare what we want to say."

"I'll be there for moral support, but you should lead the conversation."

Tess took a deep breath. "You're right. I'll take charge with your support."

I hugged her. "It's going to be okay."

"Thanks, Emma."

After Tess left, I waited up for Abby. At least I tried, but I fell asleep on the couch in my gathering room, researching land grants.

"Mom. Wake up." Abby touched my shoulder.

"Hi, honey." I yawned.

"You don't need to stay up until I get home anymore. I'm a college kid."

I stood. "As long as you're my kid, living in my home, I'll wait up."

"I love you, Mom."

"Love you, too. Now, let's go to bed."

Chapter Three

Tuesday morning, I walked to the library with a bouquet of fresh-cut sunflowers. It was already humid, but I enjoyed walking at my pace. Since adopting Cowboy, I'd been forced to move faster to keep up with him.

My hand throbbed from an early morning bee sting, and doctoring it was the reason I was ten minutes late. Surely, Tess would understand.

A group of women stood under the library's awning, chatting, and holding travel mugs.

I slowed my stride.

Faith Meier stepped away from the group. "Hi, Emma. Are you joining our group?"

"What group?"

"We're the Tuesday morning coloring and coffee group. The library provides coloring pages, pencils, and pens. We bring our own coffee, or whatever. It's been a fun way for me to get better connected in Lutz. Running the bed-and-breakfast has allowed me to meet interesting people, but they always leave." She chuckled. "I need more lasting friendships."

"It sounds fun, but I'm here to see Tess. Unfortunately, I'm running a tad late. Maybe I'll see you inside." I went to the front door and knocked on the glass.

There was no sign of life. I leaned closer to the glass and peered in.

"Tess's car is in the parking lot." Faith joined me and pointed to an electric car.

"Hmm. Have you seen her?"

"No, but she makes it a habit to arrive early. When we enter, the event is prepared for us, lights are on, and she welcomes us."

If Tess hadn't been worried about the well-dressed man and Maebell Franks, I wouldn't be concerned. I pulled out my phone. "I'll give her a quick call."

Faith looked over my shoulder.

It rang a few times before rolling to voicemail. "Okay, that didn't work."

"I'll ask the others if they've seen Tess." Faith turned, and her blond ponytail swung as she moved to rejoin the other ladies.

"Okay, and I'll call her new assistant." I looked in my phone for Laurel Holley's number and called her.

"Hello? Is this Emma?"

"Yes. I'm at the library. I was supposed to meet Tess early, but I don't see her, and she's not answering her phone. Do you know anything?"

"No. Tess thought it would be slow because it's the day after a holiday. She gave me the time off, so I'm not on the schedule. If she doesn't open at nine, call me back." She paused. "Thanks for letting me join your book club. It was a fun evening."

"I'm glad you could make it. Hopefully, I won't call you back." I ended the call and checked the time. Nine o'clock exactly.

Still no sign of Tess.

I knocked on the glass again.

Nothing.

I hurried to Faith. "I'm going to look in her car, but will you keep knocking?"

"Sure. It's that one." She pointed to the white car that I knew belonged to Tess.

"Be right back." I ran across the parking lot and stopped at the driver's door. I looked in the car. Empty. I tried the door handle, but it was locked.

I dialed Laurel again.

"You found her, didn't you?" Laurel yawned.

"No, but her car is here. Can you open the library for us? It's possible Tess fell or something and can't open the door."

"Okay, but I'm not dressed for work. Still, if she's hurt, I shouldn't waste time. I'll be there soon."

"Thanks." I leaned against Tess's car and studied the people gathered around the front of the library.

There were a few young women with children, and there was a man with a little girl. The child had dark hair like her father. Faith's group clustered closer to the door. A young man stuffed books and videos into the return box and then walked away. There was another man wearing faded jeans and a plaid shirt with the sleeves rolled up. His scuffed boots indicated he was a working man and not wearing the boots for show.

Nothing seemed suspicious, and I was happy to see men using the library.

Tess had been stressed yesterday. Today, she was a no-show. Something was off.

An expensive sports car pulled into the parking lot. The driver wore a white shirt and dark tie, and he backed into a shady parking space.

Could he be the one who'd aroused Tess's suspicions?

A black Camry careened around the corner and parked next to Tess's car. Laurel jumped out, wearing shorts and a wrinkled T-shirt. "Hi, Emma. Got here as soon as I could. Still no sign of Tess?"

"No. I'm glad you got here so fast." Acid churned in my belly. Tess had to be okay. I glanced at the sports car. The man was talking on a phone.

Brett pulled into the parking lot, going as slow as I'd ever witnessed him drive. Who knew the library was such a busy place this early in the morning?

I waved for him to pull over.

Laurel walked to the library door.

Brett stopped near me and rolled down his window. "Emma, what's going on? Tess left a message that you were going to meet with her and Aunt Maebell."

"Well, yeah. That was the plan, but I can't find Tess. Maybe sit here a minute until we figure out if there's a problem." I leaned down and waved to Brett's aunt. "Hi, Ms. Maebell."

"Morning, Emma. Did you try the hand cream like I recommended?"

"No, ma'am. But I will try it soon." I shifted my focus back to Brett. "Keep an eye on the guy in the shade over there. See if he does anything suspicious."

Brett whistled. "Guy in the Porsche? On it."

I jogged to the door and reached it as Laurel opened the thing. I said, "Do you want me to go in with you?"

She nodded. "Yes, please."

"Okay, and you might want to tell the patrons to give us a few minutes."

Laurel waved me in before facing the growing crowd. "I'm sorry y'all. We need to make sure Tess is okay before I let everybody inside."

People murmured, but I didn't wait to hear more of the conversation.

I entered the cool library and beelined it to Tess's office.

The desk lamp shone. Her brown leather briefcase and matching purse sat side by side on a credenza. There was also a stack of files and a thick reference book on the history of Texas. A bright purple planner added a pop of color to Tess's practical office. An empty flower vase had been placed next to the items. Tess knew I'd have fresh flowers with me.

I exited the office, still gripping the sunflowers.

The chair behind the check-out desk had been knocked to the floor.

Chills raced up my back.

I moved past the section of best sellers and to the reference area. A few weeks earlier, I'd helped Tess with indoor plants. We'd placed them on a bookshelf dividing the reference area from the non-fiction books. Some flowers were in Polish pottery. Tess confided she'd begun to collect pieces, and it made her happy to use them at the library. They prettied up the area, but one was missing. The bleeding heart flower had been in a blue and white French toile ceramic I'd bought at an antique sale.

The missing planter alarmed me. There was a small clump of soil on the edge of the shelf. Tess wouldn't leave a mess, if she could prevent it.

My heart thudded, but I forced myself to walk to the other side of the shelf.

Dirt surrounded the plant and broken pot. Pink petals had been smushed, and lying on the floor next to the bleeding heart flower was Tess Carranza.

I dropped the sunflowers as I fell to my knees, reaching for her wrist. My hands shook as I touched her. Tess's body was still warm, but I couldn't for the life of me find a pulse.

I screamed, "Somebody call an ambulance."

Chapter Four

Laurel ushered patrons into the community room, and the EMTs raced through the main area of the library.

How'd they get here so fast?

I'd been left alone with Tess for less than a minute, and then a paramedic pulled me away. Wringing my hands watching the scene wouldn't help anyone, especially my friend. I stepped forward. "Can I help?"

Brett appeared. "Stop, Emma. They won't let you do anything. They're the professionals, and you'll slow them down." His voice shook.

"You're right." I nodded. Crying could come later. "It seems like I should be doing something, though."

One of the men around Tess's body shot me a look. "Listen to your friend. We've been trained to rescue people. You'll only be in our way."

"I know. Sorry." Helplessness washed over me. Dizziness made me sway, and I reached out to the shelf to steady myself.

"Whoa, there. Hang on." Brett took me by the arm and led me to a reference table. We sat down, and he rubbed my shoulder. "Get your bearings. It's going to be okay."

Tears filled my eyes. I held shaky fingers over my upper lip. "I don't think she's going to make it."

He nodded. "I'm afraid you might be right. We don't know how long it's been since she was attacked. It appears she fought back. I called Jake. For moral support, maybe for me more than you."

"Trust me. I could use some emotional support, too." My voice wobbled. "Where's your aunt?"

"With the others. You know the dude you wanted me to watch?"

"Yeah. Is he in here?"

"Nope. He took off. I'm gonna be honest with you. I don't know exactly when, but it was before we got out of the car."

"Good. I'm glad he didn't see your aunt."

"Why? What do you think happened here? And how would Aunt Maebell be connected? Brett's tone was gentle.

"I think Tess was attacked." I gulped air.

"Emma, get a grip. I agree with your theory." Brett's tone remained calm. "Why didn't you want the guy in the car to see Aunt Maebell?"

"Tess was concerned somebody was trying to take advantage of your aunt. Oh, Brett. This is awful."

"Well, that's not good. Tell me what you notice before the cops get here and kick us out. Take a good look." He patted my hand. "I don't want to be rude, but we don't have much time."

Two more EMTs entered with a stretcher.

I stood and looked toward the area of the attack. Instead of focusing on Tess, I took in the details around her. At least, I did the best I could with four adults swarmed around her body. They whispered to each other, and one glanced at me, making solid eye contact.

I looked away and studied the scene. A flower pot was broken. Had it hit the hard floor, or had it been used as a weapon? By the killer? Or by Tess to defend herself? There were also the sunflowers I'd dropped.

There were faint footprints on the floor. The killer may have stepped in the dirt and made the footprints, walking around.

Or they could be from Brett and me. I'd felt for a pulse, and an emergency technician had pulled me away.

The emergency personnel were probably tracking dirt around too.

Were there any other clues to what had happened?

Tess wore a short-sleeved black blouse, a red scarf, and a black skirt. The skirt twisted around her legs. The scarf was catawampus. There were scratches on her arms, and I hadn't seen them when she'd been at my house. Defensive wounds?

23

I walked to her office, passing the check-out desk on the way. Oh, yeah. The chair had been knocked over. Is this where the struggle began? Had Tess spotted her attacker and tried to run for safety? I peered into her office. Nice and organized. Normal for Tess.

What was in the files? Did the Texas history book have information on land rights? I needed to find out more about the topic. If the police confiscated the book on the credenza, I'd research it another way. The files were what I really wanted to see, but with so many people in the building, it'd be impossible to borrow them. Plus, it might have nothing to do with her death. Would anyone notice if I entered the office?

I looked toward the paramedics. A bald man spoke to one of the younger guys. His uniform was similar to theirs but a little different. Maybe he was the head honcho.

I returned to Brett.

The building had been locked when I arrived. How had the killer gotten in and out? I whispered, "Do you think the killer might still be here?"

He shrugged and looked around. "Why?"

"The doors were locked until Laurel showed up."

"Emma." Jake's voice rang out.

I jumped.

Brett said, "We're over here, man."

Jake came straight to me and took me in his strong arms. "Oh, babe. I can't believe you found another body."

"Maybe she's still alive." I glanced toward Tess, hoping with my entire heart that she'd move and be okay.

"Shh." He patted my back.

Brett said, "You know she's not alive, Emma."

I didn't want to admit it. "She was full of life and determination yesterday."

Police Chief Matt Young entered the building, followed by three officers. His steps faltered when he spotted Jake, Brett, and me. "Why are you guys here?"

Jake said, "Would you like us to leave?"

"I'd prefer for you to answer my question." Matt turned toward us.

I stepped away from Jake. "Tess asked me to meet her and Brett's aunt here this morning. When we couldn't get inside, I called Laurel Holley."

"Who?" Matt's voice growled like a ferocious bear.

"Laurel is the Assistant Library Director. I figured she'd have a key, and she's the one who opened the door for us."

Matt looked in each direction. "Where is she?"

"She's in the community room with the patrons who'd also been waiting to get inside."

Brett said, "My aunt's in there too."

Matt stepped toward Brett. "Are you telling me there's a mob of people in the building where a crime has been committed?"

Brett's eyebrows shot up. "Don't blame me. The library lady took them in there."

"Oh, she'll hear from me. Don't you worry." Matt's nostrils flared.

"It was too hot for Laurel to make them wait on the sidewalk." I wrung my hands. "Don't be mad at her."

"You three may as well go in with them. If there was any evidence in there, it's been destroyed by now. I'll question you soon, but don't tell the others anything."

"Hey, Matt. There's dirt on the floor from a planter. The killer's footprints might be near the body, but I don't think people are paying attention to disturbing the crime scene." My voice wobbled, and I did my best not to cry.

"My crime scene. I'll caution the others. Thanks, Emma."

"One last thing. If it's okay, after you finish the crime scene, I'd like to replant the bleeding heart flower. You'll see what I mean when you go over there."

He grunted. "Great. Just great."

Without another word, we left Matt and his officers with the paramedics and Tess.

I glanced back at the scene. Nobody had pulled a sheet over her face yet. Did that mean she was still alive?

When we reached the doorway to the community room, Jake pulled me to the side. "If you're not up to facing people yet, we can stand here."

"I like that idea." I leaned against the cool wall. If I remained focused on the sight of Tess, I'd blubber like an infant. "Guys, the building was locked when I arrived. We need to figure out if the killer was lying in wait for Tess, or did she let the person inside? If the attacker was already in the building, how did he, or she, get in? But if Tess opened the door, she must've known the assailant."

Brett tapped notes on his phone. "Yeah, yeah, yeah. It must've been someone with a key, because Tess was a cautious person. But who would've done this?"

"Laurel opened the door for us, so obviously she has a key. We need to find out who else does."

Laurel popped her head out of the room full of people. "You all, I think I'll send everyone home and close the library for the day. I'm not dressed appropriately, and I'm not prepared to work."

The man in the flannel shirt stood in the background next to Faith Meier. The two were deep in conversation.

Jake said, "No. You need to ask Chief Young before letting the people go."

"Why?" Her hair was in a lopsided, messy bun.

I stared at the young blonde. She hadn't inquired about Tess. Was she heartless? Conniving? Or was she the killer? She did have a key to the library.

Jake said, "It's possible the library is a crime scene, and one of the patrons may have witnessed something and not even realize it."

Her mouth dropped open.

A young child whined from the room full of people.

Laurel glared at Jake. "This is ridiculous. I'm sending them home."

A woman entered the building and strolled toward us, juggling a purse and two tote bags. "Hi, Laurel. What's going on?"

A child squealed and ran to the newcomer. "Ms. Hope. I've been waiting for you all day!"

"Hi, Jose. I'm so happy to see you, and I have a book you're going to like." She hugged the little boy. "It's about a child who wants to be a pirate."

"Yay. I'll tell Mommy." He ran back into the community room.

The young redhead turned and looked at us. "I'm Hope Peters. Are we having story time today? I need to get set up with supplies and goodie bags."

Laurel said, "No. I'm sending all these people home."

Chief Young appeared. "No, you're not."

Chapter Five

C hief Young looked at our small group in the library's hall. "My team will question everybody. Ms. Peters, can you lead story time in one of these rooms? It'll keep the children occupied while we question the adults.

Her eyes widened. "Yes, sir."

Officer Steve Koch clomped down the hall. "Chief, what do you want me to do?"

"First, get everyone's name and contact information. If anyone thinks they saw something unusual or suspicious, send them to me. Make sure they have your business card and feel comfortable to call us at any time, day, or night. They could remember something important later."

There was a flurry of activity near the main door of the library. The EMTs pushed a gurney.

I craned my neck to get a better view, but the police chief moved sideways and blocked my line of vision. Was it possible the medics had revived Tess? Had I been mistaken in my assessment? Had they ever covered her head? I couldn't see clearly. Please, let her be okay. "Matt, is Tess going to live?"

His shoulders drooped. "I believe you already know the answer to that question. You're the one who found her, right?"

"Correct." My voice shook, and I felt weak.

"I need you to tell me exactly what happened." The kindness in his voice surprised me.

"Okay, but Matt, I also want to tell you what happened with Tess yesterday." My heart hammered against my sternum.

"Let's find a quiet place where we can talk." His gaze darted from me to Jake. "Alone."

"I get it." Jake raised in hands and backed away. "Emma, I'll be around."

"Thanks."

It didn't take long for the children to follow Hope to the back corner of the community room. Officer Koch questioned each adult, and Laurel stood beside him, for no discernible reason. One of Matt's older female officers had volunteered to question people who'd seen something. I followed Matt to one of the small rooms.

He turned two chairs so they'd face each other, and we sat.

"One of my officers swept this room, and it should be safe for us to talk here."

"Safe?" My voice squeaked.

"I mean, it's doubtful the attacker was in this room." Matt removed his notepad and pen. "You said this began yesterday."

"Yes. Something about land rights, Ms. Maebell Franks, and a well-dressed stranger hanging around the library." I lifted a finger for each issue. "Tess was concerned the man was going to harm Ms. Maebell."

"Physically?"

"No, financially, at least according to Tess. She didn't have proof of anything, and she wanted to discuss it with me."

"She should've come to me. Who is the man?"

"I have no idea." I leaned forward. "Well, maybe I have a possible clue. While I was trying to locate Tess this morning, a man drove a Porsche into the parking lot. He parked in the shade, but I never saw him enter the library. On my way inside, Brett arrived with his aunt. I asked him to watch the Porsche and see what the driver did."

"Well? Don't leave me hanging." His pen was poised over the paper.

"The guy left."

"Do you have a description?"

"He had dark hair and wore a tie. That's it." I shrugged, wishing there was more to report.

"Okay. What else? How did you get into the library?"

I launched into the events of my morning, trying to remember all the details. I held nothing back.

"Thanks, Emma. I hope you don't plan to get in the middle of my murder investigation." He stood and offered his hand to me. "What about the sunflowers?"

"I brought them." I accepted his hand in a friendly way, but pulled it back as soon as possible. "Every Monday, I try to bring fresh flowers to Tess. With yesterday being a holiday, I brought them with me today."

He crossed the room and held the door open. "I figured as much. Make wise decisions and have a nice day."

"Thanks. You, too." It was doubtful either of us would have a nice day, but it'd be rude not to act like it was possible.

I looked in both directions and spotted Jake near the entrance. Jake hadn't lived in Lutz for long, but we'd grown close during my first amateur murder investigation. Then we began dating, exclusively. At thirty-eight, it'd been nearly twenty years since I'd dated. My husband died when Abby had been an infant, and men had fallen into the category of friends. At least until I'd met Jake Hunter.

Jake had been in the Marines, and he'd hoped to join the police department when he moved to Lutz. So far, it hadn't worked out, but he'd put his investigative skills to work assisting me on two murder investigations.

"How'd that go?" Jake slid his arm around me.

"Not bad. At least Matt didn't accuse me or any of my friends of murdering Tess."

"Good to know. Would you like to go with me to Anytime Coffee House for a cup of green tea?"

"Sounds heavenly." It was a good thing I'd worked in my flower beds earlier. Now there was time to think about Tess. "Shall we walk?"

"Sorry. I was on my way to the retirement village when Brett called." He pointed to his Sequoia. "How about a ride?"

"Perfect."

He did a double-take. "Really?"

"Yeah. I'm kinda shaky from this morning's events."

"I'd be more surprised if you weren't shaky after finding your friend." He took my hand in his, and we walked to his SUV. "You probably need some protein."

"Oh, Jake. Let's go to Sophie's Bakery. We can order sandwiches and take them to the coffee shop."

"I'll never pass up a chance to go to Sophie's." Soon we were heading toward the town square.

I sat back and thought about Tess Carranza until Jake parked on the square. He turned and faced me. "Are you up to going inside? I can place your order."

"I'm a big girl."

With a tender touch, he wiped tears from my face. "You shouldn't have to cope with another murder."

I cupped his hand with mine. "Why does this keep happening? Should I just jump on I-35 and leave Lutz in my dust? Forget about crime and murders?"

"Shh. You'd also leave lifetime friends and family. Emma's Flower Farm is the result of years of dreaming and planning. You can't walk away from your life."

I sighed. "I also need to factor you into the equation."

He chuckled. "Hey, now. If you left Lutz, I'd follow you. Not in a creepy, stalkerish way, but in the way a man follows the love of his life."

My heart missed a beat. Jake would follow me. "That would make me very happy."

His lips touched mine, and my day brightened for a moment.

The sound of a car honking drew us apart.

I glanced past Jake.

The gray Porsche from the library joined the flow of traffic and headed down the street toward Heart of Texas Bed and Breakfast. I gasped.

"What?" He looked in both directions.

"I think that's the sports car from earlier. You know, the one with the man wearing a tie?"

He started the SUV. "Which way?"

"Toward the bed-and-breakfast. Do you think you can catch him?"

31

"Well, it's for sure I won't unless I try. Hang on, Sunshine." He went in the direction I'd seen the Porsche take.

Chapter Six

Jake drove us to the outskirts of town, trying to find the Porsche and the man with the tie. "How far do you want to go?"

I looked in every possible direction. No sign of the mystery man. "We should turn around. It was a long shot, but thanks for attempting to catch up with the Porsche."

"Don't give up yet. I'll take the back roads on our way to the bakery. We could get lucky." Jake signaled then turned onto a side street.

"I hope Sophie's not too busy. She said a man wearing a tie was in the store yesterday. It could be the same guy as Tess's library man." I wanted to find out more about the stranger. If Sophie was busy, my questions would have to wait.

Jake cut his gaze toward me. "Are you insinuating men in Lutz don't wear ties?"

"Um, not really." My face warmed.

"I'm messing with you. Sophie's fellow may have been the only man wearing a tie, on the Fourth of July. It's too blasted hot for that nonsense."

"Plus, it's not a work day. Why would he wear a tie on a holiday?" I adjusted the air vent so the cool air blew directly on me.

Jake merged onto the square and parked near the bakery. There were no distractions this time, and we entered Sophie's business.

My best friend looked up and smiled. "Hi, guys. Are you here for lunch? Today's special is chicken salad, fresh fruit, potato salad, and crackers with olive spread."

My stomach growled at the clean yeasty smell. "I'd like that to go, please."

Jake said, "Make that two specials."

"Emma, what's going on?" Sophie propped a fist on her hip. "You two look suspicious."

"Brace yourself." Was telling someone about death like removing a bandage? I'd break the news quickly. "Tess Carranza has been murdered."

Sophie's mouth fell open, and then she raised her forefinger. "Wait."

A lump formed in my throat.

Sophie looked toward the back of the bakery. "Katie, I need you to take over up here. We need two specials to go."

"Yes, ma'am." Katie appeared.

I handed her my credit card, before Jake and I followed Sophie to her little office. The space was cluttered with German cookbooks, recipe files, and stacks of paperwork.

Sophie crossed her arms. "I can't believe this. We were with Tess last night, and she seemed fine."

"I know, but she was worried about something."

Jake said, "Or someone."

I nodded. "That's true. Sophie, what do you know about the man who wore a tie yesterday?"

She tilted her head and frowned. "Not a whole lot. He said he's in town for business and forgot about the holiday. He mentioned that the courthouse was closed, and so was the library."

Interesting those were the places he was focused on. "What else? What does he look like?"

Sophie pulled the band out of her hair and rubbed her temples. Her face was splotchy, but she wasn't crying. "The stranger isn't as tall as Jake. His hair is dark and curly like that tall actor who played an elf in a Christmas movie."

"Will Ferrell." I smiled at her.

"Yes. The man from yesterday doesn't have hair that curly." She sank into her desk chair, and her lower lip trembled. "Do you think he's involved in Tess's death?"

"I don't know, but he's a stranger. Not that I mistrust tourists, but Tess wanted to discuss a stranger with me. It could be the same person."

Sophie reached for a tissue. "I know she wasn't a warm and fuzzy person, but people might say the same for me. I blame it on the language barrier. I try hard to understand what my customers are saying, and I want to get their order correct."

"You're nothing like Tess. She never got over her best friend's death." I reached over and patted her hand.

"Rhonda Jones. Many times, I heard Tess complain that Rhonda's killer was never caught. She blamed the husband. Nick Jones. Is it possible he killed Tess?" She pulled another tissue from the box and blew her nose.

"Anything is possible. Do you feel safe?"

"Yes, I will be okay. Katie is here with me." She rubbed her temples again. "There's so much sadness in the world. How can Tess be gone?"

I shook my head. Even though I'd found her body, it was still hard to process.

Jake said, "If the stranger returns, call us or the police."

Katie knocked on the door. "Your orders are ready. Sophie, I'm getting backed up."

Sophie stood and pulled her hair back. "Time for me to return to work."

I hugged my friend. "Please, call if you don't want to be alone."

"It might be time for me to get a cat. You be safe too, my friend."

"A cat? I hope you mean to provide company and not to protect you. Cowboy is very aware of who's good and who's bad. It's uncanny. Maybe cats can sense character, too. But I can't imagine how much protection one will provide." We left the cozy office. On the way out, we grabbed our lunches and my credit card and walked around the square to Anytime Coffee House.

Brett glanced our way and nodded when we entered, but he was waiting on a customer.

Jake pointed to the back. "Would you save that table for us? I need to run to my apartment to grab something."

"Go, ahead. If Brett has a lull in customers, what can I order for you to drink?" I tended to order the same thing, but Jake often changed it up.

"Sweet tea. I won't be long." Jake's apartment over Paige's Turn Bookshop was just around the corner from the coffee shop.

I sat at a table and looked at my phone. Tess had mentioned land rights. Or was it a land grant? Definitely something to do with land.

Brett appeared with two glasses. "On the house for two of my favorite people. Iced green tea for you, and sweet tea for my man, Jake. Where'd he go?"

"He needed to get something from his apartment. How is Ms. Maebell?"

"She's pretty shook about Tess's murder. She's known murder victims before, but she was with Tess yesterday, and they were supposed to meet this morning." He sat across from me. "But you know all that. Did you notice the paramedics who stood back and talked?"

"Instead of helping Tess? Yeah, but I thought maybe because she was dead and there was no need for life-saving actions." I took a deep breath. "What did Tess tell your aunt yesterday?"

"Not much."

"What did Tess say was the reason for the meeting?"

"Money." He drummed his fingers on the table. "Money and land, but Aunt Maebell doesn't own a lot of property. She has a little house on a small piece of land. It's closer to Houston than it is to Lutz. Years ago, our family lived in that area. Like all the cousins, aunties, and uncles. Most have left the area to find jobs in the big cities. I'm a perfect example. I live and work in Lutz."

"That must have been so cool. Was the community a compound?"

"Naw. At least I don't think so. It seemed like a neighborhood. All of us kids waited for the bus together at the end of the road." He stood. "I should get back to work, but we'll work out a time for you to chat with my aunt." He walked away.

Jake entered the coffee shop and stopped to speak to Brett. They had a brief conversation, and then Jake joined me, carrying a slim brown paper bag.

Had he paused to buy a book from Paige? "What's that?"

"A new sketchbook for you. It seems like you do your best thinking when you can write everything out and draw your little pictures." He handed it to me.

"Oh, thank you." I ran my hand over the cover. "I've drawn so many garden plans and flowers over the years, and now these pads have become useful in solving murders."

He sat down and took a drink of tea. "What's the first thing you plan to do?"

"Eat lunch." I passed one of the lunch containers to him. "After we finish, I need to consider suspects."

Jake opened the flaps on his cardboard takeout box. "Thanks for the grub. I'll pay next time."

"You're welcome, but you better not let Sophie hear you refer to her food as grub." Even though Jake was my boyfriend, I didn't expect him to pay for all my meals. We were equals in our relationship. "Let's discuss something fun."

"Such as?" He forked up a bite of watermelon.

"Your new business. Did you stay up all night coming up with ideas? Are you ready to share your business plan with me?" My face grew warm. "Um, not that you have to tell me what you're thinking."

"Of course I'll share. As a matter of fact, I'm working on goals. Celia is creating a website for me, and I've already gotten a few testimonials."

"Let me guess. The Nelle sisters?" He was so kind to the senior citizens, and they adored Jake.

He chuckled. "Well, I did work for all of them, when they moved to Lutz Village Retirement Community. Plus, I fixed some issues on the house they sold to Daniel Moore. He gave me a recommendation also."

I tapped his arm. "It's good to know somebody besides a woman with a crush on you will leave nice reviews."

"Aw, now. Ms. Ruby does not have a crush—"

I laughed. "You immediately knew who I meant."

He shook his head. "Just eat your lunch and quit picking on me."

It felt good to have a normal moment. I forked up a bite of potato salad, and we ate in silence.

At last, Jake said, "I need to go to a house in the country and draw up an estimate for a primary suite renovation. Do you want to ride along?"

"I probably need to let Cowboy out and pull weeds. Why don't you come over when you're free? I should have a list of suspects by then."

"No doubt you will, and I can't wait to see it."

Chapter Seven

I t hit me as soon as I got home. Tess's good friend, Paula Jones, might not know about the murder. I took Cowboy to the backyard and called Paula. She'd been out of town, visiting family, but I knew she'd intended to return to Lutz today.

"Hello, Emma?" Paula's voice was light.

"Yes. Are you home yet?"

"I'm almost there. I was so sad to miss book club, but Tess texted me the title of our next mystery. I'll swing by the bookstore and pick up a copy. Why'd you want to know if I'm home?" She sounded so happy. "Would you like me to lead our next discussion?"

Sadness punched me in the gut, and I sat in one of my Adirondack chairs. She shouldn't hear this news while driving. "Paula, can you stop by my house? I need to tell you something."

"You sound serious. Is something wrong?" The pitch of her voice dropped.

"Yes, but I'd rather tell you when you get here."

"Ugh, that means this is going to be bad. Can you give me a hint?"

"It is bad, and you shouldn't hear this while you're driving."

"I'll be there soon." The line went dead.

Tears flowed down my face, and I swiped at them. Poor, Tess. She might not have been warm and fuzzy, but she was passionate about some topics. We'd bonded and become good friends over our love of reading, especially mysteries. At book club, we discovered that we both had a deep sense of justice.

Cowboy moseyed over to me and rested his chin on my lap.

"Let's go inside and get you some water." July in Lutz, Texas, was scorching hot. "We both probably need to hydrate."

I led my dog to the kitchen and refilled his water bowl. After I drank a glass of water, I rinsed my face and freshened my lipstick.

The doorbell rang, and Cowboy barked.

I dreaded facing Paula, but I'd been the one to invite her over. She needed to hear about Tess from a friend. So, I placed one foot in front of the other and went to answer the door.

Paula wore a white T-shirt and jeans. "Emma, what's going on?"

"Come in, and have a seat." I pointed to the couch in my gathering room and closed the door.

My dog entered the room and lay on the floor beside Paula.

I sat next to her and reached for her hand. "There's no easy way to say this."

"Emma, you're killing me. Just spit it out."

I took a deep breath. "Tess is dead."

"No!" Paula screamed. "Nick finally got to her."

Cowboy jumped up and turned in a circle. He came to me, and I rubbed his head. "Paula, we don't know that he did it."

"Who else would it be?" She sobbed.

I grabbed a box of tissues from a side table and passed it to her. "I don't know. Why would Nick do this now?"

Paula's chin dropped to her chest. She wrapped her arms around her midsection and cried.

It seemed too soon for words of comfort. Anything I said would be irritating at this point. Shock and grief were probably competing for her primary emotion. I rubbed her shoulder.

Cowboy cocked his head and watched us. His tail swayed back and forth in a slow, rhythmic motion.

At last, the tears abated, and Paula adjusted her thick, messy bun. When she stood, Cowboy backed away.

"I have to go." Paula turned toward the door.

"You shouldn't leave when you're so upset. Please, stay. We can talk, or just sit together."

"There's no time." She turned and placed her hands on my shoulders. "I'm leaving Lutz."

"Why?" Her reaction seemed drastic.

"I'm probably next on Nick's hit list." Her face reddened.

I shivered. "Paula, we can't always assume he's the killer. I know he's scary. I've seen his mean streak, but Tess was concerned about other things. We were supposed to meet this morning."

"Oh, about the man buying up land?" She crossed her arms.

"I think so. What else do you know about him?"

"Tess was going to tell me more after my trip. There was something about land grants and maybe inheritance laws. I can't think about it right now. There's so much to do if I'm going to escape before Nick realizes I'm back in town."

"How can I help?" She'd lost her best friend, and she needed somebody. "I'm here for you, Paula."

"Will you take care of my indoor plants until Nick is arrested? Once it's safe, I can return. Until then, I'm going to hide."

"Of course, I'll take care of your plants." It seemed like such a lame request. "I'll follow you home. Do you plan to fly or drive somewhere?"

She shook her head. "I don't know, but I'll figure out my best option."

"Give me five minutes. I need to get Cowboy settled. Can you wait that long?" I didn't want her to enter her house alone, in case Nick was hiding there with evil intentions. Also, she might need a ride to the airport.

"Okay. I probably should give my family a call. In case Nick has discovered where they are, I need to warn them." She sat on the couch and pulled out her phone.

"Come, Cowboy." I led him to the kitchen and let him out in the yard. Abby was home for the summer, so she could care for the puppy, if I got home late. Despite his size, he was young.

I poured water into a travel mug and put a backup phone charger in my purse, because I wasn't sure exactly what Paula would decide. It could be hours before I returned home.

Cowboy whined at the door, and I let him inside. "Good boy. Here's a treat."

He entered his crate and turned for his dog biscuit. I fastened the door. "You be good for Abby. You hear?"

He gave a happy bark, and I rejoined Paula.

Was this smart? Was I putting myself in danger?

Maybe. I sent a text to Abby, Jake, and Sophie. I'd been in a few scrapes the past year. They could find my location by tracking my phone. Finally, I said, "Paula, I'm ready."

"Thanks. Let's go."

Chapter Eight

I stood in Paula's small kitchen and watered her violets, a spider plant, and a struggling prayer plant. They all needed to be fed. It'd be a shame for them to die, like Tess had. So, I added a few drops of food to the water.

"Hey, Paula. Do you have a key to Tess's house?"

"Yes." She grabbed papers from a drawer and placed them on the clean granite counter. Not a crumb in sight. "She has a key to my place, too. In case of emergencies, we wanted to make it easy to help each other. Only, she was murdered before I could help. I wasn't even in town." Her face turned splotchy, but she stopped herself from crying.

I rubbed Paula's shoulder. "Would you mind giving the key to me?"

She paused from opening an envelope marked important. "Emma, I know you've helped with past murder cases, but Nick is dangerous."

"I'll be careful, but there might be a clue in her house. If I have a key, Chief Young won't be able to arrest me for breaking into Tess's house, if he catches me."

"I'm not sure if that's right, so stay alert." She returned to the envelope. "But don't ever forget it's risky to cross Nick. If you investigate, even if there's a wild chance that he's innocent, he'll be furious."

In the past, I'd seen Nick's ugly side. He was one scary man. I shivered. "I'll use caution. Can I have a key to your place, too? I'll come back later and care for your plants. If you're gone for long, I'll take them home with me until you get back."

"I won't return until Nick is put in prison."

43

Goodness. She was like a dog with a bone. "Right. But suppose he's innocent? Who would be your next suspect?"

She removed two items from the envelope and placed them in an empty wallet. It looked like a driver's license and a credit card.

"Don't you always carry your license with you? I'd be afraid to drive without mine."

Her eyes widened. "Shh. Um, this is a backup. Yeah. You asked me about other suspects. What do you think about the new assistant librarian? She's meaner than some high school girls I deal with in the school office."

"That's some accusation. Do you think she's mean enough to commit murder?"

"It depends on the motive, and I don't have a clue about why she'd do it." She removed her keychain and stared at it like in a trance. "Nick might follow me."

"Do you need your car? If you want to fly or take a bus, I'll drive you to the airport or bus station. That way if Nick comes here, he'll think you're home."

She almost smiled, then her shoulders slumped. "It won't work. What if one of my neighbors sees me leave with you?"

"Good point. Why don't we both drive to the vintage sale? It won't be suspicious for you to transfer your suitcase into my truck. Somebody might think I bought it." I felt paranoid creating this plan, but Paula was scared. I respected her sense of caution. "You can go back to the entrance, I'll wait a few minutes, then pick you up. When you're in my truck, duck down, and nobody will spot me driving away with you. After we get out of town, you can ride normally. So, you need to decide where you want to go."

"Dallas Fort Worth International Airport. It'll be easier to get lost there." She removed a key and handed it to me. "This goes to Tess's front door. I need the others to drive to the market."

I palmed the silver key. "Can I gather some snacks for you while you pack?"

"Sure. I'll hurry."

There was no pantry, but I opened cabinets until I found one with granola bars. I filled a zipper plastic bag with granola bars, bags of peanuts, and crackers. Stashed behind healthy options was a stack of candy bars. I added them in case they'd comfort Paula until she got settled.

"I'm ready." She rolled a big suitcase with a smaller bag attached to it. In her other hand, she gripped a floppy hat and big black sunglasses.

"Great. How about letting me take your small bag and hat? That way we'll only transfer the big suitcase."

"Okay." She opened the refrigerator. "Good thing I've been out of town. It won't take long to empty this."

"I'll do it later. We need to get on the road." Her anxiety fed mine.

"Thanks." She grabbed two water bottles and passed one to me. "For the road."

"Paula, do you need money?" I held the bottle tight.

She shook her head. "I've been preparing for this day for years. My marriage to Nick scarred me for life. In the back of my mind, I always believed I might have to run. There are arrangements in place for such an event, and my daughter is hidden and well cared for."

I sighed. There was so much hurt and fear in the world. Paula had kept her pregnancy and the birth of her daughter from Nick. All this happened before I met Paula, and it wasn't my job to judge her. I'd do my best to protect them. "I'll see you there."

On the drive over, I left new messages with Abby and Sophie. Then I called Jake.

"Hey, Sunshine. Where are you?"

"Jake, this is top secret. I'm helping Paula leave town. She's worried Nick murdered Tess, and she's scared he'll come for her next."

"Did she say why?"

"I'll tell you more later, but I wanted you to know that I'm taking her to Dallas."

"Do you want me to come with you?"

"No, I can handle it. Plus, Paula is skittish." I gripped the steering wheel with both hands.

"Will you come back home tonight?"

"That's my goal. Why don't I call you when I head this way?"

"That's a good idea. Are you concerned about Abby being home alone?"

How had he guessed? "Normally, I wouldn't give it a second thought."

"But you never know with Nick. I get it." He paused, and I heard a Brooks & Dunn song playing in the background. "I'll bring Celia, in case your daughter isn't comfortable being alone with me."

His kindness touched my heart. "You're a nice man, Jake Hunter."

Jake chuckled. "I tend to exercise an abundance of caution, especially with young women."

"Thanks. I'll talk to you later."

"Be safe."

"Always." I signaled to turn. Was it safe to help Paula escape? Probably. It was hard to believe Nick would murder Tess after all these years. Yes, she'd gathered evidence to prove Nick murdered his first wife, Rhonda. For some reason, she could never convince the police.

Maybe on the drive to Dallas, Paula could help me understand.

Chapter Nine

"Are you sure we haven't been followed?" One of Paula's hands gripped the door, and the other clenched her phone.

"I'm not a spy, but it doesn't seem like anybody followed us." I glanced in all three of my truck's mirrors.

"Good. Emma, I've trusted you this far, can I trust you with one more thing?"

"Of course."

"I'd like you to pull into the next gas station. I want to fill up your truck and buy a prepaid phone."

"There's one up ahead." I exited off the interstate and drove to a busy convenience store with gas. "I can pay for my own gas, and I know from true crime shows there are probably cameras by the pumps. Let me drop you at the door. I'll park by the air pump."

"Thanks."

I pulled close to the door, and Paula hopped out, wearing her floppy hat and dark sunglasses.

Instead of getting gas, I sat in my truck waiting for Paula. I watched the other vehicles. No sign of Nick's obvious work truck, but could he have another car? Nobody looked familiar. Good.

Paula stepped out of the store, and looked my way. She zigged and zagged her way through the vehicles stopped for gas and hopped into Miss Daisy. "One more favor."

"Name it."

"When we reach the airport, I'd prefer being dropped off at the car rental

47

area."

"That should be easy enough to do." I was dying to ask why, but she'd tell me if she wanted. Maybe she didn't want me to see which shuttle she took. I wouldn't know for sure which airlines she was using. Unless, she planned to rent a car to drive herself to a new location.

"Also, please let my phone die and leave it at the house."

"Okay." I fiddled with her phone but wasn't able to remove the battery without a tiny screwdriver. So, I shut it off. "Are you still good with Jake driving your SUV? We can park it at your place and go into your house. We'll leave with your flowers. If anyone asks, I'll say you asked me to help make your plants healthy."

Paula smiled. "Emma, will you work with my plants to make them healthier?"

I glanced at her. Was she losing it? "Yes."

"Okay, you won't have to lie if anybody asks. As far as involving Jake, please make sure he knows my leaving is top secret. The longer it takes Nick to discover I hightailed it out of town, the longer I'll be safe."

"No problem. In the Marines, he worked some secret missions. He knows how to keep his mouth closed. In fact, we'll both be careful." I concentrated on traffic and following the signs to car rentals.

Paula looked through her purse and removed her pink wallet. "Do you have a safety deposit box or a good hiding place?"

My secret pantry would work in most cases, but if Nick broke into my home, would he figure it out? "Maybe."

"I need you to hide my license and credit cards. Like I said, running for my life was always a possibility. I have paperwork for a fake identity." Her hand shook.

"Put your wallet in my glove compartment. It'll be safe with me." At last, I arrived in the parking lot for rental cars. It didn't feel right to drop her here. "Are you sure—"

"Shh. If you're questioned about where I am, you don't know how I'm getting away. Train, plane, bus, or rental car. Emma, I truly appreciate everything you're doing." She stashed the wallet.

I found an empty spot and parked. "If Nick is the killer, why do you think he attacked Tess today?"

"I don't know. I best get a move on, though."

I reached for my door handle, intending to help her with the luggage.

Paula grabbed my arm. "Stay in the truck. I can get my stuff."

"How will you know when it's safe to come home?"

"I'll follow the investigation on social media. When I think it's okay, I'll call you." She leaned over and gave me an awkward hug. "Thanks again."

"Be safe, Paula."

She nodded, then hopped out of the truck. Soon, she had her luggage and was crossing the parking lot.

I began the trek home with a heavy heart.

In the past, Paula had asked for my help with a murder investigation. This time, I wanted to catch the killer so she'd feel safe to come back to Lutz.

I didn't believe Nick was guilty, but I wouldn't rule him out yet. He and the well-dressed stranger were the top two suspects on my list.

Chapter Ten

J ake and I stood in Paula's kitchen, gathering indoor plants to take to my house. I looked around the small home to make sure I'd gathered all of them. "I think we're good."

Jake had done everything I asked while keeping his opinion to himself.

"What's going through your mind, Jake Hunter?" My attempt at a light tone fell flat.

Jake wore a pair of gardening gloves and raised his hands. "I'm concerned you and Paula didn't consider all the repercussions of her vanishing. Suppose the police investigate Paula's disappearance. They won't find my fingerprints, but yours are all over the place."

"Hmm, I see your point. If anyone questions why I'm here, it's to take care of her sickly plants." I pointed to one with yellow leaves. "See? And her violets haven't bloomed in months."

Jake sighed. "Okay, Sunshine. Are you ready to go?"

"Yes." I handed two potted plants to Jake and placed the others in a baking dish and carried them. "Thank you for helping me tonight."

"Anything for you, Emma."

I drove us to my home. Jake's SUV was the only vehicle by the house. Abby's car had died for the final time, and she was committed to making enough money this summer to buy a new vehicle. For now, it was easy enough to share my truck.

With Paula out of town, I'd give her hours working with me at the farmers' market to my daughter. It wouldn't be a lot, but it'd help. I pulled into the driveway and parked. "It looks like the others left."

"Yeah." He sighed. "You must be exhausted. I'll help you take these inside and shove off so you can go to bed."

I slumped against my seat and faced Jake. "It's hard to believe Tess was murdered this morning. So much has happened."

His cowlick pushed a lock of hair onto his forehead. "It just goes to show we're all breathing on God's time. We need to talk, but it's late. How about breakfast?"

"I'd love that. Do you want to come over here?"

"Sure, but I'll bring breakfast with me." He leaned forward and gave me a gentle kiss.

The front porch lights came on. "Mom?"

"Oh, dear. I'm in trouble now." I hopped out of the truck. "Abby, come help us carry these into the house."

Abby jogged over barefooted. "You bought more flowers?"

"No, I'm taking care of them for a friend. She thinks they're sick." I handed her the two planters Jake had carried earlier. He'd already picked up the rest of the flowers and handed them to me. "I'll see you in the morning."

"Goodnight, Jake." I kissed his cheek.

Abby said, "Jake, I appreciate you all hanging out with me earlier."

"Give a shout anytime you need me." Jake mock-saluted her and ambled over to his Sequoia.

Once we entered the house, I locked the door and set the security system. "Where's Cowboy?"

"I think we wore him out. He's sleeping in my room." She set her pots on the kitchen counter, and I placed the others beside hers.

"Oh, you're going to spoil him. He always seemed content to sleep in his crate before you came home for the summer."

She shrugged. "Maybe I needed him to sleep with me. Mom, please tell me you are not.going to investigate Tess Carranza's murder."

"I found the body."

"I'm aware. Everybody in town is talking about it." Abby took my hand and led me to the gathering room. "Sit."

"Okay." I gulped. First, she'd called me out for sitting in the driveway with

Jake, and it was late. I braced for whatever she was about to share.

Abby sat on the next cushion and faced me. "Mom, you can't go around trying to solve murders. To be fair, you have solved two murders, but you could've died. Both times!" Her voice squeaked.

"Calm down. It's nothing to worry about."

"If you die, I'll be an orphan. Even if I had a father and siblings, I wouldn't want you to investigate." She squeezed my cold hands with her warm ones.

"Honey, I'll consider your concerns. However, I'm not making a promise to walk away. There are two men I want to investigate as suspects. I'll do as much as possible online to begin my process. On a happy note, Paula can't help me at the farmers' market for a while. Do you want to pick up her hours?"

"Does she only work on Saturdays?"

"For me? Yeah, pretty much. You'd have those hours plus the time as my bookkeeper and business manager."

"Sophie asked if I'd like to help her bake early in the mornings. If I'm careful with my time, I can do all three jobs and be that much closer to buying a good used vehicle."

Cowboy entered the room and barked.

I laughed. "He's probably not happy that we're disturbing his beauty sleep. Let's go to bed."

Abby hugged me. "Goodnight, Mom. I love you."

"I love you, too, honey. Try not to worry."

We went to our bedrooms, and my dog followed Abby.

Oh, well. Abby really had a way with dogs, and for the first time in her life, I'd rescued a puppy. She deserved all the love and devotion Cowboy lavished on her.

I brushed my teeth and reflected on the day.

Oh. I needed to hide Paula's license and stuff. I spit and rinsed before gathering the items from my purse. I entered my closet and stuck her license and credit cards in a shoebox with strappy sandals I hardly ever wore. That should do it.

At last, I fell into bed. Before I could even plot out my investigation, sleep overtook me.

Chapter Eleven

I sat on the shady back patio with Jake. We'd finished breakfast sandwiches from Sophie's Bakery and drank our coffee from Anytime Coffee House. "This is the best of both worlds."

He winked at me. "I aim to impress."

When I first me Jake, he had annoyed me. I even thought of him as a big flirt. Once I learned it was a defense mechanism, I came to respect him. We'd gone from friendship to dating pretty fast, but we were both in our late thirties. Plus, we'd experience some deadly encounters which brought us closer together. "What do you want to discuss?"

"First topic, is about my website. Is it okay for me to ask Abby to look it over? Celia did the hard work, and we'd like to get fresh eyes on it."

"You don't need to ask my permission."

His face reddened. "She's still a teenager. Don't forget, I like to respect boundaries."

He was a protective older brother to Celia, and his good intentions didn't surprise me. "Her birthday is September 1, but you're right. She'll still be in her teens. I appreciate you coming to me first. I'm sure she'll be happy to look at it." I held the travel cup of coffee. "What did you decide to name your business?"

"I'm still working on it, and I'm open to suggestions."

"I'll think about it."

"Thanks. The second thing I'd like to discuss is us."

My face warmed. "Us?"

"Yeah. We've been dating a couple months. How do you think we're doing?" His earnest expression tore my heartstrings.

"Jake, you know my history with men. My husband hid a drug habit from me, and he died young. You're the first man I've dated in seventeen years. Seventeen years. It seems like we're doing fine, but I could be wrong. What do you think?"

His frown disappeared. "I haven't had a good history with the opposite sex either, but I think we're on solid ground. However, I'm aware I don't take you out to fancy dinners, plays, trips—"

"Hold up there, partner. We went to a country music festival in June. We went water skiing with your Marine friends. We've gone to the batting cages and watched local baseball games. You've gone with me to antique sales around here. I feel like we've done a lot, including solving two murders. It doesn't get much more exciting than that." My mouth grew dry. "Are you bored?"

"Nah, but I'm a guy." He shrugged.

"Where is all this coming from?"

He stretched out his long legs and crossed them at the ankles. "Celia got into my head. She was talking about all the romantic stuff Brett does for her, and I realized you're probably disappointed."

I set my cup on the table and walked over to Jake.

He stood and gazed into my eyes.

I cupped his face in my hands. On tiptoes, I kissed him. When the kiss ended, I smiled. "Jake, I'm head over flip-flops for you. You do nice things for me every day. Breakfast is a perfect example. You also gave me a sketch pad so I could take notes on Tess's murder. You show how much you care in many ways, and I'm appreciative."

"One more of your sweet kisses might convince me." He pulled me close, and we kissed again.

My knees grew weak.

Cowboy barked, and the back door slammed.

Jake and I stepped away from each other and turned toward the house.

Abby said, "How were the peach muffins? I made them myself."

"Delicious. I'm impressed Sophie trusted you with baking. I imagined you'd be washing dishes."

She put on sunglasses. "Trust me, I washed plenty. In the past, Sophie taught me how to bake when you worked late. She claims I'm much better than you."

I laughed. "Hey, you didn't starve growing up, but she's probably right. Jake has a question for you."

Jake said, "The muffins were amazing. I'd like to pay you to look over my website. Celia created it, but she'd like somebody different look at it and see if she missed anything. Links and what have you. Things people your age know to look for."

"I'd love to. When's a good time?"

"Celia's at work now, and I know she wants to hear your thoughts. Are you free this evening?"

"Yes, but it needs to be early. I've got a feeling that my bedtime is going to be like a toddler this summer if I hope to survive early mornings with Sophia."

"I understand. We'll call you first."

"Thanks, Jake. Mom, I'll be working in your office if you need me."

Cowboy barked and followed Abby into the house.

I shook my head. "It'd be ridiculous to feel jealous that my dog likes her better than me, right?"

"You can't help how you feel, but Abby will go back to school in a few weeks."

"Yeah, and then the dog and I will both be sad. Oh, well. Do you have any suggestions on murder suspects?"

"I think the mystery man is the first person we should check out."

"I agree, but we need to figure out his name."

Jake looked at his watch. "Do you have time to run by the library now? I have three appointments this afternoon, but my morning is free."

I could always adjust my garden schedule. "Give me a minute to freshen up."

In less than ten minutes, I'd brushed my teeth, fixed my hair, and grabbed the new sketch pad Jake had given me.

CHAPTER ELEVEN

It was time to track down and question Tess's mysterious man at the library.

Chapter Twelve

In the library parking lot, I paused at the sight of the expensive sports car. "Jake. There's the Porsche."

He stopped and looked in the direction I pointed. "Same as the one you saw our suspect drive?"

"Definitely." I walked to the shady spot. There was no sign of the driver, but I took pictures of the car and the front license plate. My heart beat fast enough for me to be aware of it. I took a deep breath and tried to calm myself.

"You okay?" Jake stood with his feet shoulder-length apart and removed his Oakley sunglasses.

"For the most part. Let's see if we can find the driver."

Jake took my hand in his, and we walked into the library.

Laurel, the assistant director, helped an older couple with their books at the self-checkout station. She glanced at us and nodded.

I shot her a casual wave.

Jake whispered in my ear, "Our target is in the reference section."

I turned to look. Sure enough a man, wearing a dress shirt and tie, sat at a table. Books lay beside him, and he typed on a laptop.

"Shall we approach him together?" I looked from the stranger to Jake.

"No. If you go over by yourself, he won't be as suspicious as if we both show up. I'll observe from the table with bestsellers. Give me a signal if you need backup, or scream. Yeah, a scream always works." He winked.

"That should be effective. Okay, here goes." I took slow steps, trying to look casual.

The man never looked up from his task.

I stopped beside his table. "Excuse me."

His eyes darted to me, back to his computer, then to me again. "Yes?"

"Have we met before? You look very familiar. I'm Emma Justice." The man had wavy, dark hair with a few gray strands on the sides. His teeth were vividly white and straight. His blue eyes probably caused some women to swoon, but not me. I was a goner for Jake.

The stranger gave me a slow, lazy smile. "I'm sure I'd remember if we'd met. You're too pretty to forget."

Gag. What a line, especially for a married man. "Maybe it was at the farmers' market?"

"Never been. I'm just visiting Lutz for a few days."

I sat across from him. "Sophie's Bakery. That's probably where we crossed paths."

One side of his mouth crooked upward. "I've been there, but I don't believe you were there at the same time."

I scratched my head. "It's going to drive me crazy until I figure it out. What's your name? Maybe that'll ring a bell."

"Mason Brown, but again, I don't believe we've met." His polite tone turned suspicious, and he frowned.

I drummed my fingers on the table. "Mason Brown, you might be right. Your name doesn't ring a bell, but I'm curious. Most people come to Lutz for our antique and vintage festivals. You're working in our library. Do you mind sharing why you're in town?"

He closed the laptop and leaned forward, tapping his pointer finger on the table with authority. "I'm an attorney, Ms. Justice. I'm doing research for an upcoming case, and I charge my client by the hour. The longer we talk, the more it's going to cost my client. He's not going to be happy about that, so if you don't mind—"

"I'm curious what kind of information our little library has that you can't find online." I raised my eyebrows, hoping I looked more innocent than I felt.

"You'd be amazed. Again, I don't mean to be rude, but I must focus."

If you must announce you don't want to be rude, you most definitely are rude. Of course, I wasn't acting polite either. "I'm sorry for disturbing you. Have a nice day, Mr. Brown."

"You can call me Mason." He kept his focus on me until I walked away from the table.

With my back to the man, I motioned to Jake to stay. Once outside in the sticky humidity, I sent a text to Jake. **See what he does next. I'll wait by your SUV.**

While I stood beside the white Sequoia, I did a search for Mason Brown on my phone. I hopped from one search engine to the next and added that he lived in Texas. At last, I found something.

According to the internet, he was forty-five years old, married, no children, and worked for a small law firm outside of Houston. He lived in a new development in the suburbs of Houston. Next, I looked up the area where he resided. Wow, there was everything a person could need without getting into their car. There was even an urgent health clinic.

My phone vibrated with a text from Jake. **Start walking home. He's pacing in the foyer and it looks like he spotted you.**

Yikes.

I'm going. I took the long way home to avoid being easily seen from the library, in case Mason was still in the foyer area.

Jake pulled into my driveway behind Miss Daisy as I climbed the steps to the porch. I was sweaty, and I waited in the shade.

Jake stepped out of his SUV and joined me. "The guy made a call as soon as you left. He left his belongings on the table, so he wasn't paranoid about his stuff getting stolen. He talked to somebody like you would a boss. I think you may have shook him up."

"Good. Did you hear any of the conversation?"

"I didn't want to look suspicious, so I checked out a book by a local author. Then I pretended to read the bulletin board about July events. I gotta admit I'm impressed by all the activities."

"I'm impressed you have a library card."

He shrugged. "My sister isn't pushy about much, but she insisted I get a library card when I moved to Lutz. When I was overseas, she sent paperback books and told me to share with the others when I finished."

"It makes sense she wants you to connect with the library." Celia had been a librarian when she lived in Waco. These days, she worked at Paige's Turn Bookstore, mostly so she could be near Brett. "But you're killing me. Did you hear any of Mason's conversation?"

"You know, he mentioned land, money, and time. Like maybe they've got a deadline. It was hard to distinguish much of the conversation. He was pacing and talking on the phone until he looked outside. He came to a standstill and stared toward the parking lot. I was afraid he saw you. That's why I wanted you to get away."

"Thanks for having my back." I squeezed his hand. "Instead of going inside, I think it's time to talk to Brett about Ms. Maebell. Do you want to join me?"

He patted his chest. "Yes, but no more coffee for me this morning. I'm not sure my heart can take any more caffeine right now."

"There's always decaf, or caffeine-free tea options." I was only teasing him because he'd worked at the coffee shop when Brett had surgery earlier in the year.

"That's good to know, Sunshine, and if you need advice about your purty flowers you can ask me." He winked.

I laughed. "Touché."

"Shall we walk, or would you like me to drive?"

The day was already steamy, and I wore one of my newest blouses. "Let's drive."

On the short drive, I jotted down a few notes. "I hope Brett isn't swamped."

"Don't worry. I can fill in and let you ask your questions."

"Thanks. Is there anything you want me to include?"

"Nothing comes to mind right now, but I'll think on it. There seem to be a lot of black vehicles in town today. It's impossible to find a parking space. Good thing you enjoy walking places." Jake parked on a side street.

" This is perfect. We better scoot, because I know you need to work this afternoon."

Chapter Thirteen

A new employee was training at Anytime Coffee House, and I looked around the shop while waiting on Brett.

The bald man who'd been with the paramedics at the library sat at a table in front with a woman who wore a white blouse and black slacks. Their arms were propped on the table and they leaned toward each other. The woman took notes, and the man clenched his mug.

He must have sensed me staring because he turned and met my gaze.

My face warmed, and I spun around and walked to a table in back.

Jake held a chair out for me. "You okay?"

I sat and waited for him to do the same. "Yes. The man in front in the black polo was at the crime scene. He spoke to the paramedics. Do you recognize him?"

Jake looked up, then shook his head. "Never seen him."

Brett joined us at a table in back. His white teeth appeared when he flashed us a smile. "What's up?"

Jake pointed at me. "You're in charge."

I nodded. "Do you know the people sitting at the front?"

Jake said, "They left."

Brett shrugged. "They've been here before. Always pay cash and don't say much to me."

"It's probably nothing." I looked at my friend. "Brett, the man's name from the library is Mason Brown. He's an attorney from around Houston. Have you heard of him?"

"Aunt Maebell received a letter from a law firm, but I don't remember the names. I suspected it was a scam. If it'd been up to me, I would've tossed it."

"But?"

"My aunt likes to keep everything, especially if it looks official. Despite my doubts, it looked legit. Still, something seemed fishy."

"Do you remember what it was about?" I opened my sketch pad and started writing on a fresh sheet.

"It was an offer for some land. Aunt Maebell carries a feminine briefcase whenever she leaves home. It's at my house, and I can ask to see the letter tonight."

Jake said, "Would she give it to Emma?"

"I would promise to return it."

Brett's mouth turned down. "Are you two in a hurry?"

"Maybe." I kept my voice low. "We don't know the motive for Tess's murder. What if it's connected to Mason Brown? What if your aunt is in danger because of Mason?"

His eyes widened. "In that case, I want you to pick up my aunt and her briefcase. Bring her back here, and we'll look at the letter together."

Jake motioned for us to look at him. "Brett, you should get your aunt and bring her back here. She should be more comfortable with you, and I can work with the newbie until you return."

I shook my head. "No, you need to work."

Jake looked at his watch. "Yeah, but this is important. As soon as Brett returns with Ms. Maebell, I'll take off. What do y'all think?"

Brett pulled out his keys. "Emma's right. It will be less stressful on my aunt if I pick her up. She likes you and all that, but she's more comfortable with me."

Jake said, "Man, I get it. You two are tight."

I looked at them. "It sounds like we've got a plan. I'll see if I can find out more about Mason."

"Help yourself to the computer in my office. It shouldn't take me too long." Brett spoke to his new employee before leaving.

Jake logged onto the work computer in Brett's office before leaving me alone.

I rubbed my hands together to warm them up and then took a deep dive into Mason Brown.

Thirty minutes later, Ms. Maebell sat beside me in Brett's office. He'd made copies of the original letter from the law firm, and we read over it. The legal jargon was over my head. In fact, the main reason Abby was my business manager for the summer was so I could enjoy the flower farm part of my business. She'd handle the website, bookkeeping, and other things I didn't like until she returned to Baylor for the fall semester.

Ms. Maebell raised the original letter in her wrinkled hand. "It's a good thing I kept this. Don't you know, Brett teases me for keeping so much junk?"

I smiled at the elderly Black woman. "It's often hard to know what to keep and what to toss."

Brett said, "I'm gonna run to the courthouse, but I'll be back directly."

His aunt looked at me. "He treats me good, and I shouldn't pick on him. Brett says you believe this attorney might be involved in the librarian's death."

"I think it's possible. I wish we'd talked with Tess on Monday, instead of waiting for Tuesday morning. Have you remembered anything else Tess said that could be a clue to her death?"

Ms. Maebell crossed her legs. She wore a black top, black slacks, and a pink scarf. Her lipstick almost matched the scarf. She clutched her purse with both hands. "Tess was worried that a man wanted to take advantage of my money. I don't have a lot, and if somebody steals what little I have, well, then, I might have to live at a homeless shelter. At my age, there probably aren't a lot of jobs for me. My mind is clear, but the heat wears me out. I appreciate that the librarian wanted to help me, but I sure am sorry she lost her life because of whatever she suspected."

"Aw, Ms. Maebell, you have a lot of family who love you, especially Brett. They won't turn their backs on you. Plus, we don't know absolutely that Tess died because of this letter. It's only one possible motive. We need to investigate before looking for another motive." I pointed to the signature on the letter. "Mason Brown did sign this letter."

"Oh, dear." She looked closer at the paper, then held it farther away. "I've put off going to the eye doctor for too long. I see his name now, but I won't meet him by myself."

"I'm not pushing you to see Mr. Brown. Why don't we wait until Brett returns? He may learn something at the courthouse that will be helpful." There was no way I'd push the older lady to do something that made her uncomfortable, no matter how much I wanted to catch the killer.

"Yes. That sounds like a right good idea."

Brett stepped into the office, and I'd never seen him look so angry. "You won't believe what happened at the courthouse."

Ms. Maebell said, "We want to hear, but you best calm down first."

"I'll be right back." He turned on the toe of his tennis shoe and disappeared.

"Whoa, I don't believe I've ever seen him so mad." And I'd seen many moods of my friend. Most of the time, he was upbeat. Today, I didn't want to get sideways with him.

His aunt said, "Give him time to cool off. Tell me, how did you and Brett become such good friends?"

"We've been friends since he moved to Lutz. I worked as a pharmacy tech and had dreams of starting my own business. When he started the coffee shop, I often picked his brain. Plus, I may have been his best customer in the beginning."

"Nothing romantic?" Her eyes sparkled.

"No, ma'am. After my husband died, I was a single mother. I wasn't interested in dating."

"Until you met Jake?" She waggled her eyebrows.

My face grew warm. "Yes. He caught me by surprise."

"I thought there was a spark between you two. I've been called Cupid a time or two."

"Somehow that doesn't surprise me."

We chatted about life and romance to pass the time, but I think we were both anxious to hear what happened to Brett.

Chapter Fourteen

Brett returned to the office, carrying a glass of iced coffee in one hand and lemonade in the other. He handed the lemonade to his aunt, then looked at me. "I need to order more mint from you. The customers like when I add a sprig of mint to their drinks."

"Great. I'll get some to you soon." I jotted a note on my phone and set an alarm to remind myself. Surely, that would help me remember despite the distraction of Tess's murder.

Jake entered the room and handed a glass to me. "Green tea with local honey."

"Thank you."

Brett closed the office door, and we circled our chairs to face each other.

I took a sip of tea and set my glass on the desk. "What happened at the courthouse?"

Brett placed his hands on his thighs and rubbed them against the faded jeans he wore. "When I entered the courthouse, a man bumped me. He didn't apologize. In fact, he glared at me. By the time I found the right office, I'd calmed down."

"What did the man look like?"

"Six feet tall. Dark hair. Not fat but not skinny. Just an average guy. Nothing special about him that I discerned from our encounter."

"Okay, but you came in here mad as a hornet. Did something else happen?" I didn't believe he was still mad from the altercation.

"I asked for information on a parcel of land where Aunt Maebell used to live. I told you it was like a neighborhood—"

Jake said, "You made me think it's more like a compound."

"Yeah. Yeah. Yeah. You told me that before, and I got to thinking. What if the land was a family compound? What if it did belong to my people? Maybe that was the land the letter is referring to."

I took notes. "What happened next?"

Brett crossed his arms. "I asked the government employees about the property. One lady joked that I needed to bring muffins like Tom does if I want to get information."

"Who's that?" I looked at Brett.

"I never got a last name, but the way those women giggled and talked about him, it was enough to make me blush. It sounded like a rooster in the hen house kind of situation. It also made me wonder if the man who bumped me was the mysterious Tom."

"Why?"

"His arrogance." Brett rubbed his thighs again. "It's probably my overactive imagination. Do you all think I need to show up tomorrow with coffee?"

Jake ran a hand over his forehead. "So, they refused to help you?"

"Nah, man. They gave me the run around and sent me to another office. When I went there, the people were polite, but they didn't have the information I need."

I said, "What exactly were you hoping to learn?"

"Why are those men nosing around in our county? Aunt Maebell is not a resident here."

She lifted a finger. "Four counties touch each other right near us."

"Oh, yeah. The kids in the next neighborhood went to a different high school."

"That's right. We thought we were one big community despite the county lines."

I said, "Is it possible they want to buy land in an area that encompasses areas in all four counties?"

Brett scowled. "Who knows? I need to study the map before returning to the courthouse."

Ms. Maebell sat up. "You may have to play the game to get the right information. I'd like to suggest you take coffee and take Jake with you. Coffee is your specialty. And trust me, those women will perk up when two handsome men arrive with coffee."

Brett's eyes widened.

She held up her fingers like a peace sign. "Two handsome men trump one nondescript guy bringing muffins."

Jake said, "I'm game."

Brett stood. "It's worth a try. They open at nine. Can you meet me here a little before nine, and we'll take over coffee?"

Jake rose and patted Brett's shoulder. "I'll be here. Try not to worry."

The men walked out of the office.

Ms. Maebell's eyes sparkled. "Emma, would you be a dear and take me to the library?"

"I don't think Brett will be happy if we go behind his back."

"Leave my nephew to me. Does that mean you've agreed?"

"Only if Brett agrees." I closed my sketch pad.

"Wait right here." She left me alone in Brett's office.

I drank my tea and reviewed my notes.

It sure would be nice to know Tom's last name. It'd make it easier to dig into his background.

"Come along, Emma." Ms. Maebell held up a set of car keys. "Brett agreed, and he said you can drive his car."

I realized climbing up into Miss Daisy might be a challenge for the woman. "Okay. It looks like we're off to chase a new clue."

Chapter Fifteen

The library's parking lot was full of minivans and SUVs. "Would you like me to drop you at the front door?"

Ms. Maebell nodded. "That would be right nice. It'll give me a chance to visit the restroom."

After she walked away, I found a shady parking spot and parked. The sight of a Porsche across the way sent me hurrying to the building. I didn't want Mason Brown to approach Ms. Maebell without me.

Once inside, I spotted Mason sitting at a table with a Black woman. My steps faltered. It was a different woman.

My phone vibrated. It was a text from Jake. **Sorry I didn't say bye. Too much on my mind. Can I take you to dinner?**

Yes. No need to apologize. I added a heart to my message.

"Do you see the lawyer?" Ms. Maebell snuck up on me.

"Yes." I pointed him out. "Is there any possibility you recognize the other woman?"

"I can't decide, but I'll just mosey over and dillydally with books near them. Maybe I can get a better look." She walked away, leaving me to look silly standing by myself.

I went to the bulletin board and read about upcoming events. Jake was right. The library had a lot going on. I glanced toward the reference section.

Oh no.

Brett's aunt was talking to Mason and the other woman.

I hustled over and touched Ms. Maebell's arm. "Hey, there. What's going on?"

Mason did a double-take at my appearance. "Oh, Mrs. Justice, it's nice to see you again."

Chills broke out on my arms. I'd given him my name earlier, but his tone made me uneasy. "Good to see you, Mason."

Ms. Maebell said, "Emma, this nice young man is an attorney. In fact, he recently sent a letter to me."

The other woman stood. "I'm sorry, Mr. Brown, but I'm not interested in selling my land to you."

"Maybe you and I should chat. Mr. Brown wants to buy my land, too."

She looked at Ms. Maebell. "I don't want any part of a scheme to get hustled."

"Sister, you and I might be on the same side." Ms. Maebell loosened her scarf. "Land sakes, it's a scorcher today. Do you mind if we find a private table and compare letters? I'm assuming you got the same letter as I did."

The other woman appeared younger than Brett's aunt. Her expression softened. "There's a table near a back window."

"That sounds mighty fine." Ms. Maebell shuffled away from Mason and me. The other woman matched her pace as they crossed the room.

The attorney crossed his arms. "I don't know what you're up to, Mrs. Justice, but please butt out."

"Okay, but my friend's nephew doesn't want her talking to you unless he's present. Can you tell me what land you want to pay her for? Maybe we can clear up any confusion with a simple conversation."

He sat straighter and shuffled through some papers and maps. "It's a small tract of land south of Lutz."

"Is it in this county?"

His nostrils flared. "I can't say."

"Why do you want to buy it?"

"I have a client who wants to develop a new neighborhood."

"Does the other lady own land in the same area?" I pointed to the lady who'd walked away with Ms. Maebell.

He shook his head. "No. You see, my client specializes in developing land into planned communities. There are many areas he wants to develop.

Planned communities are the future, and it's perfectly legal to buy land and create new places to live."

Something told me there was more to it than he proclaimed. Otherwise, why had Tess been so upset? Her death meant we'd never know her suspicions, but Mason's declaration proved more than one person might have a motive for murdering our librarian. I glanced up and saw Ms. Maebell wave to me. "Have a good rest of your day, Mason." I crossed the room and sat with the two women. "Is it the same letter?"

The other woman smoothed the sheet of paper. "I'm Linda Jefferson. The letter is the same, but I don't own the home."

"What do you mean?"

"My great uncle lived in the home Mr. Brown and his people want to buy. They said because of heirs laws they need to pay me for the property."

"Did you sell to them?"

"Well, yes. Yes, I did." She held her hands together on the table. "I didn't know anything about the land, so it seemed smart to sell it. They promised me lots of money, and I sold my old clunker for a new car. I would've had enough to pay for it, if they hadn't lied. I should've waited. It was a mistake to trust them."

Ms. Maebell patted Linda's arm. "We all make mistakes. Part of being human."

Linda nodded. "I suppose you're right."

I said, "It sounds like you didn't get the money."

Linda looked at me. "No, I didn't. Mr. Brown said we had to pay back taxes. Then it was one thing after another. By the time they paid me, I received less than one hundred dollars."

Her words were like a sucker punch. "I'm so sorry."

"I blame myself."

I blamed Mason for his cruel behavior. I kept my thoughts to myself, and we spent the next few minutes giving Linda a pep talk.

At last, she said, "I'm not the only person who fell for their deceit."

My heart skipped a beat. "Do you personally know any of the others?"

Linda shook her head. "Only Maebell."

"Then how do you know?"

"Mr. Ward and Mr. Brown told me they had worked the same kind of deal with lots of people who didn't know they were property owners." She looked down at her hands. "Although they lied to me about becoming rich. There's a chance they lied about that, too. If only I could go back to the day I first met these rascals. I would've done everything differently."

"I'm so sorry, Ms. Linda." I couldn't think of any comforting words. There was no way I could pay off her vehicle or turn back time. Maybe the best I could do was be her friend.

Chapter Sixteen

When Jake arrived Wednesday evening, I was still getting ready for our date. I slipped on a sleeveless green dress and added a pearl necklace my momma had given me when I graduated from high school. She'd imagined me wearing it to college dances, but I'd never completed college. It hadn't been in the cards for me, and I was okay with that. The choices I'd made in life had led me to this moment, and I wouldn't change a thing.

Adding pearl earrings and a gold bracelet completed my outfit. I checked my hair. For a change, it didn't frizz. A swipe of lipstick, and I was ready.

Abby was downstairs talking to Jake. No doubt, Cowboy was standing between them, hoping they'd lavish more love on him.

I walked down the stairs.

Jake stood in the gathering room and whistled when I joined him and Abby. "Emma, you look beautiful."

My face warmed. "Thanks. You look very nice too."

Jake wore black slacks and a crisp white button-up shirt. "Thank you. I made a reservation at Amalfi's."

"Yum. As soon as I find my keys, I'll be ready."

Abby held out her hand. "Here they are. I found them beside Cowboy's crate and thought you might not remember where you left them."

"Thanks, honey." I took the key chain and put it and my phone into my little purse. "Jake, I'm officially ready."

Abby said, "Jake, I'm going to look at your website with Celia, but I'll probably beat you home, Mom."

"Be safe." I hugged her.

Jake said, "We'll settle up financially after we see how long it takes you."

"Sounds good." Abby gave Jake a hug, and we left.

Jake drove us to the restaurant.

The inside of Amalfi's was dimly lit with candles on tables with linen table-cloths. Soft romantic music played. The hostess found Jake's reservation and led us to a table for two in a quiet corner.

Once we were seated, I reached for Jake's hand. "This is so nice."

"I thought it was time for a date. We need to take a break from the murder and just breathe." Jake's time in the Marines had taught him to appreciate peaceful moments. He still sometimes flinched at unexpected noises, but for the most part, he didn't appear to suffer from PTSD.

It was too bad Brett hadn't come home in as good condition. His dog, Rufus, helped Brett cope with post-war stress. He also took mild medication and saw a therapist.

Jake intertwined his fingers with mine. "Did you have a good afternoon?"

"Yes. Working with my flowers always makes me feel better."

"Good evening." Ethan Tucker was Amalfi's bartender. I knew him, but we weren't close. He handed us a menu with featured drinks. "Can I get you anything from the bar? We have a few new non-alcoholic specials as well as our regular drinks."

I tapped the water glass near me. "This is all I need, but thanks."

Jake told the bartender what he wanted.

"Ethan, were you at the library yesterday morning with your daughter?" There'd been mostly mothers with young children, but it seemed like he'd been there too.

"Yes. Mia sat down for story time, but she was so disappointed the library was closed. Her mother and I will need to explain what happened, but we haven't yet." He shook his head. "Ms. Carranza was nice to the children. They softened her stern exterior. It's a real shame, but you don't want to hear my opinion. I'll send your drink over." He walked toward the bar, but there was less pep in his step.

Our waitress came over and shared the specials. We placed our orders and chatted about anything and everything.

Ethan dropped off a fruity concoction.

Jake shook his head. "I didn't expect this to look so girly, but the fruits made me think it'd be a nice way to replace the electrolytes I lost today."

I enjoyed a salad and veggie lasagna. Jake started with Italian wedding soup and feasted on spaghetti with meatballs for his main course. As usual, he teased me about my eating choices. "How can a Texas woman be vegetarian?"

"Not completely. I eat barbecue. Who can resist that?"

He chuckled. "Would you like dessert?"

"I'm full, but you go ahead."

"No—" His eyes darted away from me.

"What?"

"Your friend, Mason Brown, just sat at a table. He's with another man who might fit the definition of nondescript."

My heart skipped a beat. "Man, we'd done so well at not discussing Tess. Do you think the other man is the same person Brett saw?"

"I think it's possible." Jake frowned.

I pulled my phone from my purse. "Maybe we can do a selfie?"

"Is that code for take their picture?"

"Well, yeah. You know what? No. We're on a romantic date. It'd be silly to ruin it by trying to get a clue."

Jake shook his head. "Not silly at all. It's amazing we lasted as long as we did, without discussing the murder."

I opened the camera app on my phone and tapped the arrow for selfies. "Is he behind me?"

"Yep." Jake came to my side of the table and leaned over my shoulder.

"Smile, honey." I snapped a few legit shots of us, and then I turned my hand and took pictures of Mason and the other man.

Our waitress returned. "Would you like me to take your picture?"

"That would be so nice." I passed my phone to her, and she took multiple pictures.

"You two make a beautiful couple. Can I bring you dessert or coffee?"

We declined, and she promised to return with our check.

While waiting, I said, "Do you know anything about heirs property?"

"Can't say that I do. Tell me about it."

"Say you had a great-great-grandfather who had a house on some land. Back when he built his home on the land, he didn't make a will. Years later, he tells his children how to divide the land. They do this, but again no contract. Over time, the family grows. Some stay on the property, and others leave for various reasons. When the last person who is living on the original land dies, the government needs to decide who the land belongs to."

Jake rubbed his chin. "It's family-owned property?"

"Yes. The trick is finding the heirs. It could be as easy as finding the last owner's children or grandchildren. But it could also be trickier."

"Like nieces and nephews?"

"Exactly. That's how Ms. Linda was targeted." I stared at Mason and the other man.

The waitress returned with our check and told us to have a nice evening.

After Jake paid, he smiled at me. "I suppose you'd like to walk by their table and speak."

"Oh, Jake. You know me too well, but we don't have to." I didn't want to hurt his feelings by shifting my attention from our lovely evening to a murder suspect.

"There's no need to miss this opportunity." He stood and reached for my hand.

We walked in the direction of the other table, and I stopped when we reached it. "Hi, Mason. What a surprise."

He leaned back. "I noticed you didn't say nice."

I paused. "Oh, I get it. What a nice surprise. Have you met Jake Hunter?"

"I haven't had the pleasure." He shook Jake's hand. "I'm Mason Brown, and this is my friend, Tom Ward."

Now we had a name.

Jake shook the other man's hand, too. "You guys picked one of the best restaurants in Lutz. I hope you have a good evening."

Tom said, "You two as well."

We exited the restaurant. Jake said, "Are you up to walking?"

I often walked around town or rode my bike. It was good exercise and protected the environment. "Sure. I forgot to tell you that Ms. Maebell and I met a woman who was victimized by Tom and Mason." I shared Linda Jefferson's story with him. "She also believes there are other victims."

"That's awful. Now that I've met Tom Ward, it'll be easy enough to find out if he's the same man from the courthouse."

"Will you still go with Brett in the morning?"

"You bet. We need to decide if they intend to harm Ms. Maebell and if they're connected to Tess's murder."

"In the morning, I'll take flowers to Heart of Texas. If they're staying at Faith's bed and breakfast, maybe I can pick up a clue."

"Just be careful, Sunshine."

"You be careful too." I wrapped my arm through his arm. "If we rule out these guys, I'll have to focus on Nick Jones."

"I don't know about that, Emma. That new librarian might be worth looking at."

"Laurel Holley? I can't imagine she has a legit motive, but I'll keep her in mind." I paused. "On second thought, Paula said if Nick didn't murder Tess, Laurel might be guilty."

Chapter Seventeen

T hursday morning, I stood in Faith Meier's kitchen at Heart of Texas Bed and Breakfast. I arranged a variety of colorful zinnias in a vase for the breakfast room. "How does Zig like his law classes?"

"Good. He's used to memorizing lots of information from his acting days. Of course, it's different. Studying to become an attorney has given him purpose again. When he retired early, it never occurred to us how soon he'd become bored." Faith arranged muffins on a pretty plate and placed a vintage napkin over them.

"How old is your husband?"

"Forty-five. Way too young to retire, even though he was careful with his money through his acting career. I imagined running this place would occupy more of his time. He helps, but I have a young lady who assists with cleaning and laundry." She poured orange juice into a glass pitcher.

I rinsed my hands. "Does he like the law, or is it only a boredom buster?"

"He loves it, and he sees it as an outreach project. The goal is to focus on poor people who can't afford a good attorney." She smiled. "I'm so proud of him."

The memory of the man wearing a plaid shirt surfaced. "Who were you talking to at the library? The guy who looked like a cowboy."

"Oh, you must mean Wyatt Gardner. He really is a cowboy, as in a retired rodeo rider."

"Is he a friend?" I couldn't imagine how they'd connected to become friends.

"Kinda. He dropped out of school to help at the family farm and eventually competed in rodeos. The thing is, he doesn't know how to read. He's embarrassed that his six-year-old daughter is learning to read and decided it was time for him to learn. So, I'm his tutor. The library sponsors the program, and Tess matched us up." She glanced at her watch. "I need to carry food into the breakfast room. One of my guests is an early riser. The coffee station is the first thing I attend to, and by the time I carry food in he's already had a couple cups of coffee."

"Let me help." I carried the vase of flowers and followed her.

"Good morning, Mason. I hope you're hungry. I've got a spinach and bacon quiche in the oven, or I can prepare an omelet for you."

He looked up from his laptop. "An omelet sounds perfect."

I placed the flower arrangement on the buffet, then faced Faith's guest. "Hi, Mason."

His mouth dropped open. "You really get around. Are you by any chance the mayor of Lutz?"

"No, sir. I'm just a flower farmer."

Faith motioned for me to follow her. "Emma, Mason doesn't need us distracting him."

"Sorry, Mason. I'm not here to disturb you."

"Don't give it a second thought." He smirked.

Back in the kitchen, Faith shook her finger at me. "Don't look so innocent. You're investigating Tess's murder. Aren't you?"

I stepped close and kept my voice to a whisper. "Tess wanted to tell me something, and I'm pretty sure it's connected to Mason. Have you overheard anything suspicious?"

"Shh. Emma, please leave. I'm running a business, and he's my guest. While Mason is under my roof, I need to protect him."

"You make a good point, but I'm also concerned for you and Zig." I glanced toward the breakfast room to make sure Mason wasn't eavesdropping on us. No sign of the man. "Just one quick question. Is his friend, Tom Ward, staying here too?"

"I don't know anybody by that name. Emma, you're stressing me out."

"I'm sorry." I never wanted to upset anybody, especially a friend as nice as

Faith.

The oven buzzer dinged. Faith's blond ponytail swung when she snatched oven mitts and removed two beautiful quiches. She placed them on pretty silicone trivets.

"Faith, I'll leave, but please be careful. We don't know who murdered Tess."

"Mason is nice, and I can't imagine he's involved."

I nodded. "Are there other people here with you and Mason?"

"I've got a full house, and Zig should return from his morning run soon."

"Good." I gave her a hug. "I'm sorry for upsetting you."

"We can talk later." She pulled a knife from a drawer and began cutting the quiche.

"Bye." I left her in the kitchen, hoping she was right about Mason. But somebody had killed Tess, and they could still be lurking around town.

Chapter Eighteen

I walked away from Heart of Texas with a heavy heart. I'd seen Mason, but Faith was distressed. Shame on me, because I had gone there intending to look for a clue. Poor Faith. No doubt she'd imagined I was there as a friend. To make matters worse, nothing had been gained from me learning where Mason was staying.

I crossed the street and continued walking toward the town square. Hopefully, Jake and Brett were more successful than I'd been. At least they weren't hurting anybody's feelings.

Fast footsteps sounded behind me.

I scooted to the side and slowed so the other person could pass me.

"Mrs. Justice, can I have a minute of your time?"

Chills skittered up my spine.

Mason caught up with me.

No need to be fearful. It was broad daylight. People were driving to work, and the police station was up the street. I took a deep breath. "How can I help you?"

He stepped close enough for me to smell his aftershave. "Why are you following me?"

I gasped.

"Don't try to deny it. You approached me at the library, the restaurant last night, and this morning at Faith's place. What do you want?" His tone was angry, and he narrowed his eyes.

"Wait a second." I raised my hands. "Last night was a coincidence. If you'll remember, Jake and I were there first. When we left, the polite thing to do was speak."

His nostrils flared. "And this morning?"

"I always supply flowers for Faith and Zig." That was the truth. He didn't need to know I had wanted to discover where he was staying. I stepped back and bumped into a jogger. "Sorry."

"No problem, Emma." Paige Booker, the owner of the local bookstore, waved. She wore a white T-shirt with a drawing of Agatha Christie. Most of Paige's shirts had famous quotes, and the people in town got a kick out of them.

Seeing Paige lessened my anxiety. "I'm sorry for offending you, Mason. Have you set up an appointment with Ms. Maebell and her nephew? She might sell her land to you, if she feels like it's a fair offer."

"It'll be more than fair, considering my client is willing to pay back taxes."

"Back taxes? I don't know what you mean. Talk to Brett Tirabassi. He's usually at Anytime Coffee House." I didn't have a horse in that race, and I tried to walk away.

Mason jumped in front of me and turned, leaning down. We were face to face. Our noses almost touched. "Maybe you can put in a good word for me."

"Ms. Maebell is very smart. She can make up her own mind about you." I tried to move around him. If he didn't get out of my way, I would scream and run to the police station.

A tall Black man jogged across the street. Zig. "Morning, Emma. I'd give you a hug if I wasn't so sweaty. Mason, I hope you slept well. I bet Faith has breakfast ready. Why don't I walk with you? After a quick shower, I'll join you."

Relief swept through me. "Hi, Zig. It's good to see you. I need to get to work. Have a good day."

"You too, Emma." Zig's deep voice soothed my nerves.

I hurried away and left the two men standing together.

That was a close call, and I'd thank Zig later. I could've saved myself, but there might have been a scene.

Did Zig realize I was struggling? Or was it a lucky break that we'd crossed paths?

Either way, I was glad to get away from Mason Brown.

He'd referred to back taxes. The words singsonged in my head with each step. Mason also claimed the offer would be fair. Could that be a clue? Tess had said something about an offer and land rights to Ms. Maebell the night before she died.

What had Tess stumbled upon? Had it led to her death? Was Brett's aunt in danger? I hurried home to work in my flower gardens. I often did my best thinking working with my flowers and pulling weeds. With some luck, today would be no different.

Chapter Nineteen

After my encounter with Mason, I spent the next few hours working in the flower gardens. The land behind my fenced-in yard was also my property, and I'd begun to grow wildflowers in the area. One day when I was financially stable, I'd extend my fence to cover the entire property. Starting my business took one step at a time. I'd had a few setbacks, but supportive friends had encouraged me to not give up.

The murder investigation was the same way. I thought about my suspect list while showering. My main suspects were Mason Brown and Nick Jones, but Tom Ward and Laurel Holley needed to be investigated also.

I got dressed and headed to the kitchen.

"Morning, Mom." Abby sat at the French harvest table, eating an apple. Cowboy lay on the floor beside my daughter.

"Good morning. I'm ready for lunch. What about you?"

"Good luck. We need to buy groceries."

I opened the refrigerator door and discovered she hadn't exaggerated. "Slim pickings for sure. I'll run to Sophie's Bakery and pick up something. What do you want?"

"A nap." Abby yawned. "These early mornings are getting to me. When I wake up, I can eat peanut butter and crackers."

"Okay. I may run a few errands, but I'll be quiet when I return."

She got up and dropped the apple core into the compost bin. "I interpret your words to mean you want to find a clue to the murder. Be careful, Mom."

I hugged my daughter. "Always."

Cowboy followed Abby up the stairs.

It only took me a few minutes to walk up the street and around the square to the bakery, but I was perspiring when I got there.

Sophie glanced at me. "Perfect timing. Tara and I have been running our feet off. What can I get you?"

"Chicken salad on whole wheat with fruit, and the biggest glass of iced tea possible."

Tara said, "Unsweet tea?"

"Yes, with lemon, please."

Sophie prepared my salad. "You must have been working in the garden this morning. I think you have a few more freckles."

"I wore my big hat and sunscreen, but it seems to be the curse of being a redhead."

"No investigating?" She raised her eyebrows.

"I didn't say that. Mason Brown got mad at me." I looked around and verified the place was empty except for the three of us, and then I told her my story.

Tara handed me the glass of tea. "I've seen Mason at the library. I try to take my son on the days Hope leads story time. He also enjoys the activities with building blocks."

"It sounds like you're there a lot."

"Yes."

Sophie glared at me. "Are you questioning Tara about Tess's murder?"

Tara looked from Sophie to me.

"In my defense, I came here for lunch. But I'm not going to pass up a chance to ask a possible witness questions." I took a big drink of tea before pulling out my credit card to pay.

"Give Emma an employee discount. She helps at a lot of catering events, and she never lets me pay her." Sophie finished preparing my plate while Tara rang up my order. "I'm sorry, Emma. You should talk to Tara before we get busy again."

"Thanks."

Tara carried my plate to a table and sat, so I followed. "I'm not sure how helpful I'll be."

"Don't worry. Did you ever see Tess get into an altercation with Mason?"

"Once, I saw her tell him to take a phone call out in the lobby. She said she liked to keep the reference section quiet. Tess had quiet areas and other sections where people could talk. For instance, the room for children has windows looking between it and the rest of the library, and there's a door. It cuts down on noise, and believe me, the kids can get loud."

I pulled the sketch pad from my turquoise and white polka dot bag and took notes. "Was there any friction when she asked him to step out?"

"No. In fact, he apologized and left the main room. I was looking for a book on Texas history for a genealogy group I want to join. Mason had a book I needed. That's why I heard the conversation that day." She pushed a strand of curly hair behind her ear. "Mason was nice to me. He even shared the reference book. On the days I've been to the library, the only person I witnessed getting bent out of shape was Ethan. I don't know his last name, but he has a daughter."

"Could it be Ethan Tucker? He has a six-year-old daughter. Her name is Mia, and she has black hair like her dad."

Tara's eyes widened. "Yes. Mia is the man's daughter."

The bakery door opened, and six men walked in wearing work clothes.

"Thanks for your help. I know you need to go back to work."

"See you later." She hurried behind the counter and put on a fresh hairnet.

I ate my lunch and considered all Tara had said. She and Sophie both believed Mason was nice. I'd seen an ugly side of Mason, and I'd be careful around him.

Ethan Tucker hadn't been on my suspect radar. Witness? Yes.

I needed to find out about his argument with Tess, but I wouldn't go alone.

Chapter Twenty

J ake met me at Anytime Coffee House, after I'd run my errands. He had a couple of hours between appointments, and we drove over to Tess's house.

"I'm glad Coop is out of town this week, and I appreciate you spending so much time helping me solve the murder." I parked my truck, and we walked to the door of the modest house. I used the key Paula had given me and opened the door.

"Wait. The killer could be here." Jake entered the one-story house.

I waited on the small front porch but peeked inside. The main area was one big room. Kitchen, dining area, and family room. On the island was a large tray and multiple plants. From where I stood, there appeared to be a bleeding heart plant in bloom, a violet, and a spider plant. She and Paula had most likely bought their plants at the same time.

Jake returned. "I guess it's a good thing she doesn't have an alarm, or else we'd probably be arrested."

"No, I've got a key." I held it up. "We can't be arrested for breaking and entering."

"I saw you use it to open the door, but it'd be good not to have the police question us. The place is clear. Let's get busy. If somebody else broke in here, they left it neat."

"That's for sure, but again, I have a key. Do you want to divide and conquer?"

"I'd prefer for us to stick together. Tess has an office. We might start there, but what exactly are we looking for?" Jake stood near enough that I could smell his minty chewing gum. Unlike earlier, when Mason had stood close, I felt safe. Jake was a good man. Mason? Not so sure.

"Anything about property. Ownership and taxes. Of course, if you see Mason Brown's name or Tom Ward's name, that'll be a good clue. Where's her office?"

"In the front room." Jake led the way.

The space was efficient and organized. "I'll begin in the file cabinet."

"Okay, I can go through her desk. We can take her laptop with us in your big bag if this lasts long."

"Good idea." I pulled a chair over and opened the top drawer of her two-drawer file cabinet. "How did it go at the courthouse this morning?"

Jake laughed. "I don't know if it was the coffee and supplies or my pleasing personality, but the women weren't horrible. Brett was ticked."

I knew he was joking, and I played along. "I'm sure they were nice because of your boyish good looks. And if you winked at them, they probably swooned. Did you learn anything?"

"Tom Ward, the man we met last night, is the same man who brings them muffins."

"What does he get for his trouble?"

"Time alone with property information. They say he's a real charmer." Jake opened a drawer. "And he's a real estate agent with an emphasis on developing properties."

"Interesting." I fingered through the clearly labeled files and paused at a thick one. It was bound, plus there was a rubber band around it. The first page had a title with her name under it. "Jake, this looks like a book Tess wrote. I had no idea she wanted to be an author."

"Does she have family? They may want it."

"I really don't know. She and Paula were close, but I never met any family members. I'm going to take this with me. If it's good, Paula needs to make sure it gets published." I laid the manuscript to the side and continued to look at her files.

Jake finished the desk and walked to bookshelves filling one wall. He whistled an old country song.

I plucked out a file with Paula's name on it and placed it with the manuscript. Tess and I might be the only two people who knew Paula's deepest secrets. If the police found this, it might put Paula and her family in danger. It was going home with me. If Chief Young wanted it, I'd need to at least warn Paula before turning it over.

Jake said, "None of the books look suspicious. Is it funny for a librarian to have so many books in her home? I mean, she could've had the library carry all these books."

I cut my eyes to him. "That wouldn't have been ethical. She made her decisions based on what the community will read. I guarantee there are books at the library that Tess didn't enjoy reading."

"I understand." In a few minutes, Jake walked to the door. "I'll start in the kitchen."

"Okay. This is going to take me a few more minutes. Do you think the police took her purse?"

"It's what I would've done. She may have notes in her purse or on her phone. I'd also look for recent receipts. I'd want to get a timeline of what she did in the days leading up to her death."

"Jake, that's a terrific idea. Let me know if you see any receipts in a junk drawer—"

"I doubt Tess had a junk drawer, but I'll look."

"You're probably right. Maybe we should each do what we think is best and compare notes. Even if we overlap, we might interpret differently."

"On it." This time, he left Tess's home office without interference from me.

The next file contained receipts. Most had been paid with cash. Why keep a record of cash transactions? I added the information to my stack, then closed the bottom drawer. It'd still be interesting to know what was in the files at the library. Without permission from the police, I'd never know. I organized her laptop, the manuscript, and the files in my bag before joining Jake in the main room.

He stood in front of the open freezer. "I've read about people hiding things in their freezers. Tess only has ice and a few frozen meals."

"It doesn't surprise me. Tess once confessed that she'd rather spend time reading than cooking. I think it's the reason she always got lunch from Sophie."

"One decent meal a day?"

"Something like that." A reflection swept across the room, and I looked outside. "Oh, no. Nick Jones pulled up next door. What are we going to do?"

"Stay calm. You said it yourself earlier. We have permission to be here. Kinda. At least we have a key." Jake moved and looked out the window. "Uh-oh. He's coming our way."

Chapter Twenty-One

"What are we going to do?" I asked again, and the phrase repeated in my head, over and over.

"Nick can't do anything to us." Jake looked from me to the flower pots. "We'll say you're taking care of the plants until the will is read."

The doorbell pealed.

"Okay." My hands shook. "I'll gather the plants."

"I'll answer the door." Jake crossed the room slowly.

I found a dish towel and placed it over the items in my bag. Two flower pots would fit easily on the towel, and I could carry the other one.

"Hi, there." Jake stood at the opening and blocked Nick's ability to enter. "I hope you're not here to spray Tess's house for bugs. She died, but you probably knew that."

Nick swiped at perspiration with a faded red bandanna. "Everybody in town is talking about her death. Why are you here?"

"It seemed like a good idea to pick up the indoor plants. We can keep them alive until Tess's family comes to town. Once the will is read, we'll give them to the beneficiaries."

Nick snorted. "May as well give them to Paula. None of Tess's family probably cares."

I joined the men. "Do you know her relatives?"

"They weren't close to Tess. I met them when Paula and I were married. Why isn't Paula here taking care of things?" He glared at me.

"Um, maybe she was here earlier. I'm caring for the plants. It's what I do." Time to go on the offensive. "If you didn't come to do your pest control

91

thing, why are you here?"

"I treat the house next door. When I saw the truck in the driveway, it seemed like I should make sure thieves hadn't broken into the house."

Jake said, "We should leave and let Nick get back to work."

Nick made another attempt to look around Jake. "How'd you get in here? Did Tess have a hiding place for her key? Lots of my customers leave a hidden key for me, or they pay me to only spray outside their home. I bet she has one of those fake rocks."

"Nope. I've got my own key. She was always careful when it came to safety." My eyes filled with tears. How had a woman as cautious as Tess been caught off guard and murdered?

"Something don't add up. I'm going to call the police."

Jake said, "Go right ahead."

Nick's eyebrows shot up. "I don't have time to wait on the cops."

"We're about to lock up and leave. Have a good day, Nick." Jake turned to me. "Do you need help carrying the plants?"

"Yes, please. It'll be quicker if you help."

"I don't trust you two, but I've got better things to do." Nick stomped away.

His disappearance made it easier to breathe. "We should probably leave in case he changes his mind."

"My thoughts exactly." Jake stuffed something in the back waistband of his pants before picking up the pots that wouldn't fit in my bag, then opened the door for me.

I took one last look around Tess's home. "I wish we'd had more time to search. Do you think we can come back?"

"I don't know, but I found one little jewel you'll probably be excited about."

"What?" I set the bag down and used the key to deadlock the door.

"Hold on. Do you see Nick?" Jake adjusted his shirt at the waistband.

"I don't see him, but he could've driven around the corner and come back. For all I know, he's lurking behind a bush or something."

Jake made a show of tying his shoe while looking toward the street. "No obvious sign of Nick."

I pocketed the key and picked up the bag. "I'd say the coast is clear, but nothing would surprise me."

An official police car pulled in front of the house.

"Oh, no." I gripped the handles tight. "This is bad."

"Keep walking to the truck, put your bag in it. It looks like Matt. I'll try to head him off."

I didn't have time to question the reason for Jake's request, but I did as he suggested. Once the bag was in the truck, I looked around.

Jake walked through the grass, heading to the official vehicle.

Across the street, a neighbor sat in a swing on her front porch, watching us.

Matt exited his Charger.

I joined the men and stood beside Jake.

"Somebody reported suspicious activity at Tess Carranza's house. Did you two break in?" His voice croaked, and dark circles had formed under his eyes.

I removed the key and showed it to the police chief. "I had permission to be here, and I came and got the plants. Just because Tess is gone, it doesn't mean her plants should die too."

Matt's gaze darted from me to Jake. "Is that the story you're going with, too?"

"I'm carrying a flower, aren't I?" There was no love lost between the two men, and Jake's smart-aleck reply didn't catch me off guard. "You might want to speak to Nick Jones. He came over and asked about a key to the place."

"Explain." Matt reached for his notepad.

Jake glanced at me. "Do you want to share?"

"I don't think so. He mostly talked to you." I reached for the spider plant in the Polish pottery. The pattern was blue and white with hens and flowers. Adorable. "I'm going to stand in the shade."

I leaned against a Crepe Myrtle and watched the men discuss what had happened. The woman across the street leaned in our direction. No doubt this encounter would make it to the local gossip mill, but I couldn't worry about rumors.

Tess had been murdered, and solving the mystery wasn't a game. The killer needed to be stopped before somebody else died.

Was it Nick Jones? Would Paula be next? Or was it a conspiracy between Mason Brown and Tom Ward? Tess had been concerned that they were taking advantage of people.

I stood in the shade and prayed for wisdom and justice. There should be no more murders in Lutz, Texas.

Chapter Twenty-Two

I stood in the comfort of my kitchen and fed Tess's plants.

Cowboy paced near me.

"What's the matter, boy? Do you need to go for a walk?"

Abby entered the kitchen. "I took him for a walk after my nap. He kept stopping to eat grass. Does that mean anything?"

I shrugged. "Being a dog owner is still relatively new to me. I'll take him out back."

Abby opened the refrigerator door. "Hey, you got some groceries."

"Yeah, we should be able to manage for a few days." I headed to the back with Cowboy. He didn't walk far, but he licked grass near the patio.

"Mom, you've got company. I'll keep an eye on my pup." My daughter appeared on the patio.

"My pup." I smiled. Abby nudged me with her arm. "Mr. and Mrs. Meier are in the gathering room."

"Oh, I better get in there." I hoped Faith had forgiven me for my morning visit. I walked through the house and joined them. "Hi guys. Can I get you anything?"

Zig stood. "We're just fine, Emma, but we'd like to talk to you about Mason Brown."

Uh-oh. I sat in my comfy chair, and Zig returned to his spot beside Faith. They looked at each other.

I wasn't sure who was supposed to start the conversation, so I took charge. "Faith, I'm sorry about this morning. You're my friend, and if I want to know about your guests in the future, I'll ask you. In my mind, you wouldn't be able to tell me, like patient confidentiality, when I worked at the drug store. I never really imagined I'd have a conversation with Mason."

Faith said, "I accept your apology. Zig and I talked about the situation. If you ever believe a dangerous person is staying with us, we want you to speak up."

Zig held his wife's hand. "Mason seemed like a nice enough guy, but when I saw you with him on the sidewalk, something didn't feel right. That's why I interrupted. Did he threaten you?"

I shivered. "Part of me felt like I could get away if he attempted anything, but he accused me of following him. This morning, was a lucky guess. Other times when we've crossed paths it's just been a coincidence."

Zig said, "Tell us more. Why are you worried about him?"

I scootched to the edge of my chair and leaned forward. "On Monday, Tess wanted to talk to me about a man who had been visiting the library. He became a constant presence in the reference section. She overheard a conversation, and she wanted to discuss it with me. She told me it involved property, and he was going to take advantage of Brett Tirabassi's aunt."

Faith released Zig's hand and stood. "Brett was there Tuesday morning with an older lady. Was that his aunt?"

"Yes. Tess wanted to talk to both of us. You know how Tess always enjoyed reading mysteries?"

She looked out the window and pinched her lip. "I visited the library often every week. Tess was always helpful. I made friends at the coloring and coffee group. The last time I saw Tess alive at the library, I was looking for a book on the history of this area. Plus, I put my name on the waiting list for a new book."

Silence followed.

Zig stood and rubbed Faith's shoulders. "What happened?"

"Mason was on a phone call, and Tess asked him to take it to the lobby or outside. I chalked it up to Tess having a bad day. She and Ethan Tucker had an argument, too, and it was worse."

I thought back to what Tara had told me at the bakery. She'd witnessed the same things. "Was Mason upset?"

"He frowned at first, and then his expression cleared. He even apologized. I didn't put much thought into his reaction until today. When Zig was acting, I sometimes visited the set and observed the actors. Mason's apology almost seemed like an act." She swayed, and a tear slid down her face.

"Baby, why don't you sit back down?" Zig waited for her to return to the couch. After she settled, he sat beside her again. "What about Ethan? What did they get into it about?"

"I didn't hear the words, but his daughter, Mia, was with Tess. Ethan had fallen asleep, and Mia was wandering around without supervision. I know he works late at the bar, but what if the child wandered out of the building? I could understand why Tess was upset." She shrugged. "Again, that was my interpretation from what I saw. I wasn't close enough to hear."

Zig adjusted his hat. "Emma, what do you think? Is it safe for Mason to stay with us? I'd never forgive myself if he hurt Faith or one of the guests."

For the love of daffodils. I didn't want to tell them what to do. "Why don't you ask Chief Young?"

Faith said, "Is Mason on your suspect list?"

"Yes, but you thought he was a good guy before today. Have you met Tom Ward?"

"No." Faith crossed her legs.

Zig said, "Who is Tom Ward?"

"A real estate agent who works with Mason. No, it's more than that. He buys land himself and develops it. Can I trust you to keep this conversation confidential?"

They both nodded.

"Tom has been going to the courthouse looking up properties, while Mason has been at the library. They're working together. Ms. Maebell is one of their targets."

Zig sighed. "I'll do some research on Tom and Mason. If I find any record of illegal dealings, I'll let you know."

"Thanks, Zig."

"You're welcome. We best let you get on with your day." He stood and reached for Faith's hand.

I walked them to the door. "So, are the three of us okay? No hurt feelings? I promise to be upfront from now on."

Faith hugged me. "We're good."

Relief swept through me. I closed the door behind them and leaned against it.

My investigations were only to help the police and stop crime. I didn't want to lose friends in the process. Faith and Zig had only been here a few years, but we'd grown close. I needed to get better at walking the fine line of asking questions without upsetting friends.

Abby yelled from the kitchen. "Mom, your puppy vomited on the patio, and he's sniffing it."

"Oh, no." Now he was my puppy. "I'm coming."

"Hurry."

I ran outside to help with Cowboy. I'd have to focus on the murder investigation later.

Chapter Twenty-Three

I took Cowboy to Dr. Bushy Erb's office. The kind veterinarian reassured me my golden retriever was going to be okay. He chalked the episode up to the heat or the chance Cowboy ate something that didn't agree with him. He warned me to be careful with the hot days, and I assured him I would take good care of my puppy.

When we got home, I slipped a few ice cubes into the water bowl, and Cowboy seemed to enjoy licking them.

Tess had carried her own tumbler on Monday. I had assumed it was iced tea or water. She never gave up believing that Nick Jones murdered his first wife, Rhonda, by poisoning her. Was that the reason she carried her own drink? Although, she used to order tea with her lunch from Sophie at the bakery.

It was too confusing.

I sat at the eating table and called Brett.

"Hey, girl. What's going on? Did you talk to Zig Meier about Aunt Maebell's situation?"

"Yes, but I asked him not to discuss it with anyone. I hope you don't mind."

"Hunh. He did ask to speak to me privately."

"I'm sorry, Brett. What exactly did Zig say?" I hoped he didn't think I was a blabbermouth.

"He's in law school, and he offered to help me get to the bottom of this situation between my aunt and Mason Brown. No, to be fair, he said Tom Ward."

"Did you accept his offer?"

"Sure did. I trust Zig. He's going to set up a meeting and get back to me."

The tension in my shoulders disappeared. "Keep me posted."

"Will do. Why'd you call?"

"I wanted to hear your opinion about the courthouse this morning. Jake said you found out Tom Ward gives the ladies muffins and sweet talks them, so he can be alone with maps and records." I drew a daisy on a fresh page in my sketch pad.

"First off, they were all into my good buddy Jake. As his girlfriend, you should never let him go back there by himself."

I laughed. "Good to know." I doubted the county clerk's office would be on my radar anytime soon, but I'd keep his warning in mind.

"Anything else?"

"Not really. We know Mr. Ward has a chauffeur, and I have a view of the square. I'm keeping my eyes open in case I see him again."

"Oh, Brett. I'll text you a picture I took last night of Mason and Tom." I opened my photos app and sent the picture to Brett. "There. It's not the best—"

"It's good enough. That's the same man who bumped me yesterday."

"Hey, I wonder if Zig can get them to meet with y'all?"

"Do you think Tom's the killer?"

"Maybe. Mason works for Tom, and Tom wants the land. I'm missing something. But what?" I made bullet points on my page.

"What was his motive for killing Tess?"

"The only altercation we know about is when Tess told him to take his call in the lobby." I doodled again. "Witnesses said he didn't appear to be mad, though."

"Don't forget Tess was suspicious he was up to no good after she overheard a phone conversation. I don't think she confronted him about taking advantage of people."

"She told you and your aunt that she wanted to discuss the situation with you. Did she call you on the phone?"

"Yeah. It was Sunday afternoon. I believe she might have been working at the library." Brett paused. "Definitely at work. There was a quiet hum in the background, and then a baby cried."

"I'd love to know if Mason was at the library on Sunday. It's possible he overheard the conversation." I made a note to find out, or at least try. "Your aunt had a conversation with a lady at the library. Do you know if she learned anything?"

"They compared letters, and they were practically the same. Hey, Celia walked in. I'll talk to you later."

"Tell her hi for me."

"Yes, ma'am." He hung up.

I looked at Cowboy. He snoozed in his crate, and I walked to my office. "Abby, do you think you're too much excitement for the dog?"

"I'm usually trying to keep up with him. Maybe he ate something. He runs all around the yard. I don't know how you trained him to stay out of your flowers, but good job. Still, maybe he ate a weed."

"The vet suggested a calm diet and to be careful of the heat. I'll fix him plain chicken and rice for supper."

Abby laughed. "That could require another trip to the grocery store."

"Okay, smarty pants. I have rice."

"It's a start. Now, shoo. I need to get back to work. I'm setting up automatic bill payments for things like water and electricity."

"You'll need to teach me what you're doing before you go back to school. Do you have any fun plans tonight?"

"I'm going to meet friends for supper, but I need to go to bed early."

I walked over and kissed her head. "I hate that you're working so hard."

"It's part of learning to be responsible. I want a new car, and I'm willing to pay the price."

My heart broke a little at her words. How I wished I could give her a new car, but I was a hard-working single mom. There was only so much I could provide for my only child.

This was no time for a pity party, when a murderer was running around Lutz. "Abby, I'm going to the library. If I'm not back before you go, please leave me a note where you'll be."

"Be careful, Mom. If you're not back in an hour, I'm calling Jake and Brett."

"Oh, you're tough. I'll be back, though. No need to call the cavalry."

Chapter Twenty-Four

I stood in Tess's old office, shocked at the changes Laurel had already made. "What did you do with Tess's belongings?" Where were the files that had been on the credenza?

"Her stuff is boxed up in the storage room. The police told me not to do anything with her things."

"Laurel, don't you think that meant to leave her office alone?" I managed to keep my tone neutral despite my incredulousness.

"That's not what the policeman said." She moved from the desk chair to straighten her diploma on the wall. "I'm the director, and I need office space. This is the office of the director."

"Congratulations on your promotion." It sickened me how easily Laurel moved on.

"It's not official yet, but who else will they pick? I've been here working with Tess. I know what works and what needs to be changed. I've made a list of adjustments and will implement them as soon as it's official."

Pictures of Laurel with friends and family filled her desk and bookshelves. Besides her diploma, multiple certificates of recognition filled the walls. It was hard to like Laurel at this very moment. How could she be so insensitive? "You sure do have a lot of awards."

"I worked hard to earn each one of them. My mom was disappointed when I chose to get my masters in library science instead of going into medicine. She thought being a doctor would make me rich, but I never wanted that kind of life. Each one of my awards is confirmation that I made the right decision." Her smile faded. "Emma, is there something you need?"

I took a deep breath. "Two things. Will you remain in the book club?"

"Yes, and your second question?"

"Do you know if Tess has family? I'm taking care of her indoor plants, and they may want them."

Laurel sat back down in the desk chair and crossed her legs. Her beautiful curly blond hair hung over her shoulders. "I don't remember her talking about any relatives."

"Can you look in the employee records? Maybe she listed them as emergency contacts."

"I should probably ask Chief Young, first."

I sat in the chair on the opposite side of the desk. "Laurel, that's probably a good idea. If Tess has any living family members, they need to be notified of her passing."

She stared at me.

I pulled my phone out of my purse and looked for Matt's contact information.

She snapped out of her trance. "What are you doing?"

"Chief Young and I raised our children together in this town. We're friends, and I have his contact information in my phone. It'll be easy for me to call him. That way you won't have to trouble yourself looking up his number."

She opened a desk drawer and removed a business card. "I've got his information here."

"Do you prefer to call him?"

"Yes. If you'll step out of my office, I'll do it right now."

"Laurel, aren't you upset about Tess's death?"

"My daddy died when I was young. My mother taught me not to dwell on death. If you intend on surviving, you've got to keep moving."

"I'm sorry about your dad. My husband died when my daughter was an infant, and I understand life couldn't have been easy for you and your mom." I exited the office.

Did I trust Laurel to call Matt?

No.

I texted him. **We need to talk about Laurel and Tess's family.**

"Emma, what a surprise to find you here." Mason startled me with his quiet approach.

My heart skipped a beat. "Hi, Mason. Give me just a minute."

I texted Abby. **Send in the cavalry.**

"Mason, I'm not up to talking to you." My phone buzzed, and I looked at it. Matt had replied. "I should get this."

"You seem to be a busy woman."

"Yeah."

Where are you? Three dots appeared, indicating he was waiting on my answer.

The library. I gripped my phone, waiting for his reply.

On the way.

Mason laughed. "I prefer phone calls."

My phone buzzed again, and I looked. "I'm sorry to be rude, but this is my daughter."

They're coming. Be careful, Mom.

I thanked her, then stuck the phone in the pocket of my denim shorts. "Mason, it's hard for me to be back in the library after finding my friend's body. Can we talk another time?"

"I only wanted to warn you to be careful what you say. This is a small town, and if you start rumors about me, I might have to sue you."

I gasped. "I assure you—"

"Be careful what you say, Emma."

Laurel appeared. "The police chief isn't answering his phone."

Matt walked up behind Laurel, and I almost laughed. He said, "Are you sure you dialed the right number?"

Mason walked away.

Laurel's face turned red.

And for the first time since entering the library, I smiled. "Hi, Matt."

Chapter Twenty-Five

Matt looked at his phone. "Miss Holley, no missed calls appear on my phone."

"Um, well, I guess I could have misdialed." Laurel wrapped a strand of curly hair around her finger.

Matt held out his hand. "Let me see the number you dialed."

Laurel shoved the phone into the pocket of her red miniskirt.

"Can you explain why you were trying to reach me, Miss Holley?"

I was always relieved when the police chief questioned somebody besides me. He was intense, and it was evident he didn't believe her story.

"Well, you see, Emma wanted to make sure Tess's family has been contacted about her death. She asked me to look at her employee record for contact information in case of emergencies."

"What did you find?"

"Nothing."

I clenched my fists. "You didn't try."

Matt crossed his arms. "I think we should go to Ms. Carranza's office."

Laurel shuffled her feet. "It's my office now."

"You were told not to move her belongings." He frowned.

"I didn't move them out of the building."

From the corner of my eye, I spotted Jake entering the library. "Excuse me, please."

"No problem." Matt locked eyes with me. "I'm going to have a conversation with Miss Holley, but I want to talk to you next."

"Okay. In case you haven't noticed, Mason Brown is here too." I walked toward Jake. "Thanks for coming."

"I see our police chief beat me here." He hugged me.

"There's a lot going on. Have you got a few minutes? Maybe we can find a private place where we can talk."

"There's a table in the lobby. Brett's on the way, too."

"Celia was with him earlier."

Jake chuckled. "She's probably on the way with Brett."

We walked to the lobby and sat next to each other at a small table for four.

I reached for Jake's hand. "Mason is here, and he confronted me. I had already texted Matt about Laurel's actions. She's settling in as the library director. That's when Mason confronted me. So, I texted Abby to contact you and Brett. Both things happened simultaneously."

"Here comes Brett and Celia."

"Good. I can tell all y'all at the same time." As soon as the other two sat down, I gave them a replay of what had happened.

Celia had left her job as a librarian in Waco to live closer to Brett. "Did she get appointed as the library director?"

I shook my head. "Nothing official. If it's a government job, don't they have to post the job opening?"

"I don't know if it's an official rule, but I interviewed for my previous job." Celia massaged the back of her neck.

"Celia, you should apply." I knew money was tight for her, and if she got a job as the library director, she'd have a bigger paycheck and benefits.

She shrugged. "I'm not sure I can leave Paige after she was so kind to give me a job. It wouldn't be nice."

Brett said, "Ladies, you're losing focus. Are you in danger, Emma?"

"Mason is here, but so is Chief Young. He told me not to leave until he questions me."

Jake touched my arm. "I'll stay with her. You all can shove off."

I placed my hands on the table. "Jake's right. Thanks for coming. Mason made me nervous, especially after he came after me this morning."

Celia said, "Wait a minute. This morning? It seems like you didn't tell us everything."

"It's been a long day. Mason confronted me on the street. I wasn't too worried because there was traffic, and we weren't too far from the police station. Zig was out on his morning run, and he came over to us. He was great, acting super casual and all. He—"

"Emma, have you got a minute?" Matt stood at the end of the table. "I'd like to hear your side of the story."

"Okay, but can we talk at a table where you can watch Mason Brown?"

"Oh, boy. I doubt I'm going to like this."

"Maybe not." I walked with him to the main area of the library.

Jake said, "I'll wait for you."

I glanced back. "Thanks."

Chapter Twenty-Six

Matt dropped his notepad onto the library table. "I don't like you discussing the murder with others, but tell me what you know."

I leaned forward, intending to keep my voice soft. "Mason Brown, the man wearing a shirt and tie behind me, he's an attorney."

"Good grief. Rather than irritate my ulcer by questioning how you know that I'll accept your word."

"Tess wanted to talk to me about him and something she overheard him say. Also, do you know who Tom Ward is?"

"No, but I'm sure you're about to inform me." He rubbed his temples. "Sorry. I didn't mean to be sarcastic."

I placed my arms on the table and spoke softly, sharing my thoughts on Tess's murder.

Matt looked at the notes he'd taken, after I finished. "Who are your suspects?"

"Mason Brown, Tom Ward, Laurel Holley, and Nick Jones."

He sighed. "Tess often complained about Nick. Almost every time somebody died, she'd come to my office and ask if he was on my suspect list."

"She was friends with his first wife, and she never got over Rhonda's death."

Matt nodded. "Out of respect for Tess, I'll question him. I was a rookie when Rhonda died, and I remember how it shook the community."

"Thank you, Matt." Had he only wanted to find out what I knew? I'd expected a lecture.

"But Emma—"

Here it came.

"I don't want you to get involved in my murder investigation. For your safety, as well as my sanity." He swiped a hand over his face. "However, it's evident you're already working on the case. Experience has taught me that I can't stop you even if I try. Never confront a suspect by yourself. Jake is a good sidekick for you—"

"Matt, why haven't you hired Jake at the police department?"

He put his notebook in his shirt pocket and stood. "That's a conversation for another day between Jake and me. Make smart decisions, Emma, and call me if you need me."

I stood too. "Will you at least tell me how Tess died? Strangulation? Hit over the head?"

"I can't tell you anything." Matt walked away with a quick, determined stride. He waved to Jake before exiting the building.

Mason joined me. "What just happened?"

"Chief Young questioned me about Tess Carranza's murder."

"Why you? What did you say?" Mason glared at me.

"I discovered the body. He was asking if I remembered anything new."

"Did you?"

"No, but this conversation is over. If you have questions regarding the murder investigation, I suggest you take them to Chief Young." I hurried away.

Jake met me halfway to the door. "I was on my way to you when I spotted Mason. Are you okay?"

"Just dandy."

"Ready to go?"

"Most definitely." I kept a tight leash on my indignation, and we walked to the door.

"Wait." Laurel snatched at my arm.

My pulse stuttered. It was only Laurel. Not Mason. "What?" My question came out louder than I intended.

"Shh. Come to my office."

"Only if Jake can come too."

Her spine stiffened. "Fine."

We followed her to the library director's office. I looked at Jake. "This is Tess's old office."

He nodded.

Laurel shut the door behind us. "What did you tell Chief Young?"

I walked to the near-empty bookshelves. There was a photo of Laurel in her cap and gown at the University of North Texas. I picked it up. "Not much. What did you tell him?"

"I told him the truth about you asking me to come over and open the library."

"Are you worried about something?"

"It just feels weird." She sat in the chair and combed her fingers through her thick hair.

"Yes, it does." I returned the framed photo to the shelf. "Have you thought of anything that could help the police catch the killer?"

"No."

"What do you know about Tess getting mad at Ethan Tucker?"

"Tess believed he neglected his daughter. She was afraid the child could get kidnapped or run over if she walked out of the library. He works late hours, and he did fall asleep. Often. If she was mad at him, I believe it was due to concern for Mia, his daughter." Her fingers stopped moving through the blond waves. "Chief Young should know about Ethan. As soon as I get off work, I'll contact him. Unless, you want to tell him now, Emma."

I stepped back. "No. It'll only be hearsay, if I report Ethan. You should be the one to talk to the police."

She straightened her legs and pulled a business card from the top desk drawer. "I'll schedule an appointment."

"Laurel, is there any chance Tess reported Ethan to child protective services?"

"How would I know?"

"Well, you two work together. It seems like something you'd discuss."

She stood and motioned for us to leave the office. "I can't tell you what she did. Now, if you'll excuse me, I need to get back to work."

Jake had been leaning against the door, and his body blocked Laurel's exit. "We're the ones who were leaving when you asked us to come back here."

I slipped between the two of them and patted Jake's arm. "Let's be on our way, honey."

Jake mumbled something about entitled people, but he left with me.

Chapter Twenty-Seven

J ake and I sat at my French harvest table, discussing Tess's murder.
"I don't want to forget that Tess said something about three more people. That's related to Mason Brown." I doodled with the number three. "They needed them to sign a list or something."

"Let's table that for the moment, until Brett and Ms. Maebell have their meeting with Mason and Tom Ward."

"Okay, another thing we learned is that Laurel isn't always truthful. She lied about contacting the police, and Matt overheard her." I'd dealt with lying customers in the past. Usually, it was people wanting early refills on pain meds. With the recent murders in town, I'd come across more liars. Sometimes they fooled me, but not always.

"Good. Did Matt seem different to you today? Like, not as angry as in the past?"

I considered his question. "As a matter of fact, he did. I wonder what's going on with him? Wouldn't it be great if he's ready to hire you?"

Jake placed his hands on the table. "After my time in the Marines, it made sense to become a cop. I admit, it irritated me that Matt wouldn't hire me to begin with."

"Hey, Mom." Abby entered the room. "There's a lady on the office phone who says she can only speak to you."

"Oh, excuse me, Jake. This conversation will be continued, but maybe it's an order. I'll be right back." I hurried to the office and reached for the phone. "Hello."

"Emma, it's me. You know who."

It sounded like Paula. "Are you okay?"

"Yes. I've been watching the news and social media, but it doesn't look like anyone has been arrested. What do you know?"

"I'm working on it. Have you thought of anything that might help?"

"Not really. Our friend was nervous the past couple weeks, but she didn't talk about problems at work." There was a pause. "That's not exactly right. She thought she made a mistake hiring the assistant director. The girl might have been trying to make it look like Tess was incompetent. But that would make it more likely for Tess to murder Laurel than the other way around. Plus, you know who I think did it."

"Why are we talking in code?" I knew she'd bought burner phones. I was the one who took her to the mini-store at the gas station.

"Your phone could be tapped."

My scalp tingled. "Good grief, then you probably don't want to talk much longer. Real quick. Did our friend have family?"

"They were estranged."

Her words confirmed what I was hearing from others. "Did she have a will?"

"Yes. She wanted most of her books to go to the library and some to the high school library. I don't know who the other beneficiaries will be. Braden Stone was her attorney."

The man's name was familiar to me. "Thanks. You stay safe."

"You, too." Paula ended the call.

I walked back to the breakfast room and sat across from Jake.

He met my gaze. "Abby's in the yard with Cowboy."

"Good. She doesn't need to get involved in this situation. That was Paula on the phone. She's okay." I shared our brief conversation, including the part about Tess's will.

"Well, Braden Stone's a local attorney, and he should be able to contact whoever will inherit her estate."

"I'm surprised you've already met him." While I'd lived most of my life here, Jake was still a relative newcomer.

"I helped Coop remodel his new office. Braden liked the location, but it

114

needed updates. He also paid extra for us to put a rush on the project." Jake shrugged. "He's a decent guy."

I jotted down the information. "This is another issue beyond our control. I think we need to stay focused on our current list of suspects. Mason Brown, Tom Ward, Laurel Holley, Nick Jones, and Ethan Tucker."

Jake looked at his watch. "It's too early for the supper crowd at Amalfi's."

"But I like the way you think. We could go over and place a carryout order. While we wait, we can sit at the bar and talk to Ethan." I looked at the time on my phone. "Do you want to meet over there a little later? I need to decide what to plant in the next few days, so I'll have flowers to sell this fall."

"I have things to do also. Call me when you get to a good stopping place, and we'll go over together." Jake stood, and we walked to the front door. "I can't believe we're investigating another murder."

"Me, either. I appreciate your support, though." I kissed him goodbye then found my garden sketch pad and worked on my vision for the fall flowers. I got lost in the process until a voice pulled me from my work.

"Your daughter said I'd find you here." Matt stopped beside my patio table.

"Hi, Matt." I closed my sketch pad and sat straighter. "Have a seat. How are you doing?"

He took the seat opposite me. "Do you mean, how is the investigation going?"

"No, I'm asking about you as a person. You don't seem as angry as you have been the past few months."

His shoulders slumped. "I didn't realize it was apparent. I'm sure you remember Candace, my ex-wife."

"Of course. Is she okay?" We'd crossed paths often when she'd lived in Lutz.

"Yep. She's getting married. It's not like I imagined we'd ever get back together, but it took me by surprise." He stared at the table.

"I'm sorry, Matt." As I reflected on life the past few months, he'd seemed mad, and probably hurt. He'd even shown interest in me. I wouldn't have considered dating him, but my relationship with Jake had made it easier to turn him down without hurting his feelings.

"It's life. Whatcha going to do?" He removed his sunglasses and rubbed his eyes.

"There are a lot of women in town who'd probably be thrilled if you asked them out." My best friend came to mind.

"Thanks for saying that."

"No, really. Why don't you ask Sophie on a date? You two have a lot in common."

He lifted his hand to stop me. "I can't think about dating now. Do you know where Paula Jones is? Her vehicle is in front of her house, but nobody answers the door. She's also not answering her phone. I'm this close to busting inside to perform a wellness check." He held his thumb and pointer finger close together.

"I honestly don't know where Paula is." That was the truth. "Do you think she's in danger?"

"She might be, or it's possible she murdered Tess."

I gasped. "No way. They're best friends. Why would she harm Tess? There's no motive." My temple throbbed. "According to Braden Stone, Tess left the bulk of her estate to Paula."

"Well, the attorney wouldn't lie about that. I'm sorry Matt, but I don't know where Paula is, and if she won't answer her phone for you, it's doubtful, she'll answer my call."

Matt pointed to my phone. "Humor me."

I picked it up and called Paula, showing him her contact information in the process. I knew good and well it was still in her house. Had we wiped off our fingerprints?

"Put it on speaker, please."

I did as Matt requested.

"Hello." A man's voice answered, and I nearly fell out of my chair.

116

Chapter Twenty-Eight

Whoever was on the other end of the phone must have broken into Paula's house.

I said, "May I speak to Paula? This is Emma Justice, and I'm with Chief Matt Young. We need to speak to Paula." I was rattling.

The line went dead.

Matt huffed. "Try again."

I redialed, but this time nobody answered. "Matt, I'm worried."

"Me, too." He walked away and made a call while standing in the shade.

My brain swirled. Who was in Paula's house? How did they get inside?

Matt returned. "I've got a team going over to her place. Be safe, Emma."

"Hey, Matt. If my phone was tapped, like my business phone, it's a landline, how would I know?"

He frowned. "Don't use it, and I'll come back to check it for you."

"Thanks."

He jogged away, and I entered the house.

The siren on Matt's car sounded, and my heart skipped a beat.

Cowboy barked and raced to the front window.

"Here, boy." I sat on the couch and patted the cushion beside me. "It's okay."

The puppy joined me, and I rubbed his sides.

"Mom, what's happening?" Abby appeared.

"Chief Young is driving over to Paula's house to see if she's okay."

"Miss Jones?" Abby's voice squeaked. "Do you think she's been hurt?"

"I have no idea, but we'll trust the police to figure it out." I met my daughter's worried gaze. "Well, honestly, I believe she's safe, at least for now. But don't tell anyone I said that. Try not to worry. For now, don't answer the work phone. We need to make sure nobody tapped it."

"Arg. Mom. I was only away for one semester, and you are a completely different person. You're solving murders, putting yourself in danger, you've got a dog, and the phone might be tapped. This is crazy." Abby continued her tirade.

I didn't interrupt until she ran out of steam. She was scared, and she made several good points. At last, I addressed her issues. "I'm the same person, and I love you. I followed my dream to start my flower farming business. I felt sorry for Cowboy, and you wouldn't have wanted me to abandon him. You know I've always loved to read, especially cozy mysteries. I still host our book club meetings. See, I'm the same person, except for solving murders. That just kinda happened like adopting Cowboy."

Abby sat beside me. "It's more than that. You're more confident and ready to tackle problems."

Cowboy situated himself so he lay on both our laps.

"That hurts a little. When your dad died, I had a lot of problems to tackle."

"Did you think about putting me up for adoption?" Her eyes widened.

"No! Never. You were my greatest joy, but I needed to find a way to support us financially. Food, shelter, clothing, and someone to watch you while I worked were hurdles. As you got older, we settled into a routine. So, I see how you thought I wasn't spunky. Sometimes you need to fight harder than other times. Peaks and valleys."

She rested her head on my shoulder. "Okay. Is this a good time to tell you I don't want to keep playing volleyball?"

That was a gut punch. " That's fine, but I don't think Baylor is affordable without your scholarship." Her dad had left an inheritance for her college education when he died, but it wasn't enough by itself.

"True, but I want to be a veterinarian. It'll take longer than a business degree—"

"You never mentioned vet school before." How many years would it take?

Abby sat straighter. "During my junior year, I talked to my high school counselor, and she discouraged me. Having Cowboy around has made me realize I want to try."

"Forget about the counselor. You've got my support, but you don't need to work for Sophie and me this summer. I want you to go see Dr. Erb about a job." I looked at my amazing daughter. "Now, Abby. Don't waste one more day to chase your dreams."

She squealed and gave me a hug. "Thanks, Mom. If he hires me, do you think Sophie will be mad?"

"No. She'll understand." I smiled at my daughter. "I'm proud of you, honey."

"Let's hope he hires me." Abby ran out of the room.

Cowboy looked at me and tilted his head.

"Hey, who knew how inspiring you'd be?" I hugged my golden retriever mutt. "Time for me to get back to reviewing my murder notes. Do you have any thoughts?"

My dog leapt to the floor and shook.

"I'll take that for a no." I laughed and reached for my sketch pad of murder notes.

Who in the world had answered the phone at Paula's house? Did the phone still have charge, or had the man plugged it in? What did he hope to find on Paula's phone?

I made bullet points. Was it somebody who thought she had a clue to Tess's murder? Was it possibly Nick? There was no way he had a key to her place, and Paula was too smart to have a key hidden on her property. Or could it be linked to the reading of Tess's will?

I couldn't wait to find out more when Matt came over to check for a phone tap.

I shivered at the memory of how much my mention of the tap had upset Abby. Maybe if I could check it myself, Matt wouldn't need to come over, and Abby would be less stressed. There was no need to upset her if I could help it.I looked online for ways to detect a phone tap. Once I resolved that issue, I'd return to my investigation.

Chapter Twenty-Nine

Abby left for Dr. Bushy Erb's office, and I was on my knees, following the phone line.

"Whatcha doing?" Jake's voice held a tone of amusement.

I jumped and bumped my head on the desk. "Looking for a phone tap, but I don't see anything here."

"Good to know. Why were you worried?"

"Oh, um, well—"

"Never mind. Where's Cowboy?"

"Out back." I stood. "Sorry, I lost track of time. Give me just a few minutes to change."

"Don't worry. I'm sure we'll have time to talk to Ethan. I'll check on your pup."

"Thanks." I ran up to my room and slipped into a sleeveless midi-skirt dress and yellow platform sandals. I didn't dress up often, and this seemed like a good opportunity. A quick touchup to my hair and makeup, and I hurried back to Jake. "I hope I haven't made us too late."

He shook his head. "We're fine, and you look beautiful. Do you want to drive or walk?"

My knees shook from nervous energy. "Let's drive. It'll give me time to calm down. If we walk, I'll stress over not having much time to talk to Ethan."

"My Sequoia's on the street."

"Perfect, because I'm sure Abby has Miss Daisy." The drive to the vet clinic was too far to easily walk.

Sure enough, when we stepped outside, my truck wasn't in the driveway.

It was a quiet and quick trip to the Italian restaurant, and soon we were sitting on barstools, talking to one of my suspects.

Ethan placed drinks in front of us. "How's it going today?"

I said, "Pretty good. Tell us about you and Tess."

His eyes widened. "Tess? The librarian? She didn't care much for me."

"People have told me the two of you argued a few times."

He sneered. "Who? That little blonde who works at the library?"

"There are more people who witnessed you and Tess argue."

Ethan leaned toward us with both fists on the bar. "She threatened to call child protective services on me because I fell asleep. It's not like I left Mia in a hot car or home alone. I dozed off during story time. Can you believe it?"

Jake placed one hand on the bar. "Those would be worse, but dude, somebody could've kidnapped your daughter."

"But they didn't. The library staff knows she's my kid. Hope, the children's librarian, was always nice. Tess kept an eye on events involving kids. Nothing bad ever happened there."

No wonder Tess had been frustrated with the bartender. "Babysitting Mia while you nap is not their responsibility."

Ethan frowned. "That's what she said, too."

I met his angry gaze. Time to try something different. "Ethan, who do you believe could've murdered Tess?"

"All I know is it wasn't me." His tone wasn't as angry.

Jake said, "We're not accusing you, but did you notice anyone suspicious at the library whenever you were there?"

Ethan pushed off the bar and crossed his arms. "Tess was one uptight woman. She often told people to take their phone calls in the outer area or the parking lot. Come to think of it, she wasn't exactly mean, but she was firm. Like an unpopular school teacher. You know how years later, you realize they taught you a lot, but at the time, you dreaded their class?"

"I get it." Jake nodded.

"She was nice to the kids, though. Mia adored her." He lifted a finger, indicating he'd be back. He got a drink for a man at the end of the bar and returned to us. "In fact, no matter how mad she was at me, she never put me down in front of my daughter. I appreciate that. Most of the people at the library are locals. There are lots of parents with children, especially in the summer. There are adult events too. They even started a yoga class for seniors this summer. None of those people seem suspicious."

Jake said, "But?"

"One man never seemed to fit in. He was overdressed for the library."

"Mason Brown?" I watched his expression.

"That sounds about right."

"What about him? Could he have killed Tess?"

"I'm not going to accuse him of murder, because I don't know him. But again, I did not kill Tess."

The guy at the end of the bar signaled he wanted a refill.

"Sorry, but I need to keep customers happy. Maybe then I can afford a babysitter. I love my daughter, and I'd never let her get hurt." He walked to the other man.

Jake turned on his stool, and our knees touched. "Do you want to order takeout? Or eat here?"

"Let's eat here. My treat." We usually ate at my house, and I'd discovered Jake was probably better at preparing meals than I was. Even Abby had commented on his skills. It'd been a hot day, and I didn't feel like cooking and washing dishes.

"Oh, thanks. It'll be a legit date night."

We approached the hostess stand, and she led us to the same table as before. After she left, Jake leaned close. "I guess this is our official table."

I laughed. "I thought only rich people had special tables at restaurants. What do you think about Ethan?"

"He may do the best he can as a dad, but some alarm bells went off in my head. It's possible he needs to take a parenting class. Although, he does seem to love his daughter. So, that's a plus."

"You know, people may have questioned my parenting skills over the years. I always did the best I could, though, and I had good friends who supported me. Maybe Ethan needs friends."

"Interesting take on the situation. What about the murder? I don't see him being the one."

"Me either. Are we agreeing to take him off our list?"

"Yes." Jake nodded. "Not the best father, but not the killer either."

"Okay. Onward to another suspect."

"But first, dinner." Jake opened the menu.

He was right. Time to enjoy the evening with my boyfriend.

Chapter Thirty

The restaurant was close to Jake's apartment, so we left his SUV and went for an after-dinner walk.

He reached for my hand. "Did you check your cell phone to make sure it hadn't been tapped?"

I felt guilty for not telling him why I'd been suspicious. "Paula suggested I check. She's safe for the moment, but Tess left her most everything in her will. Now, Matt wants to question Paula. And another thing, I found out why Matt's been so grumpy. His ex-wife is engaged to get married. He's been taking it hard."

"Maybe he believed they'd get back together. I guess we should cut him some slack ."

"Even if he was hoping for a second chance, he could've handled your job application better." I squeezed Jake's hand.

"Or maybe God had other plans for me. I'm not going to sweat it, and you shouldn't either." He pointed. "There's Zig and Faith. Do you want to talk to them?"

"Yeah. Is that okay?"

"Definitely."

We walked in their direction.

Zig waved. "Folks, how are you this evening?"

His deep voice inspired confidence. I smiled. "We're good. We just had dinner at Amalfi's."

Faith smiled. "I love that place. It reminds me a little of my favorite restaurant when we lived in Los Angeles."

Zig chuckled. "It was one of the few things she liked about LA."

"He's not entirely wrong. I didn't like the smog, the traffic, or the women throwing themselves at Zig. The weather was okay, and there were some beautiful views." Faith's blond hair was loose and touched her shoulders. She smiled at her husband before turning back to us. "How's your investigation going?"

I shrugged. "Okay. We ruled out Ethan Tucker."

Zig said, "I appreciate you connecting Brett and me. There's nothing about his specific case I can tell you, but I did learn some interesting facts about Tom Ward. He likes to research people who are late paying property taxes. Once he has the information, he approaches them by saying they can't get away without paying taxes. He uses scare tactics to convince them to sell their land to him. In most cases, it works. They sell the property to Tom for a pittance, and he pays the taxes."

Jake crossed his arms. "Ah, ha. He probably wanted to pull the same stunt on Brett's aunt. What does he get out of the deal, though? I didn't think Ms. Maebell's land was valuable."

Zig grinned. "That's where you'd be wrong."

"Honey, shh." Faith gave him a gentle nudge.

We all looked in the direction of the bed-and-breakfast. Mason was headed our way.

For once, Mason didn't wear dress clothes. Instead, he ran in shorts and a tank top. When he spotted us, he stopped. "Looks like an important meeting."

Jake said, "Nah. Just a neighborly chat. It happens a lot in Lutz. In fact, it took me a while to adjust to this friendly town."

Mason's gaze bounced around our group. "All right, then. I better get back to my run." He waved and sprinted toward the square.

When he was out of earshot, we moved to a shady spot. Zig said, "From what I can deduce, Tom buys up what others think is worthless. Once he owns the land, he creates planned communities and builds expensive houses. He makes a killing on most of his projects, and he's one of the wealthiest men in Texas. Keep in mind, I'm a student. It's possible antitrust laws are being broken. The land Tom wants to buy from Maebell—oops, I need to stop there. I don't know enough, and it'll be her story to tell." I took notes on my phone. "You and Brett will protect Ms. Maebell from Mr. Ward and Mason."

"We aim to take care of her. She deserves a fair price for the land in question." His expression was serious.

"Zig, can you think of any reason they'd have for murdering Tess?"

"Not at this point."

Faith said, "It's possible Tess was going to warn the landowners. Would that be a motive?"

"If she got between those men and a whole lot of money, it might be a motive." I added this to my notes.

My phone buzzed in my purse. I pulled it out. "This is Chief Young. I probably should take it."

Faith said, "We'll give you some privacy. See y'all later."

"Bye." I swiped my phone. "Hi, Matt. Is Paula okay?"

Jake lifted his eyebrows.

I wasn't lying. In fact, I'd asked a question. So, why'd I feel rotten?

"It's hard to say. I'm about to leave her house. Her car is in the driveway, and her phone is in the house. It's barely got any charge. There are no indoor plants, but there's plant food under the sink."

"Um, I have them."

The silence that followed sent a shiver up my spine.

"Is there anything else I should know? Like is she staying at your house? I'd hate to discover she was hiding right under my nose."

"I promise she's not hiding at my house. Only her indoor plants are there. And I have Tess's plants, which, according to you, now belong to Paula."

There was another long pause, but I waited for Matt to break the silence. I angled the phone so Jake could also hear.

"Hypothetically speaking, if Paula is safe, but hiding, why would she hide?"

"Hypothetically?" I met Jake's gaze, and he nodded.

"Yeah. Is it because she murdered Tess for the inheritance? Or would there be another reason?"

"I'm confident she didn't murder Tess." So far, so good. "Maybe she heard that Tess was murdered, and maybe she left town in fear. Isn't it possible she felt like she might be next on the killer's list?"

Jake gave me a thumbs up.

"Let's go with your theory. If she left town, you know what? Never you mind. I can track her identification and credit cards. In fact, that should work whether she left town or not."

I breathed a sigh of relief. "Matt, if her phone is there, was there any sign of the man who answered it?"

"No, but the laundry room window had been pried open. Must be how the man entered. We're checking for fingerprints."

"Okay. By the way, I looked up how to determine if my phone had been tapped, and I'm good. I know how busy you are with the murder investigation, and it seemed silly to bother you. Can you share anything with me about Tess?"

"Be safe, Emma." The call ended.

"Oh, Jake. That was stressful. He knows that I know something."

"Yes, but he handled it better than expected. I guess coming to terms with his ex-wife's marriage has made him more bearable." He reached for my hand. "Are you ready to finish our walk?"

"Yeah. Let's go home and see what happened with Abby."

Chapter Thirty-One

J ake and I finished our walk when we reached my home. My truck was in the driveway, but Abby wasn't in the house. I called her cell, but she didn't answer. "Jake, I don't like this."

"Let's stay calm."

I let Cowboy out of the crate and took him to the back door. "He doesn't seem upset."

"Check Abby's room and the office. Maybe she fell asleep. I'll keep an eye on the pup."

"Thanks." I ran upstairs and entered Abby's bedroom. Empty. The ensuite was also vacant. I crossed the hall to my primary suite. "Abby, are you in here?"

More silence, but I checked anyway. Not a soul was in sight.

I hit the redial button and ran downstairs to check the last bedroom turned home office. There was no answer on her phone, and there was no sign of my daughter in the house. My ears rang.

Jake joined me in the office, and Cowboy followed. Jake said, "Does this happen often?"

"No." I collapsed into the nearest chair.

Jake knelt beside me and took my hands in his warm ones. "Don't panic. She's been in college and not used to checking in with you."

"True, but she's been home for weeks now. We have courtesy rules to let the other know our whereabouts. Do you think something bad happened to her? Has Tess's killer taken my daughter?"

"Shh. Abby's not the one investigating the murder. I'll call Matt, and you

128

contact her friends."

I nodded and searched my phone contacts. Thank goodness, I had a lot of Abby's friends in my phone, probably because she'd been one of the last teens to get her personal cell phone and had been stuck sharing one with me.

I sent out a huge group text. **This is Ms. Justice, Abby's mom. I need to speak to her. It's kinda an emergency. If anybody sees Abby, please ask her to call me. Thank you.**

Jake walked out of the room, but Cowboy stood beside me.

I called Sophie next.

"Hey, Emma. What are you doing tonight?"

"Looking for Abby. Have you seen her?" My voice shook.

"No. She's not scheduled to work again until Saturday morning. I gave her the day off tomorrow. Why?"

I explained.

Sophie said, "I'll drive around town and look for her, and then I'm coming over."

"Thanks." When the call ended, I petted my dog's head. "Where is she?"

Jake returned. "Matt's on his way here."

I met his gaze. "Am I overreacting?"

He shook his head. "I don't know, but there is a killer on the loose. If my sister disappeared, I'd probably panic too. After we find Abby, we can decide the answer to your question."

My lips quivered, and I pressed my fingers on my mouth.

Jake said, "I don't know the best way to respond. If I hug you, will you fall apart? Or will you realize how much I care about you and Abby? Should I fix you a cup of tea? Or a stiff shot of bourbon?"

I laughed. "I don't believe Chief Young will appreciate me being inebriated when he arrives, and don't comfort me right now. I might start to cry and not be able to stop."

"A cup of tea it is." He motioned for me to follow him to the kitchen.

"I'll call Brett." It didn't make sense he'd know, but I had to keep trying. I dialed his number.

"Hey, Emma. Zig has a meeting for us with Mr. Ward and Mr. Brown tomorrow morning. I'll let you know what happens."

My stomach tightened. "Good, but that's not why I'm calling. Have you seen Abby?"

"Yeah. She stopped by for a frozen coffee. She told me about her new job, and she was going to celebrate. She also said the vet pays better than you do."

"What time was that?"

"A little after five. I remember because she joked about the caffeine keeping her up all night." He paused. "You're starting to worry me. Is everything okay?"

"I don't know. She's not answering my calls."

"Hang tight. I'll get back to you soon." He ended the call.

I leaned against the counter.

"Emma." Sophie walked in the front door and hurried to me. "I'm so sorry, but I didn't see her. The town is kinda dead except for the bookstore. What can I do?"

I shrugged, then looked at my phone. "It's strange that only one of Abby's friends responded, and she's in Dallas."

Jake said, "Oh, man. Celia mentioned an event tonight. I think it was for college students. She's responsible for it, and she mentioned one of the goals was that people would turn off their phones and really connect. Do you suppose they're all at that?"

"Maybe. She does enjoy reading."

Sophie patted my shoulder. "I'll go check. You two stay here."

I shook my head. "I should go."

"I'm already out the door." Sophie walked away. "Oh, Matt. Hi. They're in the kitchen. Go on back."

The electric tea kettle clicked, indicating the water was ready.

I opened the cabinet where I kept mugs.

"I beat you to it." Jake pointed to three mugs and went about preparing tea.

Matt entered the kitchen and cleared his throat. "Sophie, let me in."

CHAPTER THIRTY-ONE

"Thanks for coming. Abby's missing. What if the killer took her?"

"Your concern is valid, but don't think like that."

My phone vibrated, and we both looked at it.

I swiped the screen and read the message. **Ms. Emma, I'm at a friend's pool, but Abby is not with us. Sorry.**

Matt and Jake looked over my shoulders.

Before I could say anything, Brett called me.

"Hey, Brett. Did you find out any news?"

"I'm at Paige's Turn Bookstore, and your baby girl is here. She said she left a note on the breakfast table. What do you want me to do? Oh, wait. Sophie's here now, and she looks worried. I better go talk to her." The call ended.

I walked over to the coffee table. Instead of food and dishes, it was covered with my murder sketch pad and business papers. Amid the mess was a square of white paper, with Abby's handwriting. "Oh, Matt. I'm sorry to have bothered you. This is so embarrassing."

"You know my kids, and I'd have been concerned too. Don't think anything about it."

Jake said, "Matt, how about a cup of green tea?"

"Thanks, but I need to get back to solving Tess's case. I'm relieved Abby's safe, though." He paused. "Emma, this could be a sign that you need to quit investigating. It's not safe."

"I'll think about it, Matt." I walked him to the door. He said Tess's case. Why hadn't he said murder? "Matt, are you sure you can't tell me more?"

"I don't want to say anything to endanger you." He opened the door.

Sophie and Abby stood on the front porch.

Matt said, "Abby, I'm glad you're okay."

"Thanks, Chief Young."

I glanced from Abby to Matt. " I appreciate your help."

"All in the line of duty. All y'all have a good night." He glanced at Sophie. "Can I walk you to your car?"

"Sure." My friend blushed, and they walked down the sidewalk.

"Abby, we need to talk." I waved her inside, and we went to the kitchen.

"Sorry about not answering my phone, but Celia asked that we all turn off our phones."

Jake said, "That sounds like my sister. How was the event?"

"Terrific. It was a summer mixer. Paige and Celia encouraged us to form book clubs and meet back each week. We'll discuss our book with the group, and then we'll form another group. It'll help us stay connected through the summer." Abby poured hot water into a mug. "And y'all won't guess who is in my group."

Jake met my gaze.

I said, "Tell us."

"Hope Peters, the children's librarian. She loves to read and wanted an opportunity to connect with other readers who might not use the library. I've seen your notes on the murder, so I asked Hope if she has a key to the library, and she does."

I hugged Abby. "It sounds like she'll be the next person I question."

Jake moved to the table and reached for my sketch pad of murder notes. "Since, you're not going to take Chief Young's advice, I suggest we add this information to your notes."

Chapter Thirty-Two

Early Friday morning, I raked the garden area where I would plant fall flowers. I removed weeds and spent plants, then disposed of them. The soil had been tested, and it was time to allow it to rest. Cowboy appeared and barked.

His happy attitude reassured me that everything was okay. "Hey there. How'd you get outside?"

"I'm home." Abby joined us and handed me a large tumbler. "You need to take better care of yourself, Mom. Try this. It's got electrolytes, and I squeezed some lemon drops in it."

I stood and stretched my back. "Thanks. What time is it?"

Abby looked at her watch. "Ten. I went to the bakery and talked to Sophie about my new job. She was cool when I told her about working for Dr. Erb, and she's not even making me give her a two-week notice."

"You're like the daughter she never had." I took a deep drink of my daughter's concoction. "Not bad." I lifted the glass to my mouth again.

"Mom, you and Sophie are not too old to get married and have children."

Water spewed from my mouth, and I coughed.

"Easy, there." She patted my back.

Cowboy barked, then moseyed away from us.

"You're almost eighteen. Wouldn't it embarrass you if I had another baby at my age?" Did a second chance at love with Jake translate into becoming a mother again?

"It depends on the situation, but I don't think you and Sophie should believe it's not possible. Did I detect some chemistry between her and Chief

Young last night? He comes in the bakery almost every morning."

"Some days I think they'd make a good couple, but other days I'm not so sure." I took another drink and managed to swallow it. "I need to finish this area, and then I'll get cleaned up and go to the library. What are you doing today?"

"I'm supposed to buy scrubs. Can I drive you to the library? I need to borrow your truck to go shopping."

"Sure, but if you're in a hurry, I can easily walk there. You know it's not that far."

"It's no problem to wait. I'll take Cowboy inside. You can find me in the office when you're ready."

"Sounds good."

An hour later, I held the library door for a woman pushing a stroller before I entered.

More parents and children stood at the check-out area, and I looked for the children's librarian.

Hope Peters was speaking to a dark-haired child.

Ethan rose from a chair and walked over to them. When the little girl hugged his legs, I knew for certain it was Mia. I turned my back to the scene and perused the shelf of current best sellers. It was not my place to judge Ethan. I'd only heard stories about his actions, including what he'd admitted to doing in the library.

"Spying on me?"

I squealed and jumped.

Ethan laughed. "Guilty conscience?"

"No. I'm here for another reason."

"Daddy, who's that?" Mia pointed at me.

He picked up his daughter. "Pumpkin, this is Ms. Emma."

"Hi, Mia. It's nice to meet you."

The child gave me a shy smile. "Hi."

Ethan said, "I'm going to take my daughter home for a nutritious lunch and a nap."

"Hey, Ethan. I'm not accusing you of anything bad. I'm sorry for asking you questions about Tess, but it's the only way I know to find answers."

He frowned for a minute, and then his expression cleared. "Don't sweat it. We're cool."

"Thanks. I hope y'all have a nice lunch."

"See you around." Ethan walked out of the library, carrying Mia.

Had we become friends? It was hard to tell, but it was time for me to question a possible suspect.

Hope was picking up scattered books and toys.

"Excuse me. May I speak to you for a moment?"

The redhead straightened and turned to face me. Her hair was a vibrant shade, while mine was strawberry red. Hope wore a gray T-shirt with cartoon characters on it. "How can I help you?"

"I'm Emma Justice, and I was friends with Tess. It's hard to process what happened. Can I ask you a few questions?"

"This is a good time, if you don't mind tagging along with me. I like to keep my area organized. It makes it easier when I help a child look for a book."

"I don't mind at all." I picked up some random blocks.

"Justice? I may have met your daughter last night, but you don't look old enough to be her mother."

"If you're talking about Abby Justice, then you met my daughter. She went to the bookstore event."

"Yes, that's her." Hope put books on a cart and toys in a plastic basket. "I try to have as many washable toys as possible to cut down on germs. These will be cleaned before children can play with them again. You didn't say how I can help."

"Do you have a key to the library?"

"Sure do."

"Who else does?"

She rolled the library cart to the first aisle. "Laurel has a key."

"What about janitors? Pest control? County officials?"

Hope's eyes widened. "I can't answer your questions, because I don't know. Are you a policewoman?"

"No. I'm a flower farmer. You should come by my booth at the farmers' market tomorrow."

"Oh, that's why I recognize you. Tess had you bring flowers into the library every week."

"Right, and I helped her with the potted plants near the reference section." I cleared my throat. "I also found her body."

"I remember seeing you. What a heartbreaking morning." She made a circular motion with her pointer fingers. "Did Tess give you a key to the library?"

"No. I just brought flower arrangements when the building was open."

Her head bobbed more than nodded. "That makes me think she didn't give a key to the pest control man. I don't know about janitors, though."

"Fair enough. Who do you believe murdered Tess?"

She leaned over the cart and whispered, "I'd hate to make a wrong guess and get somebody in trouble."

I moved closer to the younger woman. "If you know anything, you need to tell the police, or I can tell them for you. Don't put yourself in danger."

"But—"

"Seriously. The police are smart, but they need help from the public. If you think you might know something, tell them. They can decide if it's important or not."

"What if I get fired? I love my job."

"Hope, isn't Laurel the only person who can fire you? Or can the board of directors?"

"I'm not sure. Tess hired me, and when she died, Laurel took charge." She looked over my shoulder, and I turned.

Laurel stood at the end of the row of books, staring at us.

Chapter Thirty-Three

Hope pushed past me and walked to the new library director. "Laurel, will we still order flowers from Emma? If so, what do you think about helium balloons once a week in the children's area?"

I approached the two, impressed with how quick Hope recovered from Laurel's surprise appearance. Maybe working with children had taught her to respond fast to surprises.

"I will need to study the budget before deciding." Laurel turned her gaze on me. "Why did you ask her when you know I'm the director?"

"Good question. You're always so busy, and Hope was picking up from story time. I just walked over here and started talking to her. Since you're here, will the library trustees post the job opening for the director's position, or did they officially give you the job?"

"I'm sure they'll make an announcement soon. Excuse me, I need to take care of library business." Laurel lifted her chin before walking away.

Hope placed her hands over her stomach. "That was too close for comfort."

"Yep. Can I take you to lunch?"

She shook her head. "It's too risky."

"Are you more worried that Laurel will fire you or that she murdered Tess?"

Her face reddened. "Laurel is very ambitious, and she pushed Tess to make some big changes. I can tell she has a passion for books, but it's almost like she's out to prove something."

"But do you believe she's capable of murder?"

"She's mean, but it's hard to imagine she murdered Tess for a job. Although, I don't know Laurel well."

What did that mean? "Are you implying there could be another motive to kill Tess?"

"No. I better get back to putting away the books. Please, leave."

"Okay, but contact me if you want to talk. Better yet, call Chief Young." Her blank expression didn't inspire confidence. "If you're at the farmers' market tomorrow, stop by, and I'll give you something. It'll be a thank-you gift for talking to me today."

"Sure." Hope returned to the library cart, and I entered the main library area.

There was no sign of Mason. Was he still meeting with Brett, Ms. Maebell, and Zig?

The July heat wrapped around me, and tightened my lungs, making it hard to take a deep breath. My sunglasses fogged, and I waited on the sidewalk until they cleared.

My phone vibrated with a message from Brett. **Can you meet at Anytime Coffee?**

Yes. I chose to walk the route with the most shade trees, even though it was technically longer. I'd worked up a good sweat by the time I entered the coffee shop.

"Hey, girl. I fixed you my July quencher. No caffeine, and I hope you like it. Let's sit back there." He pointed to a table we'd sat at before.

I walked to it. "Where's your aunt?"

"She's at my place with Rufus watching over her. I don't know how I'd have survived the past few years without my PTSD dog."

"Remember how skeptical you were at first?"

"Boy, do I. But I'm a believer now. You know, Aunt Maebell seems calmer with the lab around her, too."

"I'm not totally surprised." I sat. "How did this morning go?"

"Zig's appearance seemed to throw off Mr. Ward and Mr. Brown, but they soon recovered. They offered Aunt Maebell five thousand dollars for her land. Zig pushed that it should be more. They argued they'd pay the back taxes. You won't believe what happened next."

"What?" I sipped the cool drink.

"Aunt Maebell had her tax records, a cousin brought them to us late last night, and my aunt proved she was only two months behind on her taxes. It was because she'd been traveling to visit other relatives. She told those men that it wouldn't be any problem for her to catch up on the tax issue."

"Good for her." I smiled. "How did they respond?"

"After some back and forth, Zig told the men they needed to up their offer."

"And?"

"They explained why the land wasn't valuable. That's when Zig told them we knew about their intention to turn it into a planned community."

I gasped. "Who did most of the talking?"

"That Tom Ward fellow. Occasionally, Mr. Brown told him to stop talking, but in a nicer way. Ward is for sure the boss, though. The two of them whispered for a bit, and then Ward made an acceptable offer. Mr. Brown will draw up the contract, and we'll sign it later today." He drummed his fingers on the table. "Oh, yeah, we're not allowed to tell other landowners how much they're paying my aunt."

"What will happen if you do?" I took another sip of the quencher.

"Breach of contract? They can sue us. To be honest, when Aunt Maebell and I give our word, we'd never go back on the agreement."

"I know you're honest, Brett. The sale will be in the public records. Any of the other landowners can look it up."

Brett's fingers stopped moving. "Not everyone is as educated in matters of the law."

"But y'all figured out what Tom Ward's plan was."

"True, but we had Zig on our side, and you and Jake kept encouraging us. We're blessed." He stared at the table. "You remember I told you how many people left the area?"

"Yeah."

"Some of the homes have been abandoned for years. Many original owners have passed on, and it's hard to guess who the property belongs to now. It could be distant relatives who have no sentimental attachment to the land. It makes me wonder."

A familiar figure entered the coffee shop.

"Brett, hold that thought. Chief Young is here."

"Cool." He looked over his shoulder. "We're not busy. The new guy should be able to handle his order."

Matt headed in our direction.

"He's coming our way, but he seems to have chilled out recently." I looked up and smiled. "Hi, Matt."

"Mind if I join you?" He placed his hands on his belt.

Brett said, "Have a seat. Can I get you a drink?"

"No, but you can answer a few questions about Tess Carranza's murder."

Chapter Thirty-Four

Brett's head jerked back at the police chief's comment. "I don't know anything about Tess's murder."

"Did you recently have an argument with her?" Matt pulled a little notepad from his shirt pocket.

"No." Brett glared at Matt.

"That's not the way I heard it."

The men looked like a bull and a matador, with the way they stared at each other.

I raised my hands. "Hey, guys. We're all friends here."

Matt kept his eyes on Brett. "It's been reported to us that you and Tess argued at the library."

"Man, I hardly ever go there. I've taken my aunt a few times. Oh—" Brett closed his eyes.

"Did you remember something?" Matt leaned forward.

"Maybe. I wanted to look at a reference book, but every time I went to the library, Mason Brown had it on his table. He refused to share it, and I talked to Tess. I was frustrated, but I wasn't angry with her. I just couldn't beat the dude to the library with my work schedule."

I pressed my lips together, knowing Matt wouldn't appreciate my interference.

"Did you raise your voice? Yell at her? Possibly threaten her?"

"No. No. No. I told her it didn't seem fair that Mason always got the book I needed to look at. I asked if she could put a hold on it for me or something. She said they didn't do that with reference books. I asked if she could hide it, so Mason wouldn't get to it first. Man, you know what a stickler Tess was. She didn't like my request."

"Is that when you threatened her?" Matt narrowed his eyes.

"I did not threaten Tess. Where are you getting your information?"

"Can't say." He leaned back in his chair.

I said, "If it was Laurel Holley, I'd take her comments with a grain of salt. In fact, she pushed Tess to make changes. The two of them didn't agree on much, and with Tess gone, Laurel can do anything she wants. Taking Tess's job is one of Laurel's motives."

"Just one?" Matt turned his face toward me.

"I've heard there may have been more than work conflicts, but I don't know what they were. I'm trying to persuade my source to talk to you, but she's scared."

Matt tucked the notebook back into his pocket. "By referring to her as a source, I suppose you're not going to reveal her name. Brett, if you think of anything else, let me know. Try to keep a lid on your temper, and we'll avoid talks like this."

"Understood." Brett nodded.

Matt took off.

I finished my drink. "Who do you think saw you at the library?"

"Laurel. She's the one with the curly blond hair, right?"

"Yes."

"It must've been her, and she exaggerated to Chief Young."

"It doesn't surprise me. She wanted to deflect the focus from herself, but Matt's smart. He knows you, and her accusations could backfire. I bet Matt will take a harder look at Laurel."

"At least he didn't tell me not to leave town. He's right about one thing. I need to get my temper under control. It's possible I need to take Rufus with me more places, but not everybody will appreciate me bringing my big black Labrador ."

I patted his hand. "Don't work yourself up. If you need Rufus, you should take him with you."

"You're a good friend, Emma."

"Should I worry that my girlfriend and my best friend are holding hands?" Jake's smile seemed forced.

"Hi, honey. Matt questioned Brett, and—"

Brett stood. "I'm innocent, but he told me to get my temper under control. Your girl just felt sorry for me."

"She does have a tender heart." Jake sat and scooted the chair close to me.

"I best get back to work." Brett walked away.

Jake looked at me. "Have you had lunch?"

"No. Do you have time to eat together?" I knew Jake had been dumped by a woman when he'd been fighting as a Marine. She'd married his best friend at the time. I never wanted to hurt Jake, and I'd never betray him.

Jake looked at his watch. "Sure do, and then I'm going to put in a garbage disposal for a family in town. Shall we eat here?"

"May as well, and I'll tell you what I've learned about Tess's murder case." I touched his face. "Jake, I know you were joking earlier. But just in case there was a kernel of truth in your comment, I love you. Nobody else. I've never felt this way about anybody before. Not even my husband. Our relationship failed, and I'm so incredibly thankful for the second chance I have at love with you."

He leaned forward and kissed me. "I love you, too, Sunshine. You know, you are the sunshine—"

I laughed. "That's too corny to finish. Let's order."

Chapter Thirty-Five

"Mom, I've got two words for you. Bloom bar."

Was this how Tess had felt with Laurel, when the younger woman suggested new ways to run the library? No. Abby had my best interests at heart. "Bloom bar? What is that?"

"It's a way to bring in additional income. You take flowers to special events. For instance, a birthday party or a wedding shower. The host will contact you—"

"Do I have to prepare food and drinks?"

"No, but I've got an idea if that's requested." Abby took my hand and led me to the office. "Sit."

I sat behind my desk, and Abby touched some keys. "I was afraid you might be resistant. Here's my official presentation."

"I'm not opposed to your suggestion, but I need to understand."

Pictures popped up on the screen. "The host will tell you how many people are attending. You'll probably want to start with something simple like using Mason jars for vases, and the guests can create floral arrangements. There should be a simple contract, including how many flowers will be provided per person. For instance, if you're going to a fantasy theme or fairy tale, you might want to take supplies to create hair adornments. You'll also need to take things like scissors, ribbon, jars, and whatever you normally use for flower arrangements."

I watched the presentation with a mixture of excitement and anxiety.

"What do you think?" Abby's smile was contagious.

"The farmers' market is always on Saturday, and that's when I make the most money. Wouldn't that be when most people want to have their parties?"

"My research shows most parties are in the evenings and weekends. In the fall and winter, there won't be as much business at the farmers' market. It's a good opportunity for you to increase your income throughout the slower months."

"I'll consider your suggestion. It sounds like it could be fun."

"When you're ready, Paige and Celia would like to host your first event at the bookstore."

I gasped. "When did you talk to them?"

"Last night at the store's big event. They agreed to limit the number of attendees, and they've got tables and chairs. The only thing you'll need to bring will be yourself and the flowers."

It couldn't be that simple. "Do you have sample contracts?"

"Yes, but you may want an attorney to look at forms before you start using them. These are very basic."

My mind drifted to the library. "Can you make a flyer for me? This could be a way for me to talk to Laurel again without seeming suspicious."

"Mom! Is this about the murder?" Abby crossed her arms. "You need to focus on your business."

"You're right. I talked to your new friend, Hope. She was nice, but she seems scared of Laurel. Did she share much about work?"

"Obviously, it's useless to tell you to quit trying to solve Tess's murder." She sighed. "Hope didn't tell me much about her job. If you can give me a few minutes, I'll make a flyer. Please, have your first event at Paige's Turn Bookstore. They were so nice about it, and Celia's practically family."

I got out of the seat. "Hey, now. We're not talking marriage."

"Yet. Don't worry, Mom. I like Jake."

"Good grief." I left the office and freshened up for my return trip to the library.

Abby had flyers ready when I came back downstairs.

I said, "You've got a real knack for business, but I don't want you to spend so much time helping me that it distracts from applying to vet school. Do you know—"

"Mom, stop. I've checked it out. This fall, I plan to take organic chemistry, physics, biology, and animal nutrition. With labs, it'll be a full semester. Dr. Erb said he has guest lectured at the university before, and he can help me prepare for animal nutrition this summer."

"That's very nice of him."

"Yes, it is."

Twenty minutes later, I was seated in the library director's office, facing Laurel. "What do you think?"

"You'd do this in a community room?"

"Yes."

She stared at the pretty flyer. "I'd prefer it if we can tie this to a book or a book series. Otherwise, I don't believe it'll work."

Her rejection unleashed my competitiveness. "Oh. Maybe you can help me figure out what you mean. There's a knitting group, and a yoga class. How do they relate?"

"Many cozy mystery series involve crafts." She continued telling me why my bloom party wouldn't be popular. Part of her explanation made sense, but part of it was malarky. She shot me a satisfied smile.

"What about gardening and flower arranging books? I'm not trying to be argumentative, but I'd like to understand better."

She put the flyer on her desk. "Those could work. Right now, we're in an upheaval because of Tess. Give me time to decide."

"Speaking of Tess—"

"Oh boy, here we go."

"Have you thought of any other possible suspects?"

"I didn't know Tess outside of work. She didn't get along with Ethan Tucker or Nick Jones. He's the exterminator. She also had words with an attorney. He just walked in." Laurel pointed toward the reference area.

I turned, and sure enough, Mason was in the building. "They had words, but nothing serious?"

"I don't think so, but that guy's a little too cool to be real, if you know what I mean." Laurel pressed her lips together.

"I'm not sure that I do."

"He acts like he agrees with you, but he's going to do what he wants. After he's caught, he'll pretend that he misunderstood."

"That's an interesting analysis. If you think he possibly murdered Tess, be careful. Don't get in a situation where you could be alone with him. I suspect he might have a mean side if he doesn't get his way." In fact, I'd seen his ugly side, but I didn't know how far I could trust Laurel to keep her mouth shut. "I'll let you get back to work."

"Thanks for the warning, Emma. I promise, I'm not the killer." Her comment hung awkwardly in the air like a broken ceiling fan.

"See you later." I closed her office door behind me, and I stood for a moment, unsure of my next move. If I confronted Mason, what would I say? Nothing came to mind, so I walked toward the library exit.

"Emma, wait a minute." Mason had come after me.

Chapter Thirty-Six

"Emma, wait." Mason grabbed my arm. "Have you talked to your friends?"

"Let go of me." I gritted my teeth.

One finger at a time, he released his grip. "Sorry, but I wanted to speak to you."

I stepped back, straightened my shoulders, and lifted my chin. He would not intimidate me, at least not in a public place. "Next time, just holler. What do you want?"

"Your friends. Did they tell you we offered Ms. Maebell Franks more money to buy her land?"

My pulse throbbed in my temple. Was this a trap? Brett had claimed they couldn't disclose the amount Tom paid for the property. I needed to play this smart. "I hope you gave her a respectable sum of money."

He placed one hand on his chest. "I didn't buy it. My client did. I thought you should know that your friend didn't get cheated."

"Thanks for sharing. Does this mean you plan to leave town soon?"

"Not quite yet. I'll see you around, Emma. Who knows? I might stop by the farmers' market tomorrow."

"Bye, Mason." On shaky legs, I left the building. Thank goodness I'd driven Miss Daisy. I hurried to my truck and sped away, checking to make sure Mason didn't follow me.

Once I got home, I set the alarm. "Abby? Are you here?"

"Yes, ma'am." She walked down the stairs, and Cowboy followed. "Did you set the alarm?"

"I did." I looked through photos on my phone and showed my daughter pictures of Mason Brown and Tom Ward. "If you see either of these men, go another way. If they follow you, call the police. Go to a public place or scream. Don't be afraid of causing a scene."

"Mom, you're scaring me."

Cowboy barked.

"I'm a little spooked myself, but promise me, you won't engage with them."

"Okay." Her voice trembled.

I hugged her. "Thanks, honey."

"What are we going to do about transportation, when I start my new job next week? I haven't made enough money to buy a decent car yet."

"For now, you can either drive my truck, or I'll give you a ride. I want to add some things to my murder notes, and then I'll start getting organized for tomorrow. Do you want to help me at the farmers' market when you finish working at the bakery?"

"Sure, but is there any chance this is a paying gig?"

I laughed. "Of course."

"Why don't I start supper?"

"I love the sound of that." I sat down and updated everything I'd learned today. There were more details for every suspect on my list except for Nick Jones. Besides the incident at Tess's house, we hadn't crossed paths. Was it intentional on his part, or only a coincidence? Could Nick have been the man to answer Paula's phone when Matt insisted I call?

Today, Matt had questioned Brett. It wasn't fair that he was looking at Brett during another murder investigation. It also wasn't nice of me to think about Nick every time a person was murdered in Lutz.

Still.

I turned to the page on Nick Jones. He had a bad history with Tess. Was it possible she'd finally pushed him too far with her accusations of killing his first wife?

I didn't know, but I wouldn't remove him from my list yet.

Chapter Thirty-Seven

Saturday morning, I loaded the back of my truck with buckets, coolers, flowers, vases, and other supplies I needed for the farmers' market. It didn't seem like enough, so I hurried to the backyard to cut a few more zinnias and celosias. The colorful blooms should be popular.

Because I'd sold out on the Fourth of July, I wasn't sure how sales would go today. I returned the shearers and gloves to the potting shed and turned to leave.

Ow.

A sting on my ankle drew my attention, and I looked down.

Fire ants crawled on my tennis shoes and onto my ankles. Ack! I ran to the patio and dropped the flowers onto a chair.

I swiped at the ants, kicked off my shoes and socks, and practically did a dance to get the ants off me. At last, I didn't see any more of the aggressive insects. There wasn't time to destroy the ant mound, but maybe I could call Nick Jones. Was I that desperate?

I gathered the flowers, a pair of flip-flops by the back door, and I jogged around the house to my truck. In minutes, I was at the farmers' market parking lot. I opened Miss Daisy's tailgate, and reached for my backpack. It contained my credit card reader and cash. It wouldn't do to let the bag out of my sight.

Jake crossed the parking lot and grabbed the stand that would hold my metal buckets of cut flowers. "I was starting to worry. You're always early. Is everything okay?"

"I stepped onto a fire ant mound, and they attacked." I pointed to my ankles with white pustules on them. "It was careless, but the ants weren't there yesterday. I'm so aggravated." I reached for the fresh-cut flowers.

"Ouch. Have you put anything on the bites to soothe the stings?" He followed me to my designated area.

"There wasn't time. I was about to head this way, but at the last minute, I decided to cut more flowers." I tried to ignore the pain. "It was so silly."

Jake rubbed my shoulder. "Brett's running the coffee truck this morning, and the new guy's at the shop. This is a test to see if he can manage on his own."

"I hope the new guy works out."

"Me too. Let me help you set up, and then I'll make a baking soda paste. It should provide some relief."

"I've got baking soda at the house. Would you mind going there? It'd also be great if you brought my cowboy boots or my rubber gardening boots. No, they'll make it hard to massage the area around the bites. How about clean tennis shoes? Not the ones I kicked off in the yard because there may still be ants in them. I sure don't want you to get stung. Oh, please don't let Cowboy out there until I do something about the mound."

Jake raised his hand. "Take a breath, Emma."

I met his concerned gaze and laughed. "You probably think I'm losing my mind."

"No, but you do seem frazzled. I'll bring the rest of your supplies while you get organized." Jake had his serious moments, and this was one of them.

"Thanks, Jake." The manager of the market provided tents and tables for vendors, and I went about organizing my space. With Jake's help, it didn't take long before I was open for business.

Jake propped his hands on his hips. "If you give me a key, I'll run over to your house. Is Abby home? I don't want to startle her."

"No, she's working at the bakery." I handed my keychain to Jake and pointed out the one he needed. "The alarm is set."

"I remember the code. Be back soon." He gave me a quick kiss before jogging away.

I stood near the entrance to my area and spoke to people going by. I sold some arrangements and stems, which I wrapped in nice paper and tied with a bow.

In the distance, I spotted Nick. He was with a woman, but I didn't recognize her. They held hands, but she seemed more excited than he did. She pointed to a tent with colorful hand-woven blankets. Nick went with her, but he looked in my direction.

I waved.

He frowned.

A group of young women approached me and asked about my flowers.

I focused on them instead of Nick. "I'm considering running bloom bars in the fall. There'll be more information on my website soon."

They promised to follow me on social media. They also spent money at my booth. I counted it as a double win.

"Hey, Mom. Why are you wearing flip-flops? I thought it hurt your feet to stand so long without good support." Abby stepped into the booth and stored her purse.

"True, but I got bitten by fire ants. Jake's going to bring my tennis shoes over soon."

"Oh, man. Sorry about that. What should I do?"

"Would you man the booth for a minute? I need to ask somebody a question."

"Yeah, but should I be worried about you?"

I patted the pocket of my overall shorts. "My phone is on me, but I want to ask Nick about the fire ants. He's over there."

Abby looked in the direction I pointed. "Be careful, Mom."

"Always." I walked toward Nick and the woman.

He released her hand and met me in the middle. "You better not accuse me of murdering Tess ."

"No, that's not my intention." My heart raced.

"What then?" Spit flew out of his mouth.

"I've got fire ants in my yard, and I thought about you. Do you have any natural ways to get rid of the mound?"

He glared at me as if he didn't believe me.

I lifted my leg and pointed to my ankle. "See?"

He leaned close. "Yep. You probably should take an antihistamine. As far as natural options to get rid of them, try boiling water. It can help. I have a product, but it's not natural. If you change your mind, give me a call." His voice held a tone of authority.

"Thanks. Since you mentioned Tess, who do you think murdered her?"

He glared at me. "I'm sure you think it's me, but why don't you consider Paula? Or maybe one of the library patrons. She wasn't the friendliest person."

I didn't defend Tess, because it'd only lead to an unnecessary argument.

Nick said, "Give me a call if you want me to use my product on the mound. Don't call if you have questions about the murder. I know nothing about it."

Chapter Thirty-Eight

I sat at a picnic table in the food area of Lutz Farmers Market, with my foot propped on Jake's leg. He applied the white paste around my ankles. "How does that feel?"

"Nice. It's cool, like it's removing the fire. It's helping me not scratch." I reached for my shoes and socks and put them on.

"That was my intention."

"I spoke to Nick, and he was very defensive."

"You what?" He removed his Oakley sunglasses and stared at me. "I guess it shouldn't surprise me. What happened?"

"Before I said a word, he proclaimed his innocence in Tess's murder. Then I told him about the fire ants. At my request for a safe and natural way to get rid of them, he suggested boiling water."

"Hmm. I've heard of boiling soapy water and pouring it on the mound. Maybe it's the heat that does the job."

"Could be." I stood. "Thanks for your help this morning. What are your plans today?"

"I'm presenting a closet remodel to a new family in town in about an hour. After that, I'm going to fix a ceiling fan and change smoke detector batteries for a lady who recently had knee replacement surgery. I'm going to enjoy being a fix-it man."

" Have you come up with a name for your business?"

"No, and I need to do it soon before I can move forward. Celia needs the name to finish my website."

"Fix-It Jake? Hunter the Handyman? Jake the Handyman?"

"Stop. I like Jake the Handyman. Let's mull it over a few days, and next week, I'll do all the legal work necessary to begin my business."

"I was saving the best for last. What do you think about Jake of All Trades?"

He laughed. "Very cool. That's officially my favorite. Any other suggestions?"

"No, those were my top four."

He pulled out a blister pack with pink tablets. "These are diphenhydramine. If the bites bother you too much, you should take one."

"Thanks, but they'll make me sleepy."

He held out the pack of medicine. "It won't hurt to hold onto it, in case you change your mind."

I took his offering. "Thanks."

"I'll walk you to your booth on my way to the parking lot."

"Thanks again for your help this morning."

We walked together hand-in-hand until we spotted quilted journals for sale. An older woman sat behind the display, reading a magazine.

Jake stopped walking and stared at them. "Lands sake."

"What?"

He pulled me away from the crowd, before looking in both directions. He whispered, "Emma, I've got Tess's diary. At least I had it. I meant to give it to you, but we were interrupted by Nick and the police."

My heart beat faster. "Have you read it?"

"No. In fact, I'm not sure where it is. I need to look."

"Please, Jake. Tell me you didn't lose it."

"No, way." His reply lacked conviction. "I'm going to find it. See you later."

"Bye."

Jake gave me a quick kiss, then ran off.

I rejoined Abby, who was busy ringing up a man wearing a baseball jersey. I took care of a young woman who was expecting company and wanted to fill her house with flowers to welcome them.

Soon, a woman approached me. "My daughter is getting married in August. We already placed an order with the local florist."

"Okay." I smiled. "Is there some way I can assist?"

The woman was taller than my five-nine. In addition, she wore wedges. "My daughter recently decided she wants to wear a ring of daisies around her head, and she wants something similar for the bridesmaids and flower girl."

"I'm primarily a flower farmer. Do you want me to provide the flowers for them?"

"Can you make the crowns?"

"Maybe. Do you want a wire as the base? Or do you prefer for me to find a way to weave the flowers together by their stems? That's trickier and may not hold up to all the wedding day activities."

The mother of the bride opened her purse and retrieved a business card. She wrote on it with a permanent marker. "This is my direct number. Please, call me next week. That will give me time to question my daughter and find out exactly what she wants. I'm a real estate agent, and I know people frequently change their minds. If we hire you to do this, I'll put our request in writing. That way you won't need to worry that we'll come up with a different idea and refuse to pay you. The bride is my youngest daughter, and her daddy spoiled her. She tends to be flighty, but I won't punish you if she changes her mind."

I took the card and put it in my pocket. "I can't ask for more than that. By the time we talk, I'll have some specific ideas to present to your daughter."

"Thank you. Also, I'd like to buy those three arrangements. I have an open house later today, and they'll be perfect." She gave me her credit card. "I don't suppose you can provide cookies?"

I laughed. "Sophie's Bakery is the best option in town for treats. She's on the square."

We finished our transaction, and Abby walked over to me. "What was that all about?"

I updated her on the opportunity to do the wedding.

"Mom, I'm proud of you. I really think you need to do more than the farmers' market if you're going to succeed."

A knot formed in my belly. "I'm keeping an open mind, because I want

156

this to be my career." This had been a year for second chances. I'd planned and prepared for becoming a flower farmer. I'd found a second chance at love with Jake. His presence in my life has been an unexpected blessing.

My thoughts leapt from love back to work. Tom Ward was a successful businessman and real estate agent. Tricking people into selling their property for a pittance was one way he'd become rich. How far would he go? Would he murder Tess so he could make more money?

It was time to look harder at Tom.

Chapter Thirty-Nine

After the farmers' market, I delivered my leftover flowers to the church and the retirement community. The retirement place was on the outskirts of town and required driving.

The itchiness had returned, and I took one of the pink tablets Jake had given me.

How was I going to research Tom? I knew he was a successful businessman who developed wealthy neighborhoods. Some might argue he wasn't stealing land from poor people. After all, he paid them. It wasn't like he was breaking laws on that front. Or was he? Maybe I could learn more by searching for victims like Linda Jefferson.

Whoa. I'd gotten off track. I wasn't going to investigate his financial misconduct. My goal was to find the person who murdered Tess. My heart broke for Linda, but at this point, I could only be her friend.

Instead of going home, I drove to Heart of Texas B&B. Maybe Zig could give me some guidance.

I parked on the street and walked to the front door. I knocked. It was always a challenge for me to decide whether to knock or walk inside. The place was a business and a home.

The door opened, and Faith waved me in. "Hi, Emma. I saw you from a distance at the farmers' market. It looked like you were busy."

"It was a good day. How are you?"

"Busy. We have a family staying here, and they have three teenage boys. They are loud, fun, and hungry. They're probably younger than Abby, or else I'd find a way to introduce her to them. What's up?"

I followed her to the kitchen. "I'd like to talk to you and Zig, but it needs to be a private conversation."

Faith poured two glasses of tea and handed one to me. "Is it too late in the day for you to have caffeine?"

"Not today. I just took an antihistamine." I explained about the ant bites, and that reminded me of Cowboy. "Excuse me one minute. I need to text Abby. My puppy needs to stay out of the problem area."

Please don't let Cowboy in the backyard because of the ants.

"Relax a minute. I want to put out some snacks for our guests, and then we can look for Zig."

My phone vibrated, and a text from Abby appeared. **No problem. We went for a walk, and we're chillin' in my room.**

I drank the tea and clamped my teeth to avoid a yawn.

Faith returned. "I bet my husband's in his office. If there's a golf tournament on TV, he'll be watching it." She grabbed her glass and led me to Zig's office.

"How's law school going for him?"

"He loves it, and helping Brett and Ms. Maebell got him jazzed." She knocked on a closed door. "Honey, it's me. Emma's here."

"Come in." He stood. "Hi, Emma. Have a seat."

I took a leather chair, and they sat next to each other on the matching couch. He muted the television. "The Texas boys are doing good today."

I glanced at the screen and recognized the man putting. "Good."

"Are you here to discuss the murder?" Zig leaned forward and rested his arms on his thighs.

"Yes. Was it awkward to represent Brett and his aunt because Mason is staying here?"

"I'm not licensed, so I didn't represent them. Brett asked me to go as a friend. It didn't seem to faze Mason. The most upset I've ever seen the man was the morning he confronted you on the street."

"Don't worry. I drove today." I yawned. "Sorry."

Faith said, "Before the antihistamine knocks you out, what do you need?"

"I want to investigate Tom Ward. What's his history? Has he ever hurt another person? Physically, that is. Did he know Tess personally?"

"Hold up." Zig lifted his hand. "I know the answer to the last question. Tom dealt with the county clerk ladies. Mason stayed at the library. They would go together to inspect land they were considering."

I took notes on my phone and would update my official notes on Tess's murder later. "Okay. Brett was happy with the final offer."

"Good. Me, too." Zig rubbed his chin. "In my opinion, Mason is Tom's fixer. He does research and makes things happen."

"Do you think Mason murdered Tess?"

"Not really. If I did, he wouldn't be staying with us. Even if I had to cancel everybody's reservation in order to kick him out. I'd use an excuse like the air conditioner was on the fritz."

Faith looked at her husband. "You'd lie?"

"If it was the only way to keep you and our guests safe, I'd get creative with the truth. I've been told I'm a good actor." He ran his hand up and down her back.

"I won't argue that." She leaned into him. "Emma, I've never had trouble with Mason. He's always the first guest to come down to breakfast, and we've had quite a few conversations. If you're his friend, he's loyal. Mason grew up poor, and the guys met each other in high school. Tom was rich and introduced Mason to powerful people. In fact, Tom's father paid for Mason's college and law school."

I gasped. "In exchange for what?"

"He worked for Mr. Ward's corporation for a time. He got paid, and each year he worked there, they shaved off a significant amount of his debt." Faith folded her hands together. "Mason is loyal to Tom and his family, even if he doesn't agree with everything they do."

I whispered, "Let's suppose Mason didn't kill Tess. If he knew Tom was guilty, would he remain silent?"

Faith shrugged. "I honestly don't know."

My heart beat faster. "I need to talk to Mason and figure out where he draws the line on friendship and loyalty."

"No." Zig shook his head. "No. No. No. It's not safe. Next time he confronts you, it could take a dark turn. Stay away from Mason."

"Please, listen to Zig." Faith squeezed my hand.

There was a knock on the door, and it opened. Mason stepped in, and we all froze.

Chapter Forty

"Pardon me." Mason's gaze circled the room. "Zig, I was hoping to have a private conversation with you. It looks like I interrupted—"

Had Mason listened to us at the door?

Zig stood. "Come on in. Emma's a friend, and we were just catching up."

If Zig had told me he was a retired NFL player when we'd first me, I would've believed him. Professional basketball player, too. He was probably the tallest man I knew. His charm and deep voice made it believable he'd been a successful movie star. Still, if I was a man, I wouldn't want to make Zig mad.

Faith stood. "Emma and I can continue talking in the kitchen and let you two have your privacy."

Mason nodded. "Much appreciated."

I trailed behind Faith, hoping to hear a bit of the conversation.

Mason closed the door behind us.

Once we were in the kitchen, Faith refilled our glasses. "It's killing you not to know what they're discussing."

I laughed. "Am I that transparent?"

"To me? Yes."

"I'm so glad we're friends." I took a big gulp of the tea. "Do you think Zig'll tell me about their conversation?"

"If Mason asked him to keep it private, Zig won't say a word."

"I figured as much. He's an honorable man." I yawned. "Do you think Mason was snooping on us?"

"I hope not, but we weren't loud. If he tried, it's doubtful he heard anything."

My eyes grew heavy. "I should've known that antihistamine would knock me out. I think it's time for a nap. See you later."

Faith shook her finger at me. "There's no reason for you to investigate. You're one of my closest friends, and I'd hate for something bad to happen to you."

"Thanks." I gave her a quick hug then left.

The house was quiet when I got home. In case Abby and Cowboy were snoozing in her room, I collapsed on the couch and fell asleep before kicking off my tennis shoes.

* * *

"Emma." A hand touched my shoulder. "Emma, wake up."

I turned and opened my eyes. "Jake? Why are you here? What time is it?"

"It's almost seven." He knelt beside me.

I elbowed myself to a sitting position and bent my legs so Jake could sit on the couch. "It's still Saturday, right?"

He chuckled. "Yes."

"Good. I should have taken half the dose of diphenhydramine. The twenty-five-milligram tablet wiped me out."

"The heat and stress could have added to the drug's side effects." He sat beside me. "How are the bites?"

"At the moment, they're not bothering me." I fought the lethargic feeling. "You know, Tess's theory was that Nick Jones gradually poisoned his first wife. Whenever Rhonda was in the hospital, she began feeling better. Then she'd go home and get worse again. What kind of poison could he have given her to act so slowly that she didn't realize what was happening?"

"Was it ever proven that the woman was poisoned?"

"I'm not sure." I yawned. "Let's talk about something nicer. Have you had dinner?"

"No. What if I order a pizza?"

"Perfect. How was your day?"

"Exciting. Let me place our order, and then I'll tell you about it." Jake pulled out his phone and opened the pizza app. "Vegetarian?"

"Yes, please." I appreciated his suggestion. If he was alone, Jake would probably order pizza with meat toppings. "We should do half-and-half."

"It's good." He finished the order and looked at me. "There's a piece of land for sale on the outskirts of town. It's before you get to the big ranches."

"With a house? Do you want to buy it?"

His face reddened. "I'd like you to see it. It's a small farm with a three-bedroom cottage."

I turned to face him better. "I'm confused. Who is the house for?"

He reached into his pocket, then dropped to one knee. "Us. Will you marry me?"

I screamed and took Jake's face in my hands. The sleepiness vanished. His squished face smiled.

The doorbell rang.

"Emma, is everybody okay in there?" Zig's voice carried into the gathering room.

"Yes!" I answered Zig first, and then I gave Jake the biggest kiss I'd ever given him. "And a big yes to you!"

He whooped and leapt to his feet.

Zig knocked on the door. "I'm coming inside."

The door swooshed open, and Zig stood in front of us.

Jake smiled. "She said yes. We're getting married."

"Oh. Alrighty. Congratulations." Zig reached out and shook Jake's hand, and then he gave me a hug. "I'm sorry to interrupt your special moment. I panicked, thinking Emma was in trouble. Congrats again."

Jake said, "Give me one moment to make it official." Jake reached for my hand and slipped a diamond solitaire on my ring finger. It sparkled in the fading sunlight, and I couldn't remember being happier than this moment.

"Oh, Jake. It's beautiful." I kissed him again.

Zig backed away. "My news can keep until later."

Jake slipped his arm around my shoulders, and we looked at Zig.

I said, "No. Please have a seat. We want to hear what you have to say."

"It won't take long." He remained standing. "You can eliminate Mason from your list of suspects. He was in Houston with his wife, who was in the hospital. She had a seizure and fell on the concrete. She ended up with a concussion and broken shoulder."

I'd seen Mason on the morning of the murder. "When?"

"It happened last Saturday."

"I saw him in the parking lot Tuesday morning."

"Mason said he arrived in town that morning for a meeting at the bank." Zig stuck his hands into the pockets of his khakis. "I tend to believe him."

"I trust your instincts, Zig. Mason Brown is off my suspect list."

"Good. I best move along, but I'm happy for you two. Congratulations again."

Abby and Cowboy walked in the front door. "Congratulations on what?"

I held up my hand, flashing the ring at my daughter. "We're getting married."

Abby screeched and flung herself at me. "Mom! Whoohoo!"

Cowboy barked, and the men laughed.

I patted my daughter's back. "It sounds like you're okay with me marrying Jake."

"The only thing that would make me happier is if you'd quit trying to solve the mystery of Tess's murder and married Jake."

Chapter Forty-One

I placed the leftover pizza in a plastic storage container. "Do you need more to drink?"

Jake looked up from my sketch pad of murder notes. "I'm fine."

Abby said, "I'm going swimming at a friend's house tonight. Can I take your truck?"

"Sure. Text me when you head home."

"Yes, ma'am." She turned to Jake. "I'm glad you're marrying my mom. Does that mean I can call you Dad ?"

"Abby, nothing would make me happier." He crossed the room and hugged her.

I choked up and turned around before I busted into tears of happiness.

Cowboy stood at the back door and barked.

"Oh, the ants. Boy, I'll take you out front." I leashed my golden retriever and led him to the front yard.

When we returned, Abby was backing out of the driveway. "Bye, Mom."

"Have fun, honey." I waved and went inside. "Jake, I need to start boiling water for the ant mounds." After removing the leash, I went to the kitchen.

"I'm one step ahead of you." Jake pointed to the stove where two pots of water began to bubble.

"What a way to celebrate our engagement." I laughed, but really felt bad.

He shrugged. "I don't need a party, as long as we're together."

I wrapped my arms around his neck. "I completely agree. What do you think about contacting Tom tonight? Maybe he can schedule a time for us to see the house and farm you were talking about."

166

"You are so devious, but I'm on to your ways. Do you want to see the place or grill Tom about the murder?"

"Both. If I only wanted to tour the property, I'd prefer another agent. How did you find out about this place?" My thoughts drifted back to the agent whose daughter had changed her mind about wedding flowers.

"The owner is getting the place ready to sell. I replaced a toilet and fixed a leaky sink in the primary suite." He rubbed my back. "I don't want you to think the house is nicer than yours, but there's more land to grow your pretty flowers. There's a small barn, and I think it's more practical than your flower shed. She shed. Whatever you call that little building."

"Potting shed. Jake, I'm happy to look at it with an open mind. Wherever we decide to live, it should feel like home to both of us."

"I like your home, and we've created some good memories here since we met. There are two main reasons to consider another house. Does it make sense for your business? And if I move in here, will you and Abby feel like I'm intruding on your space?"

"We wouldn't feel like you're intruding, but let's look at the farm." The water was almost at a full boil. "Can we afford it?"

"I've got money saved for a down payment because I'm a frugal man. Even though Matt didn't hire me, I've been able to save money."

"Do you feel like Jake of All Trades will be secure?"

"Yes. You made me a believer, but if business isn't good, I can work for Coop. I've learned quite a bit from him. I'm putting all thoughts of being a cop behind me."

I nodded. "Good employees are hard to find, and Coop may call you a lot."

"True. I'll call Tom and set up a time to see the farm. There's no pressure. If you don't like it, speak up."

"Yes, sir. The water is boiling. I think we're supposed to pour it on the ant mound."

Jake frowned. "I don't know if it'll kill the ants immediately, but if they run out of the mound, you better be prepared to run."

"Why'd you fix two pots of boiling water?" I turned the burners off.

"I didn't know how much it'd take. Do you want me to do it?"

"No. I'd rather you call Tom, but please keep Cowboy inside."

He crated my puppy then held the door open for me. "Be careful."

"You bet." If I had a dollar for every time somebody told me that, I'd be able to buy two farms.

Wearing oven mitts, I carried the heavy pot to the mound and held it as far from my body as possible. I poured it on the ant hill and ran. If another ant bit me, and Jake witnessed my Texas two-step, he might take back his lovely proposal.

I examined my body for ants. No sign of the critters, so I headed inside with the empty pot.

"Thanks for your time, Mr. Ward. We'll see you at one o'clock tomorrow afternoon." Jake ended the call. "I had no idea you could run so fast."

"We've got the rest of our lives to get to know each other better." I put the pot in the sink.

"Should we have a list of questions ready for our meeting with Tom?"

"Definitely." I found another sketch pad. "We need to be prepared with murder questions and inquiries about the farm if we decide we're interested. If Tom doesn't live here, how can he sell property in Lutz?"

"My belief is real estate agents follow state laws and can sell property anywhere in Texas."

"What if we fall in love with the farm? We'll add to his fortune—"

"You're worried about a potential killer making money off us?"

"Well, yeah. I think we made a mistake calling Tom."

"Hear me out. This will be the least hostile setting to ask him about Tess. There's a good chance he's innocent."

"Even if he didn't commit the murder, it doesn't seem like he plays fair with property owners." My stomach tightened.

"Maybe we can figure that out too." Jake leaned a hip against a counter. "Do you want me to cancel?"

"I'm not sure. There's another thing we haven't factored into our debate. We're going to be out there by ourselves with him. If we say, or do, the wrong thing, he might decide to kill us too."

"Oh, babe. You're overthinking this. We'll put safety precautions in place."

CHAPTER FORTY-ONE

He took me in his arms.

I couldn't imagine what kind of measures he intended to implement, but I didn't want to argue, especially since he'd just popped the question. Tomorrow would be soon enough to evaluate our plan.

Chapter Forty-Two

Sunday afternoon, Jake parked his SUV under a shade tree at the farm we were about to tour. "This will be fine. Brett knows we're here, and if he hasn't heard back from me in an hour, he'll call the police."

"I made a similar arrangement with Sophie. She's having lunch with Chief Young, but she promised not to say anything unless I missed our check-in."

Jake pointed to an approaching figure. "Here comes Tom."

"Hopefully, I'm not too nervous to get a good feel for the place."

"We can always do a second tour. Let's go." Jake opened his door, and a wave of hot air filled the vehicle.

I stepped out and took in my surroundings. Flowers were growing in an enclosed area to the right of the light blue cottage. Closer to us was a field of sunflowers. I met Jake in front of the Sequoia. "Look at all the beautiful sunflowers. They self-seed, so I won't have to start from scratch."

"It can be a slow transition if we move here, because you've already got seeds planted for fall flowers. We don't have to move as soon as we buy the farm, and that's if we buy it."

I touched my engagement ring with my thumb, reassuring myself we were truly engaged. "That's a good idea."

"Hi, Jake. Emma, nice to see you again. I'm glad you called me about this place. The owner doesn't have an agent, but he was willing to let us have a look-see." Tom shook our hands. "Turns out to have been a good thing we met the other night. Shall we begin in the house?"

I nodded. "Can't wait."

"The place was built in the 1930s, but there have been updates through the years. There are three bedrooms along the left side of the house, and the rest of it is an open floor plan." He opened the front door for us.

From the big front porch, I entered the living room. From there, you could see through the dining area to the kitchen. The layout was similar to my current home except there weren't all the walls.

Jake said, "Your eating table should fit there easily."

"Good. I'd hate to give it up." My French harvest table was probably my favorite piece of furniture.

Tom walked us through the house, pointing out features like a modern laundry room, his and her closets, extra storage, and much more.

"Before we tour the land, do you have any questions?" Tom rolled up the sleeves of his dress shirt and unbuttoned the top button.

Jake crossed his arms. "My friend Brett told me you'd been fair with his aunt. If we decide to make an offer, how will you deal with the current owner?"

"I'm not sure what you're implying, but I'm always fair."

I said, "My friend, Tess Carranza, was disturbed about an area you're developing between here and Houston. Did she ever talk to you?"

He squinted his eyes. "I won't pretend not to know who you're talking about, and I'm sorry for your loss. However, it was none of her business, and it's none of yours. You should only care about how I deal with you. Do I make myself clear?"

Jake stepped between Tom and me. "I won't let you talk to my fiancée that way. There are other real estate agents and more farms that we can consider. Let's go, Emma."

I backed toward the door, keeping my eye on Tom.

His expression cleared. "No need to be hasty. I had nothing to do with the librarian's death."

I said, "Do you have an alibi for Tuesday morning?"

"As a matter of fact, I do. Our mutual friend, Mason Brown, can vouch for me."

"Really?" Referring to Mason as my friend was a stretch. It seemed convenient that one man who'd been on my suspect list, could now be a witness for another person of interest.

"Yes. I drove him to Houston for a family emergency. With the crisis averted, I drove us both back to Lutz." He lifted his hands in an innocent gesture. "Go ahead, and ask him. You won't offend me."

"Where was your chauffeur?"

"It was his weekend off."

If nothing else, the man was smooth. "Did you meet Tess?"

"I don't believe so, but I saw a picture of her on the news." He pointed to my purse. "Are you going to call Mason?"

I stared at the man. "I don't have his contact information on my phone."

Jake touched the doorknob. "It's probably time to shove off. Emma and I need to talk and decide if we want to look more at this property. Sorry if we wasted your time, Tom."

"Give me a call if you change your mind." He motioned for us to leave, and then he locked the door and followed us out. "Are you sure you don't want to look at the land?"

"Why not?" I paused on the front porch, imagining a swing with my rockers. Planters would look inviting on the white railing, and hanging baskets with red geraniums would appeal to visitors.

Jake did a double-take, and the agent did too.

Tom said, "Good. So, there are two barns and a shed. The owner hasn't had animals on the farm for years, except for barn cats and dogs. Because of health issues, the vegetable garden is mostly weeds. You can find wildflowers in the other gardens." Tom walked us around the property.

I said, "What if it turns out to be too much land? Can we sell off tracts?"

"It'd be smart to check at the courthouse—"

"Do you know positively that one person owns all this? I'd hate to make an offer, then find out it belongs to multiple people. Is that something you can find out?"

Tom pulled a hanky out of his pocket and wiped his perspiring face. "I do property searches all day long, but you know that."

"Never hurts to ask."

"Tom, thanks." Jake reached for my hand. "Emma, we should think about everything we've seen and maybe get a cool drink."

"Sure, honey." I waved to Tom, and we made the long trek to the SUV. I hoped we looked more casual than I felt.

Once inside the vehicle, Jake rolled down the windows, and turned on the air conditioner full blast. "Let's get the hot air out, and then we can talk." He drove down the hard-packed dirt road, and my hair tangled in the breeze.

I pulled a band out of my purse and secured my hair into a ponytail. "There are so many possibilities here, but it's going to require a lot of hard work. My big yard, or small flower farm, is about all I can manage. There's so much more land here. What did you think of the house?"

Jake reached the highway and pulled out. "It's not huge, but it seems doable. If we later decide it's not big enough, I can add on to it."

"That seems like a lot of work."

With the touch of a button, the windows went up, and only cool air circulated. "It'll be easier in the winter months, but it's doable."

A car horn tooted, and Tom whizzed past us in his red Mercedes.

An old pickup truck barreled toward us in the other lane.

Jake slammed on the brakes.

Tom cut in front of us.

I screamed.

The Sequoia screeched to a halt, and Jake cursed.

The Mercedes sped away, but the farmer in the old truck stopped in the middle of the two-lane road to check on us.

"Durn fool could've killed us all. You folks okay?" The man swiped his face with a white handkerchief.

"Yes, sir, but you're right. It's a blessing nobody was hurt." Jake continued speaking to the man while I worked to calm my racing heart.

Chapter Forty-Three

Sophie and Matt were drinking iced coffees at Anytime Coffee House when we entered.

Brett looked up. "Man, I was just about to report you missing. What happened?"

Sophie crossed the room and hugged me. "I told Matt how worried I was. I'm glad you're safe."

"Thanks, but we need to tell y'all what happened."

Matt said, "It sounds like we need a bigger table. Do I need my notepad?"

I nodded. "Probably so."

Before long, Brett had fixed an iced green tea for me, and a healthy drink for Jake. He set them on the table and pulled over a chair and joined us.

Matt clicked his pen. "Shoot."

"Jake and I went to see a farm that's for sale, and Tom Ward showed it to us."

"Have you two lost your minds?" Matt scowled.

"Maybe, but we learned Tom has a witness for the estimated time of the murder." I gave him an uncertain smile.

"Who?" The police chief growled.

"Mason Brown." I told them what Tom had claimed.

Matt rubbed his chin. "I was certain he was wrangled up in this case some way. I guess I should've given him more credit."

Jake raised his hand. "Not too much credit. He passed us at a speed far above the posted limit, and another vehicle was coming at us. If I hadn't stopped, we could've been seriously hurt."

I reached for Jake and Brett's hands and squeezed them. "I don't know how you guys put one foot in front of the other after whatever you experienced overseas. I may have PTSD after this experience."

Brett looked at me. "Cowboy may come in handy in more ways than you ever imagined."

Jake tightened his hold on my hand before facing Matt. "The other driver stopped and checked on us. I asked him to report the incident. Tom may not have murdered Tess, but four lives were endangered today because of his foolishness."

Matt said, "This is my only afternoon off, but I'll have one of my officers speak to Mr. Ward."

Brett stood. "How about gingerbread cookies? My treat. I know they won't be as good as yours, Sophie, but we're celebrating Christmas in July. They're even shaped like snowmen."

Sophie said, "They sound delicious, Brett."

Jake laughed. "Did my sister put you up to this? She loves Christmas, and it sounds like something she'd suggest."

"I can neither confirm nor deny the inspiration. Be right back."

"Excuse me while I report this." Matt walked across the room.

"And then there were three." I pointed to each of us left. "Sophie, we didn't mean to crash your date. We'll leave you two alone."

"No, it's all right for you to join us." She ran a hand over her hair and blew on her bangs.

I pushed out my chair. "Nope, because we'll discuss murder and bad stuff. We didn't mean to interrupt, and you look beautiful. Let's go, Jake."

"I'll get to-go cups, and we'll be on our way."

Matt and Brett returned at the same time.

Brett set a plate of decorated cookies in the middle of the table. "Enjoy."

I said, "Matt, the bleeding heart plant from the library is doing fine in the new pot. Is it okay if I return it to the library?"

"Don't see why not, but don't stir up trouble."

"What? Me?" I placed my hand on my chest. "I'll behave, but if you decide I should snoop, let me know. Do you have any updates on Tess's murder?"

"Stay out of my case, Emma."

Jake nudged me. "Let's go before you get yourself arrested."

"Very funny." I took my stainless steel tumbler from him and walked outside.

He joined me. "I topped off your drink."

"Thanks. What would you think about us taking the plant to the library while it's on my mind?"

"And before Matt decides it's not a good idea?"

I laughed. "Yeah. That too."

He pointed to the Sequoia. "Everything is close, but let's drive in this heat."

Clouds filled the sky, and the humidity was thick, making it a challenge to take a full breath. "Good idea."

It didn't take long to swing by my house, grab the plant, and go to the library.

On the short drive over, I said, "This is a bleeding heart plant. If it was a person, people would think it was softhearted or liberal. Tess was very black-and-white, but deep down, she was soft. She loved her patrons and books. I wish I had known her before Rhonda Jones died. Had the death of her friend caused her to put up walls?"

"I don't know." Jake parked in the shade, and we walked to the building. Jake opened the door for me. "Are you going to tell Laurel, or do your thing and leave the flower?"

"I guess the polite thing is to let her know." My purse slipped off my shoulder, but I couldn't adjust it while my hands were full. Laurel was laying out informational brochures on a back-to-school program.

"Mason is here too." Jake pointed to a table where the attorney worked on a laptop.

"It'll be interesting to see his reaction when he spots us. I wonder if Tom told him about our house tour." I tried to slide up my purse without spilling the contents. In my hurry, I'd left it unzipped.

"Let me." Jake took the leather strap and settled it on my shoulder.

"Thanks."

Laurel turned and saw us. "Hi, Emma. I haven't agreed to pay you for flowers yet."

"Oh, Tess bought this before her death." I'd repotted it in a bright yellow container, because the original had broken during the attack. T "Chief Young allowed me to save the plant, and if it's okay, I'll place it by the others."

She sighed. "As long as it doesn't cost the library anything, go ahead."

"Thanks." I headed in the direction of the shelf, but Mason stood and blocked my path.

For the love of daffodils. Could nothing be simple?

Chapter Forty-Four

"Emma, Jake." Mason nodded at us.

I tightened my grip on the flower pot. "Hi, Mason."

"You all upset Mr. Ward today. You wasted his time, showing you around some farm. He's a busy man and doesn't have time for your shenanigans." Mason gave us a smug look.

Jake advanced on the attorney. "Your client drove recklessly, and we could be in the emergency room right now. There was another driver who was endangered, too. The incident has been reported to the police."

Mason's expression morphed. He frowned and narrowed his eyes. "Great. Just great."

I said, "Mason, we heard your wife was in the hospital last week. I hope she's doing better."

He rubbed his neck. "Thank you. I'll feel a whole lot better when I can return to Houston and help. Her mom and sister are pitching in, but she's more relaxed when I'm the only one at home with her."

For the first time, I believed Mason. "That makes sense to me. Let me know when you leave town, and I'll give you some flowers to take her."

"I appreciate that. The best way you can help is if you quit accusing Tom and me of murdering Tess Carranza and committing other crimes."

Jake frowned. "There's no denying he risked four lives on the highway earlier."

"I'll speak to Tom. Anything else?"

I said, "Besides the man who fell asleep during story time, can you think of any other people who might have had a conflict with Tess?"

"Why ask me? I don't live here."

"You've camped out at the library for days, and something tells me you're very observant."

He studied me for a moment. "If you've ruled out the dozing dude, how about the guy who took her out to dinner?"

Whoa, Tess had a date recently? "Um, like a date? Who was the man?"

Mason looked in each direction, then motioned for us to huddle. "This might not sound good, but let me assure you that I'm not bragging. Neither do I want to tarnish the image of your friend. Tess may have had a little crush on me in the beginning. As soon as I suspected, I made sure she realized I was married. In her defense, some days my fingers swell, and I take off my wedding ring before running."

Jake said, "Did you see her on your runs?"

"No, but once my fingers swell—"

"There's such a thing as silicone bands that many athletes wear." Jake shook his head.

"Oh."

I wanted Mason to return to his original thoughts about Tess. "Please, keep going."

Mason sighed. "Where was I? Oh, yeah. Tess. It was easy to understand why she thought I was single. I won't share the embarrassing details, but I told her a few of my friends had tried a dating website, and it worked for them. I even shared the specific site. She tried it, and a few days later, she had a dinner date."

His response didn't jive with what Tess had told me on the Fourth of July. "Did you two discuss your research?"

"Not exactly. One day, after I walked out to take a call, she was looking at my stuff. You know, papers and my laptop. I watched for a moment before confronting her. Tess asked me about my business, and I couldn't tell her. Clients deserve discretion, plus it's the law."

"How did it make you feel to see her looking at your work?" I watched his expression and tried to decide if he was honest or a good actor.

"I was ticked, but she was furious, accusing me of stealing from poor

179

people. She didn't understand. I'm an attorney. It doesn't matter if I agree with everything my clients do."

Arguing with Mason would waste time, but I thought Tess understood exactly what was happening. The plant grew heavy in my hands, and it was time to change topics. "Let's go back to the online dating site. Did you see her date?"

"Got a glimpse of him. Older and bald. Seemed to be in decent shape. We never discussed how the dinner went." He looked at his phone. "I've got to take this."

Older and bald?

There'd been a bald man with the paramedics. I'd never seen him before. Something had seemed off about him. Was it possible he and Tess had gone on a couple of dates? Was he shocked to get called out to her murder? Or was there something else? I'd put some thought into the stranger later.

Jake and I walked to the area where the flowers had been displayed, and I set the repotted bleeding heart on the shelf.

Jake said, "The guy has an answer for everything."

"You're right." I touched the soil in the other pots. "These are dry. I'm going to get some water."

"Wait, did Tess mention dating to you?"

"Not a word, and it seems strange that she told Mason. Unless maybe she was trying to prove to him other men were interested in her. I'll be back." I entered the empty employees' break room and filled a large plastic cup with water. If Laurel had been in the room, I would've asked her about Tess's love life. Instead, I returned to Jake and the flowers.

Jake pointed to the now-empty table. "Mason took off in a hurry."

"Wonder what that's all about?"

"My guess is Tom's involved, but I'm going to look at the reference books he left out while you water the plants." He walked to the table.

I watered the Swiss cheese and spider plants. I turned the bleeding heart to get better sunlight. In the process, I knocked my phone on the floor. "Great."

I knelt to pick it up.

My mind flashed back to Tuesday morning and the sight of Tess. Her scratched body had been so still. Her normal perfectly styled hair had been a mess.

I fell back against the shelf. My body shook. Poor Tess. She'd fought for her life in the place she loved best. This library had been her pride and joy. Time and much thought had gone into her decisions on what to buy. They weren't always the most popular books in America. No, many focused on Texas. But if a patron requested a book, she'd get it for them, even if she borrowed it from another library. The situation with Mia and Ethan was for Mia's protection. She had a big soft spot for children.

I'd been the first to find her warm body. Why couldn't she have been alive?

I looked at the non-fiction books next to me.

They were biographies. I pulled one out, then another. It seemed fitting to check out and read a book in her honor. I tugged on a thick book. It slid out.

Clink.

I swiped a tear with the back of my hand to see better.

A piece of the blue and white French toile ceramic that had previously homed the bleeding heart plant glistened on the floor in a ray of sunlight.

Chapter Forty-Five

The shard of blue-and-white French toile sent my heart into overdrive. It was from the broken pot at the crime scene.

I leapt to my feet. "Psst. Jake."

He sat at the table in the reference section vacated by Mason. He didn't flinch.

"Jake," I whispered louder.

Nothing.

With a louder-than-normal voice, I said, "Jake."

He jumped and looked at me with a frown. "Shh."

I motioned for him to join me. No way I was walking away from this clue. "Hurry."

Hope rushed to me. "You're disturbing the others."

"Hope, did you hear me from the children's area?"

"No. I'm in charge of everything today since we're short-staffed. Laurel is flitting around doing who knows what."

Jake joined us. "What's wrong?"

The librarian's eyes widened. "Please, don't tell me there's another dead body ."

This was going sideways real fast. "I found a piece of evidence. At least I think it may be connected to Tess's death. Do you have rubber gloves?"

"Yes, give me a minute." Hope walked away.

"What's the evidence?" Jake popped his knuckles.

I pointed to the piece of the ceramic. "It looks like the same pattern as the broken flower pot by Tess's body."

Jake knelt on one knee like when he'd proposed and leaned down for a closer look. "I agree. We need to contact Matt."

"Will you do it? I want to speak to Hope when she returns."

"Sure. I'll be in the entry area, but holler if you need me." He stood and walked away with his long-legged stride.

"Here you go." Hope held out one pair of nitrile gloves and put another pair on her delicate hands. "We use these when inspecting valuable books."

I wiped my cold hands on my shorts before sliding my fingers into the purple gloves. "Is there any chance you know how to test for fingerprints?"

"No, but we can look it up. If Laurel questions me, I'll tell her it's research for an activity with middle school kids." She stared at the fragment. "Will the police be mad?"

"I'm not sure, but they cleared the crime scene." My stomach churned. "Honestly, Chief Young might get mad. Let's give Jake a minute to join us. He's calling the chief now."

An older woman shuffled over to us with a walker. "You two are blocking my way."

Hope said, "There was a spill. Please, give us a minute."

Her knuckles whitened on the handles of her walker. "My ride won't wait all day on me."

"We'll hurry, ma'am. Or is there something I can grab for you?"

"No, I like to look at the books myself before deciding."

Aw, a woman after my own heart. With gloved hands, I picked up the book and a piece of pottery. "I'll finish watering the other plants later."

Hope turned from me to the other lady. "I believe the coast is clear. Is there anything specific you'd like to check out?"

I made my way to the break room and crossed paths with Jake. "Did you talk to Matt?"

"No, but I left him a message."

"He must've been serious about his time off. I guess he's working around the clock on this investigation." I set the items on a table. "Do you know how to pick up fingerprints off something?"

"Please tell me you don't want to look for fingerprints on that."

"Um, why don't you finish watering the plants for me?"

Jake ran a hand over his face. "Oh, Sunshine. We could get in serious trouble for this, but I know what to do. I learned how in a lab."

The butterflies in my belly multiplied. How far could I test my friendship with the police chief? Would the action earn me a lecture, or would he throw me in jail? I took a deep breath and placed my hands on my belly. "I'm smarter than that. We'll find other clues that won't get us tossed in the clink."

Jake pulled me to him. "Good thinking."

Hope entered the room. "Emma, I'm not going to be able to fingerprint the potter. Laurel's watching me like a hawk."

"Actually, we decided it might interfere with Chief Young's investigation."

"Good." She gave us a lopsided smile and left us alone.

Jake's phone sounded, and he pulled it from his pocket. "It's Matt."

"Put him on speaker. I want to hear his reaction."

Jake swiped the phone. "Hey, Matt. You're on speaker, and Emma's with me."

"This better be important." His growl lacked bite.

I said, "I found a piece of evidence at the library. We thought you'd want it."

There was mumbling, before he replied, "Sophie's with me. We're on the way."

Jake hit the end button and looked at me. "It sounds like more than meeting for coffee to me. Do you think they're on a full-fledged date?"

"Here I am thinking about solving Tess's murder and ignoring my best friend. I should know what's going on with her and Matt."

"Does she know we're engaged?"

My face warmed. "I haven't had time to tell her."

"You better before she hears it from somebody else. She'll be hurt." He looked past me. "Here they come."

Matt entered the breakroom. "Why are you wearing gloves, Emma?"

Sophie hung back at the door frame.

I waved to her and then looked at Matt. "I didn't want to contaminate the evidence."

He spotted the box of gloves and tugged on a pair. "I don't usually carry these on my day off, but I should."

"That's what I found, and it matches the broken pot that was near Tess."

He looked at it. "I agree. Walk me through how you found this. If the crime scene team missed this, there could be more evidence."

"Follow me." I took him to the plants and told him everything.

Matt said, "Thanks, Emma. The library will close early since it's Sunday. I'm going to get the team back out here."

"Why don't I give Sophie a ride home?"

His shoulders sagged. "I'm sorry, Sophie. Do you mind?"

"You do not need to feel sorry. You are the police chief, and I understand."

"I'll make it up to you." His gaze locked with hers for a moment longer than necessary.

"I'll look forward to that."

I said, "I was going to finish watering the other plants."

"Nope, you're leaving." Matt pointed to the door.

His demand made sense. "I've ruled out Mason Brown, but in case you haven't, he was at the table where Jake is now. His fingerprints are probably on the table, chair, and books. Not that I'm telling you how to do your job, but just in case you wanted to know."

"I've been doing this job for a while now, but thanks for the tip. Also, did you speak to Mason?"

"Hey, he confronted me about Tom Ward. We told him about Tom's recklessness, and a little later, he left."

"Understood." He turned to Sophie again. "I'll talk to you later."

"Bye, Matt."

I pulled off my gloves and dropped them in a trash can. "Sophie, I've got some news to share when we get outside."

She grabbed my left hand. "Does it have anything to do with the diamond ring?"

I laughed. "Yes. Jake proposed last night."

Sophie squealed and hugged me.

Jake joined us, and she hugged him too.

Matt glanced our way.

Sophie lifted my hand in the air and pointed to my finger. "They're engaged."

Matt smiled. "Congrats, guys."

The three of us left the building, talking about our upcoming wedding and pushing aside the sadness of Tess's death for a few minutes.

Chapter Forty-Six

After taking Sophie to her home, Jake and I went to my place and walked Cowboy. "Jake, we'll have to make this short because of the heat. I want to be smart, but until all the fire ants are gone, it's risky to let him run free in the backyard."

"Oh, for sure. I'd never do anything to hurt your pup." He rubbed the dog's head. "That sliver from the planter was a surprise. Pressing forward, what's next on your investigation?"

"I've never really questioned Nick. It seems like the logical step. Don't you think?"

A muffler backfired on a truck, and Cowboy lunged.

"Heal." When he obeyed, I gave him a treat. "Good boy."

"Hey, Cowboy's doing better. And you thought you didn't have what it took to own a dog." He chuckled. "Say, have you heard from Paula recently?"

"No. I'd like to ask her about Tess's will. I don't believe she committed the murder, but what if there was another person who expected to inherit everything? Tess had a nice home and car. What if somebody killed her, expecting to be named in the will? I don't know who this person might be, but Paula probably has an idea."

Cowboy sniffed a mailbox, and we stopped.

Jake said, "Suppose you put that on the back burner until she calls you again. Have you read Tess's diary?"

"You haven't given it to me yet."

"For crying out loud. What's my problem?"

"Hey, now. You're starting a business, looking for property, and you proposed. It's easy to forget."

Cowboy began walking.

"I still can't believe it." Jake adjusted his Oakley sunglasses. "When life moves at the speed of light, it's hard to keep up. When we get back to your place, let's check the SUV, because I was sure I brought it to you. Do you believe Matt agrees with your list of suspects?"

"Maybe. He's acting cagey on this investigation." I guided Cowboy to the grass, so a lady could push a double stroller past us. Jake joined us in the shady spot.

"Thanks." She waved and kept moving.

"You're welcome." A warm breeze reminded me to keep my puppy hydrated. I poured water into my hand and held it out for him to drink. We repeated the process two more times. "I'm sure a bowl will work better than my hand."

"No doubt. The tractor store carries pet supplies." Jake crossed his arms and rocked back on his heels. "Back to the murder. You've ruled out Ethan, Mason, and Tom. We're left with Laurel, Nick, and a potential unknown person who might think they'd be in Tess's will."

"Three down. Three to go." I replaced the top on the water bottle. "I'm going to ignore whatever Mason and Tom are doing. Somebody else can deal with them because they're distracting me from the murder investigation."

"I agree. They're a waste of your time. So, Nick's next."

I dreaded that conversation. "Yes, as much as I don't want to talk to him, it's got to be done."

"I'll go with you. If it's true that he murdered his first wife, and he abused Paula when they were married, and he possibly murdered Tess, you don't need to approach him alone."

Relief lessened the tightness in my shoulders. "Thanks. Now we need to come up with a way to approach him."

Cowboy tugged on the leash, and we walked toward my house.

"If we move to the farm, I won't be able to take Cowboy for walks like this." I watched him trot with his head held high looking forward. "Although, he can run free in the fields."

"It was just a thought, and we don't have to decide today." Jake's casual stride matched my pace.

"I'm intrigued, and it'd be fun to have a place that's new to both of us as a couple."

"Family." Jake took my hand in his. "Abby is part of our family."

I leaned my head on his shoulder. "I love you, Jake."

"I love you, too." He gave me a quick kiss. "Now, let's solve Tess's murder, so we focus on our future."

"What a brilliant plan."

Cowboy barked, and we finished walking to my house.

My house. Not Jake's. If we could figure out the financial side of us moving to the farm, it'd be nice to have a fresh start as a couple and a family. Abby had given me one good idea with the bloom bar. I also knew about a flower farm that allowed people to come cut flowers on their own and pay. It worked on the honor system. I should look into that.

Jake interrupted my musings. "Let's check out your fire ant mounds. If they're still around, we should give Nick a call."

"I hope my earlier comments to him about not wanting chemicals won't stop him from replying." I unlocked the door, and Cowboy ran in first.

Jake said, "Hold up. I forgot to look for the diary."

"I'll be in the backyard." I gave Cowboy a treat and secured him in his crate before going to the yard.

Ants scurried around the area where I'd been stung.

Jake walked out the back door and joined me. "The hot water didn't kill the ants?"

Hot water. "Evidently not. Do you suppose Tess got in hot water with—"

"With who? If we can figure out an alibi, we'll be closer to catching the killer." Jake rubbed my shoulder.

"I'll go ahead and call Nick. At least we think we know his alibi. Revenge." I tapped his number into my phone and called.

"This is Nick."

"Oh, hi." The fact he answered so fast surprised me. "This is Emma Justice. I'd like to schedule an appointment with you to look at my fire ant mounds."

"Thought you didn't want chemicals."

I gave a dramatic sigh. "There may be no other option. That's why I need to get your opinion."

"Are you home now?"

"Yes." My body stilled.

"I'll swing by and look over your situation." He made five syllables out of the last word.

"Thanks, Nick." The call ended, and I looked at Jake. "He's on the way."

"Good. Together, we'll try to decide if he's guilty. At least guilty of murdering Tess. We may never know if he killed his first wife."

Chapter Forty-Seven

Nick sprayed chemicals on the fire ant mound in my backyard. Jake and I stood on the patio, watching from a safe distance.

Jake said, "He seems to take his work seriously."

"True. Tess always believed Nick poisoned his first wife, but why murder Tess?"

"If he's innocent in wife number one's murder, that cloud has hung over his head for years. That's enough to make anybody angry."

"Shh. Here he comes." I gave my best impression of smiling. "Is that it?"

"Give it a few days. If another mound appears, I'll come back and do a second treatment for free." He reached toward his shirt where a pocket might be. "Sorry. I'm not in uniform."

"That's okay. I'm just happy you took time to come here on your day off."

"I'll send you the bill." He glanced back toward the mound. "Might be best to stay away for a few hours."

"Hey, Nick."

His head jerked, and he frowned. "I told you—"

"No, wait." I lifted my hands to ward him off.

Jake advanced on Nick. "For an innocent man, you act mighty guilty."

"If you'd been accused of murder as much as I have, you'd be jumpy too."

I said, "I only wanted to thank you."

Nick snorted. "Hmm. You're welcome. Do you mind if I wash my hands in your house?"

My pulse leapt, pounding in my neck. I wanted to say no, but Jake was with me. Was it safe?

"Um, sure."

I walked inside and led him to the downstairs powder room. He set his work items on the hall floor.

Cowboy barked, but I had to ignore him.

Jake hurried to the table with all my murder notes and gathered them into a pile. "Your office?"

"Yes."

The toilet flushed, and then water ran.

"No, just throw them in the cabinet."

My puppy kept barking.

Jake tossed my stuff in with pots and pans.

Nick reappeared and looked at Cowboy. "Good thing he's locked up. I don't take to dogs biting me anymore. That costs people extra. Well, I'll be on my way."

My dog growled.

"Thanks again. You can go out the front door. I don't want the ants to attack you if any are alive."

Nick gathered his work supplies and walked in front of me. He paused in the gathering room.

A purple journal lay on the coffee table. It matched Tess's daily planner that the police probably confiscated.

Nick stared at it.

I couldn't think of anything appropriate to say. All the comments racing through my brain would make the situation more awkward.

Jake stepped around us and opened the door. "See you later, Nick."

The man practically backed out of my house.

Cowboy grew quiet.

Jake closed the door and leaned against it. "That was bad."

"Yeah." I hurried to the window. "He's moving as slow as molasses, and he's staring this way."

"Get away from the window."

"Yikes." I dropped to the floor. Smooth. Real smooth.

Jake chuckled. "Girl, you're something else."

"Would you believe I don't function well in a crisis situation?" I crawled to the coffee table and snagged the diary.

"If that's true, you need to quit investigating murders. Trust the police to catch Tess's attacker." Jake looked out the window. "Nick's sitting in his truck. We should move to the kitchen."

I debated crawling all the way not to raise Nick's suspicions more.

Jake held a hand to me.

I took it and stood. "It's time to read the diary. Maybe the answers will be in here. At least, we might discover who she went on a date with."

The doorbell rang.

"For the love of daffodils. Is he back?" I hurried to my secret pantry and hid the diary behind boxes of cereal and granola bars.

Jake said, "The pup's not barking."

"You're right, and he has a sense for bad people."

The doorbell rang again, and I went and answered it. "Hi, Faith."

Nick's tires squealed as he pulled away from the curb, but he wasn't in his work truck with the bug on it. He was driving a white sedan.

Faith stood on my porch, but Zig wasn't with her. It was another man.

It was the rodeo rider who couldn't read.

Chapter Forty-Eight

"Hey. Is Jake here?" Faith smiled.

"Yes. Come in." I mimicked her smile and hoped I didn't look as confused as I felt.

Faith and the rodeo rider followed me to the kitchen. "Jake, Faith's here. And I'm sorry. Remind me of your name."

"Wyatt Gardner, ma'am." He removed his cowboy hat and nodded.

"Where are my manners? Wyatt, this is Emma Justice, and that's Jake Hunter." She didn't touch the man. In fact, she kept an acceptable distance between them.

The men shook hands.

Faith said, "First, Zig knows we've come to talk to you."

"Good. I'd never go behind his back. What's going on?" Jake crossed his arms.

My face warmed. If we'd gone to Faith's place, she'd already be serving us refreshments. "Let's sit in the gathering room. Would anybody like something to drink? I've got pretzels to snack on, too." I needed to get something better to serve people, but handling unexpected company had never been my strong suit.

The cowboy turned the hat in his hands in a circular motion. "I'm good, thanks."

Faith was already walking to the gathering room, and we followed her. She sat in the blue chair, and after we all were seated, she said, "Jake, Wyatt needs a job. Word around town is you're starting a handyman business."

"Yes. Jake of All Trades. It's not official yet." He rubbed his chin. "Wyatt, tell me your experience."

"Just so there's no embarrassing situations later, you should know I'm learning to read. I dropped out of school when I was young, to help my parents on the farm. Then I rodeoed on the circuit to help pay bills. That farm's been in my family for generations, and we fell on tough times. The rodeo helped save the place."

"Gotcha. What other work experience do you have?"

He placed the hat on his knee. "Old houses need lots of maintenance. We also built a primary suite on the main floor for my parents when it got to be too hard for Momma to climb the stairs. I can get a long list of references for you. Many of the farmers know me, and there are plenty of people on the circuit who can vouch for me. I'm a hard worker, and I'm honest."

Why didn't I know this kid? "Did you grow up here?"

"Yes, ma'am." He told me where their property was. "My mom and sister usually have a booth at the farmers' market selling canned goods. You might know them."

Jake said, "I've also flipped houses with Coop Henderson. How would you feel about that?"

"Sir, if it gets me a paycheck, I'll feel right good about it."

"How old are you?"

I'd been wondering the same thing. He looked young, but there was also a weariness about him.

His shoulders slumped. "Thirty-two."

"You need to call me Jake. Not sir. Give me your number, and I'll call you later. We'll for sure find work for you. Is there anything else?"

"Yes, sir, I mean Jake. There was a fellow parked on the street when we came here. In a white car. Do you know who he is?"

I scooched to the edge of the couch. "Do you mean Nick Jones? Heavyset with dark hair."

"Yes. He was driving a Malibu. I saw him at the library the day Ms. Tess died."

I gasped. "You did? Like in the parking lot or in the actual building?"

"In the men's restroom at the library." He nodded. "He was washing his hands. Seemed weird."

"Why was it weird?"

"Do you know how many guys walk out while still zipping their flies and never slow to wash their hands? My parents taught me cleanliness was next to godliness. So here was this dude. I thought he must either be real godly or real guilty of something."

"Again, why?" I held my breath, anticipating something big.

"Because he pumped soap into his palms, washed his hands, rinsed, and started all over. When he noticed me, he dried off, but he didn't leave."

Jake said, "Did he speak to you?"

"Nope. I skedaddled out of there real quick like. He was giving off some bad vibes."

"Oh, Wyatt. You need to be very careful. If Nick was involved in the murder, you could be in danger."

Jake stood and paced. "He knows Emma is trying to solve Tess's death. Now he's seen you come to the house."

"But I brought him here to talk to you, Jake." Faith's voice rose. "I try to care for people. Putting somebody in danger has never happened to me before."

"Nick doesn't know why you're here."

I fell back onto the couch. "Wyatt, have you told the police what you witnessed?"

"Naw. They asked specific questions, then sent me away. I'm not scared of that scumbag, and he better not show up on my land. I've spent most of my life protecting my family from one thing or another. Mr. Jones will be no different. If you'll excuse me, I best head home and prepare."

Jake touched his arm. "I still need a way to contact you."

Wyatt recited his number, and Jake tapped it into his phone. "You'll hear from me in the next couple of days."

"Thank you, sir, I mean Jake."

Faith said, "We haven't worked on reading yet."

"If it's all the same to you, I'll reschedule. It's time to prepare. Do you want a ride?"

Faith shook her head. "No, you go on."

"Gardner out." Wyatt put his hat on and left the three of us staring after him.

"I guess I should leave, too." Faith glanced at her phone. Her fingers tightened on it, and she moved the screen closer to her face.

Jake said, "It's a scorcher today. Can I give you a lift?"

Faith dropped her phone and covered her mouth with both hands. She sank into the nearest chair.

"What's wrong?" I crossed the room and knelt beside her.

"Mason is dead."

Chapter Forty-Nine

My breathing hitched. Mason was dead? "Faith, are you sure?"

Faith nodded. "Yes. Zig said the police are searching his room at the B&B right now. That's how he found out."

Jake said, "Does he know what happened? A car crash? Heart attack?"

"I don't know. Maybe I will accept your offer to drive me home, Jake."

"Sure. Let's go." Jake met my gaze and raised his eyebrows.

"I'll join you." Was he hoping I'd calm Faith if she started to cry? "Can I bring Cowboy?"

"May as well." Faith picked up her purse and reading workbook. "Wyatt's a fast learner. I'm sorry we didn't have our lesson today. Jake, I can vouch for him."

"Good to know."

I got Cowboy on a leash, and we drove Faith home. There were four law enforcement vehicles parked in front of the bed and breakfast. One was angled to block the driveway that led to the back of the big house.

"Oh, there's Zig." Faith pointed.

Jake pulled over and stopped.

I turned to look at Faith in the back seat. "I'm sorry about Mason."

"I thought he was on your suspect list for Tess's murder." Her voice sounded defeated.

"He was, at first. Tom said they were together on Tuesday morning. If they were telling the truth, neither one of them was a suspect. Mason and I were not enemies, and I sure didn't wish for him to die."

Zig opened his wife's door and motioned for her to slide over. When she did, he hopped in. "Jake, take us somewhere safe. We need to talk in private."

"My house?" My voice squeaked.

Cowboy whined, and I stroked his side.

Zig shook his head. "No. The police might look for us there. We need to figure out this situation first."

Jake pulled onto the street. "I've got a key to Anytime Coffee."

"It'd be hard to hide there with the big windows."

Faith grabbed his arm. "You're scaring me, honey. What happened to Mason?"

"He was murdered. Plain and simple." Zig sighed. "And it happened on our property."

I snapped my fingers. "Let's go to the retirement village. Ms. Ruby will be happy to let us meet in her place."

Zig said, "I don't want to put her in danger."

"We'll figure out something. Trust me."

Jake signaled to turn. "Buckle up. Lutz Village Retirement Community it is."

Cowboy barked.

"Maybe we should take him back home."

"Good idea." Jake turned the opposite way and glanced in his rearview mirror.

I called Ms. Ruby and explained what I knew. "But I'd rather not put you in harm's way. Is there a meeting room where you host guests? Maybe we could—"

"Nonsense. They are very nice rooms, but they aren't private. Let me think a minute."

Jake parallel parked in front of my house, then jumped out with the puppy.

I looked at Faith and Zig and gave them the thumbs up.

Ms. Ruby said, "Here's what we'll do, Emma. You come to my apartment. I'll leave the door unlocked, but the place will be empty. Take as much time as you need, but lock up before you leave. I'll set out cookies and help yourselves to anything you need."

"Ms. Ruby, you're the best. I can't thank you enough."

"Nonsense, dear. You always bring me flowers, and you and that young fellow don't ignore us when you see us in town. He's a keeper if you ask me." Her voice held a playful note.

"Oh, I've got some exciting news. Jake proposed, and you and your sisters are invited to the wedding."

"Congratulations. I can't wait to hear the details, but that conversation will have to wait. Take care of business today."

Jake slid back into the SUV and handed me my sketch pad of murder notes. He whispered, "Thought you might need this."

I smiled at him. "Thank you."

"Emma, you still there?"

"Yes, ma'am. Thanks so much. We're on the way." We ended the call, and I looked at the others. "Okay, everything's set. We're going to Ms. Ruby's place."

"We may have picked up a tail. Let's see if I can lose it."

I looked back, and Zig and Faith had their heads turned too. A shiny black SUV was behind us.

Jake cleared his throat. "Guys, that's not very subtle."

The Meiers apologized.

"Sorry." I faced forward. "Do you know the back roads well enough to get to the retirement community and lose those people?"

"Maybe not compared to the local cops, but my gut tells me this might not be local."

Zig said, "Maybe you should let me out. It's probably either the Feds or the person who murdered Mason."

Faith gasped. "The Feds? No way you're jumping out. We're sticking together."

Jake said, "Relax. I have no intention of dumping Zig off, but if you all believe in prayer, it might be a good time."

I leaned back in my seat, watching the other vehicle keep up with us from a distance. I closed my eyes to pray, and before I knew it, Jake was parking at the retirement community. He backed into a shady space between two pickup trucks.

"Did you lose them?"

"Sure did, at least for now. I'm not parking close to Ms. Ruby's apartment in case they wander onto the property."

Zig patted his shoulder. "Good job, my man."

It wasn't long before the four of us were sitting in Ms. Ruby's living room. Just like she'd promised, there was a plate of cookies. I really needed to up my game of hostess duties.

The living room was on the small side. There was a loveseat, with an oval coffee table in front of us. On each side of the loveseat were two chairs with arms. The furniture was spaced out, making it easy to maneuver and not fall. The furniture was colorful with big flowery patterns.

Faith said, "Shall I get us some drinks?"

I laughed. There'd never be any possibility of getting ahead of Faith in the hostess department. "I'll help you."

Zig and Jake went through the apartment, closing the curtains.

When we entered the kitchen, I looked at Faith. "It was scary enough when we were dealing with Tess's murder. Now Mason is dead, and somebody is following us."

"The guys think the Feds are involved. What in the world?"

"If Mason and Tom were involved in price fixing, the Feds would investigate."

"This is bad, Emma. Bad, bad, bad." She shook her head. "We're normal, law-abiding people. You've helped the police solve murders, but this is way out of my comfort zone."

"Honey, believe you me, this is out of my comfort zone too." I patted her shoulder. "But Zig has no motive to harm Mason. If necessary, we'll prove he's innocent."

"How?"

"I'm not sure, but you just need to keep the faith."

Faith's eyes widened, then we both laughed.

Despite the moment of lightness, the situation was serious. I had no idea how to catch Mason's killer, but it'd never stopped me before.

Chapter Fifty

At last, Zig, Faith, Jake, and I sat in the living room. Using a pillow as a lap desk, I opened my sketch pad and started a new page with Mason Brown's name at the top. "What do we know about Mason's death?"

Zig rubbed his hands together. "His body was found behind the house. On the driveway. Another one of our guests found him and called for emergency help. I was unaware of anything happening because I was studying in the den. For me, the sound of sirens was the first indication there was a problem."

Faith sat beside him on the loveseat and rubbed his back.

Zig said, "I went outside and followed the firemen to the body. Mason wore his normal clothes."

"So, probably not a heat stroke from running in town?" I took notes on everything Zig told us.

"Nah. It was a button-up shirt and dress pants."

Jake said, "We saw him at the library earlier, and I figured he was going to see Tom."

"Why?" Zig turned his hands palms up.

"Mason accused us of making Tom mad, but I told him how Tom nearly ran us off the road." Jake rubbed his eyes. "When I mentioned a witness, Mason seemed distraught. Next thing we knew, he was gone."

"He never entered the house, which makes me think he was attacked when he got out of his car. He liked to back into parking places, and his body was near the front end of the Porsche."

I did a rough sketch of the sports car with a body in front of it. "I'm curious how long he was there. Had he already met with Tom?"

Zig said, "No way of telling that I know of. I was deep into studying property law."

Jake moved to the window. "That's interesting, because Mason and Tom were focused on properties. But you know that because you went with Brett and Ms. Maebell to a meeting with Mason." He peeked out the curtain.

"Sure did. In fact, Mason and I had a few discussions about property and heir laws. We couldn't discuss the case specifically, but I asked a lot of questions. Mason was happy to answer until I got into the moral issues behind what Tom does. At that point, he got downright uncomfortable." Zig looked at Faith. "I sure could go for a cup of coffee."

"Why sure, darling. We started a pot and it should be ready. Anybody else?"

Instead of my comforting green tea, I'd join Zig in drinking coffee. Even in the dog days of summer, there was comfort in a hot beverage. "Yes, please."

Jake stepped away from the window and followed Faith into the little kitchen.

I said, "Did Mason mention any issues he had with Tom?"

Zig rubbed his hands together. "He never discussed clients by name, and I understood. He said he'd gotten jaded over the years, but after his wife's recent hospital stay, he wanted to get back to the basics. He also said I inspired him."

"How?"

"My enthusiasm for the law and wanting to help others reminded him of why he became an attorney in the first place. I didn't question him, but maybe I should have. He just admitted he needed to make some positive changes in his life."

My heart raced. "Hear me out. What if our encounter with Tom made him realize how bad his client was? He was upset when he left the library. Is it possible he confronted Tom and told him he wanted out? He wasn't going to do Tom's dirty work any longer?"

"Go on. It makes sense to me." Zig held his hands together and nodded like a bobblehead.

Jake returned, carrying a glass of water. He looked out the window once more, and then he sat down.

I said, "It's possible Tom came after Mason, intending to convince him not to quit. They may have argued, and before you know it, Mason's dead. But who would be following us?"

Jake closed his eyes for a moment, as if deep in thought. "We all think Tom might be committing a crime."

"Right." I sat straighter. "Mason's wife had a brush with death. He's inspired by Zig. He's tired of Tom. And he decides to report the crimes to the authorities. That would explain why the FBI is following us."

Jake said, "Let's hope it's the FBI and not mobsters."

Zig shook his head. "Does Tom seem like the kind of guy who does his own grunt work?

Faith handed a mug to me. "I doctored it up for you."

"Thanks."

Zig took the other mug from her. "Thanks, hon."

Faith sat beside her husband.

I sipped my coffee and gave Zig a moment to enjoy his. It was strong and sweet, but not too sweet. I took another sip before interrupting the silence. "You seemed worried earlier, Zig. Why?"

"More than likely, Mason died while I was home. It's possible the police will think I did it."

Faith held her hands together in her lap. "Why, that's just silly. Besides, isn't it possible Mason's death was an accident?"

"I don't think so." Zig faced his wife. "There was a tire iron to the side of Mason's body."

"Coincidence?" I hoped so.

"Nah. It was my tire iron, with my initials engraved on it. It was a prank gift from a friend who teased me that I was too good to change my own tire. That's why my initials are on it. Not many people have a name that starts with the letter Z."

I gulped. "How did the killer get it?"

"It was in the garage on the workbench. Anybody could've taken it." He took another sip of coffee. "Do you think I need an attorney? Like a real one, not a student such as myself?"

Jake said, "It's probably good to have one on standby, and don't say anything to the police without your attorney present."

He lifted his hand. "That much I know."

After setting my cup on a coaster, I doodled on a fresh page. "Is there any possibility the same person murdered Mason and Tess?"

Jake stood. "If so, we have a serial killer."

"If that's the case, we have a different motive for Tess's murder."

"You narrowed down your list to people in Tess's life with a possible motive. That seems most likely to me, but I can't think of a reason for Laurel, Nick, or the unknown mystery date to have a beef with Mason." Jake looked out the curtain again. "There's a black SUV. They can't know where we are exactly, but Zig, you better get your ducks in a row."

Zig stood and walked toward the bedroom. "Excuse me. I need to call one of my professors who still practice law."

I joined Jake and took pictures with my camera.

"What are you doing?"

"Maybe we can read the license plate." I moved away and looked at my phone. "It's too fuzzy to make out."

Faith joined us. "I don't know why I'm so scared. Zig is innocent."

I gave her a one-arm hug. "Of course. Nobody who knows your husband would believe he killed Mason." Even if his tire iron was the murder weapon.

"I'll clean up our mess." Faith moved away.

I looked over my notes. Were the murders connected? That was the looming question. Before Mason's death, I'd decided to focus on Tess. Her life and her past. If I could determine who murdered her, then it would become clear if the deaths were linked.

Who was in the black SUV? It looked official, like what I'd seen in movies.

Zig leaned on the doorframe between the bedroom and living room. "My professor, the practicing attorney, is on her way here. She wants to hear my story, and she thinks we need to go to the police station. I appreciate all you've done for me, but do you think Ms. Ruby will mind if we stay a little longer?"

"Both of her sisters live here, plus she has friends. She'll be fine hanging out with the others." I texted her to confirm, and then we waited with Faith and Zig until his professor arrived.

The attorney was a stylish woman with dark shoulder-length hair, and she took charge the moment she entered the apartment.

Jake and I left them alone.

We walked to the door nearest where the Sequoia waited for our return. Too bad the black SUV had us blocked.

Chapter Fifty-One

J ake and I balked at the sight of the vehicle that had been following us. Jake said, "Go back in."

We backed up and stood in the shadows. My pulse swooshed through my ears. "This case is going to make me old or kill me. Not sure which."

"Shh. There's a library around the corner. We can hide there until it's safe."

I followed him to a room with comfy chairs and two walls with bookshelves, full of paperbacks and hardbacks. Flowers comforted me, and books came in second place. Knowing we couldn't escape now had frozen my brain. What should we do?

Jake said, "I'll warn Zig. Will you call Matt and see if he knows what's happening?"

I nodded. Call Matt? It was doable, even if I wasn't sure what to say. I found his contact information and called.

"Emma?" His voice came through loud and clear.

"Yes." My voice sounded brittle.

Jake glanced at me, then kissed my head.

His gesture made it easier for me to breathe. "Matt, somebody is following us. I don't know if it's law enforcement or bad people."

"Give me a minute to find out."

"Okay." I looked over Jake's shoulder.

He said, "I decided to text in case he's ignoring calls."

"Matt's checking."

"Good. I'm going to close the plantation shutters in case those guys are walking around the campus."

"Emma, you there?" Matt's words were fast and clipped.

"Yes. Did you learn anything?"

"Yes. There are two agents tasked with following you."

"Me?" My voice squeaked.

"Officially, Zig Meier. It appears you and Jake gave Zig and Faith a ride to Lutz Village Retirement Community. They're looking for you now."

"Jake and I are together. If we walk outside, will they shoot us?"

"Probably not. Where's Zig?"

"He's speaking to his attorney, but you've got to know he didn't kill Mason."

Matt said, "I can't say anything about Mason Brown, but I'll let the agents know you're walking to Jake's Sequoia now."

I swiped my phone and looked at Jake. "Matt knows we're in your SUV. Those are FBI agents, and they're looking for Zig. We're supposed to go outside."

Jake sighed. "Something's fishy, but I don't know what."

"Yeah. If they don't arrest us, I want to focus on Tess again. With federal agents involved, there's no need to waste time looking at Mason's murder."

"Agreed." He reached for my hand, and we walked outside.

Standing beside the official vehicle was a man and woman. Both dressed in black from head to toe.

I gulped. If they arrested me, I wouldn't last twenty-four hours in prison.

* * *

I couldn't remember ever being so happy to walk into my house. "Home, sweet home."

"Amen to that." Jake locked the door behind us.

The security system beeped, and I tapped in the code. "Weird."

Cowboy and Abby greeted us in the gathering room.

"Where have you guys been? I fixed burgers, and they're staying warm in the oven." With hands on hips, Abby frowned at us. "You scared me."

"I'm sorry." I gave her a big ole hug. "Honey, you won't believe our afternoon."

Jake said, "For her safety, we're not supposed to talk about it."

"Mom, seriously?" Abby pushed back, and Cowboy barked.

I knelt and rubbed his sides. "I wasn't chasing a clue—well, maybe earlier, but Jake's right. We can't discuss the other stuff."

"Does it have to do with Nick Jones?" She crossed her arms and swayed from foot to foot.

"What about him?"

"He stopped by, claiming he'd dropped his wallet earlier. I told him it wasn't in the house, but he could look in the backyard. He wanted to walk through the house, but he gave me the creeps."

"So?"

"I told him he could go through the gate at the side of the house and look, but I wasn't allowed to have men in the house. I locked and bolted the door, then set the alarm."

That explained the beeping alarm when we entered.

Jake said, "Good girl. Instincts like that will keep you safe. Also, if you'd like me review self-protection moves, let me know."

"Thanks, Jake. We should eat before the burgers dry out." She headed to the kitchen, and we followed.

I washed my hands and set the table. "Abby, did Nick go in the back and look for his wallet?"

"I didn't watch, but the cameras didn't indicate he was back there. I know they don't pick up all the motion, but it seems like he would've moved around the yard quite a bit if he was searching. Do you think he killed Ms. Tess?"

"Possibly." I folded paper napkins.

"Hey, I ran into Hope Peters, the children's librarian, at the coffee shop. We sat together for a bit. She said Laurel is letting the power go to her head. She's bossing people around like she's been in charge for years instead of days. So, I asked her if she thought Laurel would've killed Tess to get the top job, and she said maybe."

"I appreciate you asking, but I don't want you to be in danger."

"We were in a public place. Brett and Celia were in the shop, and I was driving your truck. It seemed safe enough." She put mustard and pickles on her bun. "Did you hear somebody died at the bed-and-breakfast?"

"Yes." Jake filled glasses with ice. "It was one of their guests."

Abby's mouth dropped open. "Come on, y'all. Why do you know that? No, don't tell me. Just please, quit investigating murders."

I made no promises. Instead, I changed the conversation to Abby's new uniforms for work.

"Scrubs, Mom. There's no official uniform, and I'm going to miss wearing T-shirts and shorts for you and Sophie. I bought five different colors of scrubs, and I can mix and match them. One set has puppies and cats on them. If there'd been a set with golden retrievers, I would've bought them." She chatted about clothes, pets, and the clinic. Her nervousness was obvious, but so was her excitement. My heart swelled with pride. It'd be awesome if my daughter found her calling at a young age.

I was thirty-eight and just pursuing my passion, but I didn't regret my years focused on raising Abby. She was my biggest blessing.

Jake smiled at me, and he didn't interrupt Abby either. It was the most normal thing we'd done in almost a week, and it felt good.

Chapter Fifty-Two

I pulled the colorful scrubs from the dryer and hung them up for Abby. She'd reluctantly gone to bed, after I promised to finish the laundry. Monday would be her first day at the vet clinic, and I didn't want her to yawn the whole time.

Jake had gone to his apartment with a headache. I'd never known him to feel bad, and it left me unsettled. Had the day been too much drama? Or maybe it was related to weather.

Last year, I'd been a boring single mother raising a daughter. Never would I've imagined I'd be helping solve murders . Jake had worked with me on my amateur investigations, and we'd grown close faster than I ever would've imagined.

I looked at the sparkling engagement ring. Who would've guessed I'd meet a wonderful man like Jake and fall in love? Life was good and would get better once Tess's killer was apprehended. The FBI could handle Mason's case without any assistance from me.

I gathered my sketch pad, murder notes, and Tess's diary, turning out lights as I worked my way to the office. One issue nagged me. Matt hadn't shared much of anything concerning the murder. Oh, well. I wouldn't give up.

The house was quiet, and I got comfortable on the pink loveseat. Abby had found it at a yard sale, and she'd been so excited to add it to my office. She'd also bought a fuzzy pink shag rug and angled it on the wood floor in front of my desk.

Cowboy joined me and lay at my feet.

I reached for Tess's receipts and worked my way through the neat stack.There were many from Sophie's Bakery, but she ate there almost every day for lunch. So, it wasn't a surprise. Most of the others made sense until I came across one from Amalfi's.

It was for a glass of red wine, lasagna, and half of a serving of tiramisu. I placed it to the side and continued through the pile, looking for anything else unusual.

At last, I looked at the receipt again from the Italian restaurant. Half of a dessert? Did that mean she'd split it with someone? Was it possibly her date with the man from the website? I took a picture of the receipt to share with Jake later.

I put all the papers in an envelope with Tess's name on it, and then reached for her diary. The purple leather was soft.

I opened the book, and Tess had printed her name in the front.

The first page had been dated January 1.

This will be my year to try new things. I'll be fifty soon, and I don't want to die knowing I never tried something different. New. Exciting, maybe? My goal is to try one new thing a week. I plan to start at Sophie's Bakery. For a week, I will try her daily special every day, even if it sounds horrible. I am also going to be kind more often to people who irritate me. Not killers. Not Nick. Normal irritating people. Those are the ones I'll be kind to.

Interesting. She'd added plants in the library, including the bleeding heart. It seemed as if one of her goals for the year was to have a more tender heart. It could be why there were different opinions about Tess.

I flipped through the pages. Tess hadn't recorded her thoughts every day. It was more sporadic. The first week, she wrote down all the daily specials she ate. She included how she liked them. I took a picture and texted it to Sophie along with a note explaining what it was. Knowing my best friend, she'd be asleep, but it might be a nice message to wake up to on a Monday morning.

Cowboy growled. Deep.

Chills raced up my spine. "What is it, boy?"

He raced to the back door, continuing to growl.

I jumped up, gripping the diary in one hand and my phone in the other.

Most of the lights were off, and a burglar might suspect the house was empty. I began turning on lights inside and outside. I double-checked the security system. It was armed. Good.

I went into the hidden pantry and found my baseball bat.

In case there was a problem, and somebody broke into my house, I'd be able to protect myself.

Cowboy barked again. He raced to the front door then back to me.

"Shh. What's going on?" I didn't want him to wake up Abby, but if there was a bad person outside, I wanted them to leave. Better to let the puppy bark.

There was a crash, followed by the sound of glass falling on the floor.

I screamed.

The security system wailed.

"Mom!"

"Hide, Abby."

Footsteps thudded.

The front door squeaked open, then slammed shut.

My heart leapt into my throat.

Cowboy barked and lunged toward the front of the house. I dropped my phone and the diary in my effort to keep him under control.

More footsteps. Not as heavy as before.

Was the intruder leaving? Or had the burglar brought reinforcements?

Chapter Fifty-Three

Using all my strength, I closed Cowboy in the office. I needed to protect him and Abby.

"Mom!" Abby screamed over the blaring alarm.

"Hide."

"Mom, he's gone. I watched him run up the street from the window." She placed her hands over her ears. "Can you turn that thing off?"

"Maybe." I went to the system's command panel and punched in a variety of codes.

My phone rang. "Hello."

"Mrs. Justice?" A male voice inquired.

"Yes." I didn't recognize the voice.

"I'm calling from your security company. Are you safe? Your alarm was triggered."

"I know. Somebody tried to break in. No. Somebody did break into my house, but he's gone." I wiped away tears. "I can't turn the siren off."

"I can help. What's your code word?" He asked a series of questions before giving me the secret number to punch into the panel. "Help is on the way, but I'll remain on the phone until they arrive."

Silence followed. Blessed relief.

Cowboy barked like crazy, breaking the moment of quiet.

"Thanks. Hold on a second." I pointed to the office door. "Abby, can you calm him down?"

"Hey, I need somebody to calm me down, too." A laugh slipped out with a note of hysteria.

"Oh, honey. I'm sorry this happened." I gave her a one-armed hug.

"Ma'am?" The voice over the phone interrupted.

"Yes. Sorry. I was talking to my daughter. I'm going to be fine, and I need to make a call. You've been wonderful."

"You can hang up on me, but I can't disconnect."

Ugh. That sounded rude. "Oh, in that case, I'll stay on the line." I picked up Tess's diary.

Abby reached the doorway of my office.

"Wait. Honey, can I use your phone? I want to call the police chief." I held out my hand. "And will you stay on the line with this nice gentleman? He's from the security company."

My daughter turned and traded phones with me.

I called Matt, and Abby managed to get Cowboy under control in my office. She really had a way with our new puppy.

"What? It's still my day off." Matt's voice was rusty as if I'd woken him up.

"Sorry, but somebody was here. They broke into my house. The security people alerted the police, but I wanted you to be aware of the situation. You know, it could be linked to the murders, and that's why I called you directly. Go back to sleep, your people will update you in the morning. Sorry for waking you up."

"Stop. Is the perp gone?" Background noises indicated he was moving. The bed squeaked. There was the sound of water running in a sink. Keys jingled.

"Abby saw the person run toward the square."

"I'm on the way, and I'll make sure my people are watching in town for a suspicious character on foot."

"Thanks."

A siren blipped, and a police cruiser screeched to a halt in front of my house. "Matt, one of the officers is here."

"Good. You and Abby are safe now."

My heartbeat seemed to be returning to normal. I needed to call Jake. He'd be hurt if I didn't. I hated to wake him up, though. I tapped his contact information and called.

"Emma? What's wrong?"

"I'm fine, but somebody broke into the house. A police car just arrived, and Matt's coming. I know you're—"

"I'm on the way too."

"Thanks, Jake." Avoiding broken glass, I stood at the entrance of the gathering room. Glass was on the couch, the table, and all over the floor. My mind flashed back to earlier in the day. There was something different, but the image couldn't cut through the lingering fear.

Cowboy ran to me, and Abby was close behind. "He got away from me."

I reached out and realized the diary and Abby's phone were in my hands. I set them on the dining table and then rubbed the golden retriever's head. "Everything is okay now."

There was a knock on the front door. "Ms. Justice, this is Officer Koch. I'm coming inside."

It hadn't occurred to me that the intruder left the front door wide open. Hadn't it slammed shut?

Had somebody snuck back inside? Or had the wind blown it open?

"We're safe. My daughter and puppy are with me."

The uniformed policeman entered the house, holding his weapon. "You're sure they left? I can do a sweep of the house."

"My place is small. I was in my office when the person broke the front window. Cowboy, my puppy, and I ran this way. I thought I heard the front door open and shut, and assumed they left. You know what, maybe you should check upstairs. You know, since the door was open when you arrived. Be careful."

"Stay down here." Officer Steve Koch was around ten years younger than me. He and I were about the same height, but he was muscular. I had full confidence he'd find an intruder if one was hiding upstairs.

My legs shook, and I collapsed into a chair at the table.

Cowboy laid his head on my lap, and Abby sat next to me.

She pointed to the journal beside her phone. "What's this?"

I reached for the purple book. "That's Tess's diary."

A kaleidoscope of images filled my mind.

The gathering room in its normal state. Jake had put the purple book on the coffee table. Nick had been in my house to wash his hands earlier in the day. Nick had stared at the journal. He'd also returned and told Abby that he'd lost his wallet. Was it a coincidence that the very day Tess's diary appeared in my house, and the day Nick saw it, was the same day my house got broken into?

"Abby, I think you were very smart to prevent Nick from entering the house earlier."

Footsteps clomped down the stairs in a running cadence. "The upstairs is clear, and the chief radioed. He's here. So, is Jake Hunter. Chief Young will question you, but can you give me any kind of description of the person who broke in here?"

"It's possible Nick Jones is the person who broke into my house tonight." My heart raced again. Was it fair to assume it was Nick? "Or maybe not."

Abby said, "I got a glimpse of the person running away. I believe it was a man. He's bulkier than you."

Officer Koch wrote in his little notebook. "Thanks."

Glass crunched like somebody was walking on it.

Matt and Jake appeared behind Officer Koch.

Cowboy gave a happy bark and then moseyed over to Abby.

Jake hugged me long and hard. His racing heart confirmed I wasn't the only person dealing with fear. "I'm so glad you all are safe."

Matt said, "Nick Jones, huh? Koch, put out a BOLO, and take another officer with you to Jones's house."

"Yes, sir." He left us alone.

Matt looked toward the kitchen. "Any chance I can get a cup of coffee? Something tells me this will be a long night."

Chapter Fifty-Four

Monday morning, I rubbed my gritty eyes while watching Abby pack lunch to take to her first day of work at the veterinary clinic. The night before, Matt had allowed her to share what she knew, and then she'd gone to bed, taking the puppy with her.

Abby poured coffee into an insulated travel mug. "Do you mind if I finish this?"

"Help yourself. I'm so sorry you didn't get much sleep last night." I yawned.

"I got more than you. Wish me luck today. I'm so excited, and I don't want to make any mistakes."

I gave her a quick hug. "You're going to be amazing. I love you."

"Love you too, Mom."

I handed the truck keys to her, and she left with a tired smile.

Cowboy stared after Abby with his tail down.

"It's going to be okay. I'll check on the ant mounds, and if the fire ants are gone, you can play in back." I slipped on my gardening shoes, headed outside, and walked around the yard.

I cut flowers to take to Heart of Texas Bed and Breakfast, the coffee shop, and the bakery. Once there were enough, I checked the mounds. No sign of the ants, but were the chemicals still active? Could they make my puppy sick? How long did poisons hang around? It had to do with the half-lives of the chemicals, but I didn't know what Nick had used. It didn't seem smart to ask the exterminator, especially since he may have been the intruder last night.

Maybe I needed a good rain to diminish the danger to Cowboy.

In the meantime, I'd keep him out of danger.

After a quick shower, I prepared to make my flower deliveries. Instead of using my normal bags, I packed a backpack, including Tess's diary. No way I'd leave it alone, and it was less likely to get stolen, tight against my body.

Cowboy took himself to the crate.

"You are so smart." I tossed him a treat and secured the door. "I'll be back before you know it."

It didn't take long to walk to Heart of Texas. It was just up to the square and down another street. Faith answered the door. "Come in."

"Hi, Faith. I brought some flowers."

She sighed and plopped into the nearest chair. "Everybody checked out of here, what with the murder and the police all over the place. Don't get me wrong, I appreciate how hard law enforcement is working, but it's not good for business."

I sat near my friend. "Have they told you anything?"

"No, but the FBI was here along with local law enforcement. You know how they were following us? They're in charge now." She sighed. "Zig is torn up, feeling guilty that he couldn't put a stop to the murder. We argued, and we never argue. When I said something like he might have gotten killed too, he told me that he wasn't a coward. I know he's not a coward, but the conversation got out of hand."

"Where is Zig now?" I hoped he hadn't been arrested.

"He's meeting with his attorney in the office. There's no reason for him to be a suspect in Mason's death."

"He's a good man with a kind heart. It's going to work out."

"I sure hope you're right." She stood. "I won't need flowers this week, but I'll pay you."

"No, you won't, and when you have guests, I'll bring over fresh flowers."

"Thank you." Faith's shoulders drooped, and I couldn't remember a time when she hadn't taken me into her kitchen.

"If you need a friend to talk to, let me know."

"Thanks." She twisted her mouth. "Maybe I should go to the library. Getting out of the house will help. Right?"

"Definitely. Call me if you want. I'm a good listener." I left and walked to the bakery.

Sophie saw me the minute I entered. "Hi, Emma. I appreciated your message this morning. What would you like?"

"Avocado toast on sourdough bread, please."

"Sit down, and I'll bring it to you."

I placed some money on the counter and took a seat at the corner table. I pulled the diary out of my backpack but laid it flat on my sketch pad, hoping nobody would realize it was a purple journal. This time, I began reading in June. If the murder was connected to an event in Tess's life, maybe it'd be mentioned in the most recent pages.

"Whatcha reading?" Sophie sat beside me.

I whispered, "Tess's diary. It could be the reason my house was broken into last night."

"What?" Sophie's voice squeaked.

"Oh, yeah. Soon after I texted you, somebody smashed my front window and came into the house."

"Oh, Emma. Tell me more." Her eyes flashed.

I shared all I knew. "It's possible Nick did it."

"You stay away from him." She shook her finger at me. "He's very dangerous."

I took a bite of avocado toast. "Yum. This is even better than last time."

"I used it on a new recipe for multi-grain bread, and I sliced it into thicker pieces before toasting." Her smile diminished. "Are you trying to distract me from talking about Nick?"

"Maybe." I avoided eye contact.

"I should get back to work, but this conversation will be continued."

"I brought flowers."

"Thank you. Enjoy your food. I can arrange the flowers in a vase."

I handed a bundle of daisies to Sophie, and she went behind the counter.

I finished my second breakfast and read a few pages of the diary. I promised myself only one more entry before leaving, and I turned the page. The writing was short, but powerful.

I must apologize to Paula. I don't know how to fix what I've done, but somehow, I will make things right.

What had Tess done? I wished I could ask Paula, but it was impossible to reach her.

The bakery was filling up, and I hid the diary in my backpack.

The next person to walk into the bakery was the bald man from the murder scene. I checked my items and walked to the man. "Hi, I'm Emma Justice. I found Tess Carranza's body last week at the library."

His eyes widened.

"Yeah. Surely, you remember. I saw you there talking to the paramedics. Are you the supervisor?"

"Do you have a complaint?"

"Oh, no. Nothing of the sort. Your people were very respectful." We scooted up in line. "Do you by any chance know how she died? Did she suffer? Or was it quick?"

"Sorry, but I can't discuss the situation." He reached the counter and ordered a cup of coffee and the daily special.

I placed cash on the counter. "My treat. Thanks for being a public servant."

He shook his head. "I can't let you do that."

I glanced at my friend across the counter. "Bye, Sophie." I left with a wave to my best friend and smiled at the supervisor. He'd never shared his name. In fact, he hadn't shared anything. Still, his work to protect our community deserved appreciation. I was glad to buy his lunch even if he hadn't told me a thing.

Onward with my investigation. I couldn't wait to read more of Tess's diary, but I needed privacy.

Chapter Fifty-Five

I took a detour on my way to Anytime Coffee House. I climbed the stairs to the courthouse office where Tom Ward liked to hang out. I walked up and down the halls, gathering my courage. At last, I entered the county clerk's office.

"Good morning. How can I help you?" A young man wearing glasses greeted me. A group of women huddled around a table in back, eating muffins.

My brain froze. "Um, good morning. I'm Emma Justice, and I grow flowers."

"Yes, ma'am. My mom always buys from you at the farmers' market. She's a real fan. I'm Hayden Peters."

I shook his hand. "Nice to meet you."

"So, how can I help?" He glanced over his shoulder, then back to me. "Your best bet is to trust me. This job is temporary. I'm saving up for law school, and I plan to work my way up the ranks and run for governor one day. As you can see, I'm not shy. Your taxes pay for them to—well, you can see. One part of my platform will be to curb waste."

I laughed. "Hayden, you'll have my vote every time you run for office. So, I may be interested in buying a little farm on the edge of town. Is it possible to look at a land map and see what exactly connects to the property?"

He seemed to think my request was reasonable. "Where is the property?"

I gave him the address.

Hayden frowned. "That's the same property Mr. Ward requested to see."

My heart skipped a beat. I leaned close and whispered. "Is Mr. Ward here now?"

"Yes." Hayden kept his voice soft.

"Thanks for the warning. I'll come back another time."

"I understand wanting to be cautious." He handed me a basic white business card. "This is my number and extension. Call before you come next time, and I can let you know if the coast is clear."

"I appreciate it. By the way, just between us, Mr. Ward is dangerous. Watch your back." I hightailed it out of the courthouse before Hayden could ask a question.

I texted Jake. **Tom is at the courthouse looking at the property information for our farm.**

Three dots appeared. **Our farm. Nice. But get out of there.**

I'm going to Anytime Coffee.

Good. Be careful.

You, too.

I entered the coffee shop and waited in line. It gave me time to catch my breath. When I reached the counter, I pulled out a reusable travel cup and a bouquet of daisies. "Hi, Brett. I'd like iced green tea, please. And a vase for these."

"Emma, take a breath. Jake texted me that you might be stressed." Brett reached under the counter and soon handed me a vintage clear vase. "What's going on?"

I gave him my credit card. "You've got too many people in line for me to unburden myself. I'll arrange these, and then sit in back."

"I'll be over yonder directly with your tea." He palmed my credit card, and I walked to the restroom and filled the vase with water.

At the table, I arranged the daisies.

Brett walked up and set my drink and credit card on the table. "Why are you wearing a backpack?"

"Shh." I handed the vase to him. "What do you think?"

"Beautiful. I'll be right back." He spoke to patrons as he moved through the coffee shop.

I shrugged out of the arm straps on my bag and sat down to enjoy my drink. The cosmos were left that I'd planned to give Faith. The library seemed like a good place to stop next. Although it'd seem weird not to see Mason.

The door to the coffee shop opened, and three men and a woman, all wearing black suits, entered.

Brett moved behind the counter and offered to take their orders.

I observed the team of four agents.

They placed their orders and sat at a table near the wall. Except for extremely good posture, they seemed like normal people. Yesterday, two of them had scared me.

Faith texted me. **I'm at the library. The FBI isn't looking at Zig anymore, but they are renting rooms from us now.**

Seemed like the perfect time to leave. **I'm coming to you. Sit tight.**

I gathered my belongings and walked to the counter. "Brett, I've got to go. See you later."

"Bye, Emma." He looked up. "Wait, where are you going?"

"The library. Faith is there." I raised a finger. "I'll be careful."

"Good girl."

I walked slowly past the agents, but I didn't hear anything noteworthy. So, I busted it out of there and hurried as fast as possible in the July heat.

Chapter Fifty-Six

Faith and I sat in a small conference room at the library. She helped me arrange the pink, white, and purple cosmos in three small vases. After examining her handiwork, Faith said, "If I'd known the FBI agents were going to stay with us, I would've kept your flowers earlier."

"I'll bring you more later today or tomorrow morning. Tell me what happened." I took a drink of my green tea and dabbed the perspiration on my face with a tissue.

"Two of the agents talked to Zig and his attorney, and they decided to consider other suspects. Because Lutz doesn't have many nearby hotels, they're staying with us."

"Have you picked up any clues?"

"They're a quiet bunch, but I heard them mention Tess's name. That doesn't mean there's a connection between their attacks."

I nodded. "And it doesn't mean there's a serial killer. I get it."

"Even though Mason died on our property, with law enforcement around, I feel safe. Why do you think the federal agents are investigating Mason's murder?" Faith twirled her ponytail around a finger.

"Tess thought Mason and Tom were taking advantage of landowners. Maybe they're running a scheme that involves federal laws." I shrugged. " Would you mind to watch my stuff for a couple of minutes? I want to ask one of the librarians a question."

"Sure."

I took a vase of flowers with me and placed it on the circulation desk before tracking down Hope. "Hey, I need to talk to you."

"Good, because I was going to call you after work. Where are you sitting? I want to show you something."

"I'm in the little conference room with Faith Meier."

"Give me two minutes." Hope walked toward her office, and I rejoined Faith.

"Hope wants to show me something. You're welcome to stay."

Faith looked at her watch. "I've got time."

I pulled out my sketchbook but kept the diary hidden in my backpack.

Hope entered and closed the door with a firm click. "I'm using my ten-minute break. The other day I mentioned to you an experiment I wanted to try with the children. After the police left, I roped off the reference area. When everyone left for the day, I practiced checking for fingerprints." She pulled up a paper with fingerprints featured on it. "This one is mine, and this is Laurel's. Not that we're guilty of anything bad like murder. I saw Tess take a book one day after Mason left. She put it in her office instead of back on the shelf."

"Why would she do that?" It seemed significant to Hope.

Hope sat beside Faith and leaned close to us. "Mason was the first patron in the library that day. Tess had pulled the book out, but I think it was for herself to read. Mason stopped when he saw the book and took it to his table. Tess went over and pointed to the book. They didn't exactly argue, but she wasn't happy when she left empty-handed."

Faith placed her hands on the table. "Are you saying Tess took the book to her office after Mason left? What was the book?"

"I wasn't sure until I started my fingerprint experiment, and trust me, I was curious." Her eyes sparkled, and she pulled out a book in a sealed bag. "This is it. *Rural Texas Land.* I fingerprinted it. This sheet shows the prints I pulled off. These belonged to Tess, and I believe these prints were Mason's."

"That's good work." I looked at the swirls and lines. "Isn't it amazing?"

Faith nodded. "It sure is. We're unique individuals."

Hope's shoulders sagged. "Now that Mason has passed, there's probably no point to the fingerprints."

"Hold on." I lifted my hand. "After Tess's death, when the crime scene people left, was there any kind of a mess or leftover clues that they didn't think were important?"

She sat down and reached for her phone. "I'm married, and one day my husband wants to be an attorney."

Faith gasped. "My husband is in law school now. He loves it."

Hope gave her a weak smile. "We're both working and saving our money so he can afford to go one day."

"It'll happen. Maybe I can help you look for scholarship opportunities." Faith took a blank sheet of paper from Hope's stack and wrote on it. "That's my number. I can meet you here, or you can come to my place, and we'll find scholarships he qualifies for. Has he been accepted anywhere yet?"

Faith never stopped taking care of others. I zoned out of their conversation and pulled the pages of fingerprints closer. I snapped photos of them with my phone. When they grew quiet, I said, "This is good work. Do you have anything else?"

"As a matter of fact, I took pictures of the mess they left behind." She handed her phone to me. "This is the chaos we had to deal with. I thought Hayden would be curious in case he goes into criminal law. He wants to help people, and I don't know exactly what that will look like, but it seemed like a good idea to take pictures."

"Hayden? Does he work at the County Clerk's office?"

"Yes. It's been a learning experience."

"I met him today. He's very nice." I swiped through the photos. "Can I forward these to my phone?"

Faith said, "Me too. The more eyes we have on them, the more likely one of us will find a clue."

"Help yourselves."

I entered the necessary contact information, then forwarded all the pictures relevant to the murder. "Hayden's lucky to have you on his side." Hope's eyes sparkled again. "He's amazing."

"You are, too." I gave the phone back. "It's past your ten minutes. Why don't you take this vase of flowers to the children's area, and the small one might look nice in your office. I'll help."

Faith said, "I'll wait here for you, Emma."

I carried both flower vases and put one on a public desk and the other in Hope's office. "If you think of anything else, please call me. My focus is on solving Tess's death."

"You got it. Thanks for the flowers."

"Have a good day." I left and returned to the little conference room.

Faith stood by the table, reading Tess's diary. The one thing I was trying to keep hidden.

"What are you doing?"

Chapter Fifty-Seven

Faith jumped so hard her ponytail slapped her face. "Oh, Emma. I accidentally kicked your backpack, and this fell out. I was going to put it back, but the cover is so soft. I wanted to see who made it. I'd like one for myself. That's why I opened it, and of course, I saw Tess's name. How did you get her diary?"

"Shh." I yanked the book out of her hand. "This could contain the answer to Tess's murder. I started reading it last night, but then the person broke into my house. I really wonder if it was her killer."

"Take it easy. This room could be bugged, or have a security camera, or who knows what? Let's talk somewhere private."

"And safe." I put the items in my backpack. "Sorry, I overreacted."

"No problem. It's no wonder you wanted me to keep an eye on you know what." She pointed to the backpack, but we'd talked about it. If somebody listened to our conversation, they knew. "Did you drive?"

"No, I walked."

"Let me drive you somewhere safe." Faith pulled keys from her purse.

"It's hard to know what's safe these days."

"True. Come on."

I gathered my bags and travel mug, and we left the building in search of a secure place.

Faith drove to Paula's house, but there was a police cruiser parked behind her blue RAV4.

"Keep going. I bet it's a welfare check." Oops. That might sound suspicious. "I haven't seen Paula recently. Have you?"

"I usually see her at our book club gatherings, so no. I thought she was on vacation." She drove ever so slow down the street. "We drive this big SUV because Zig is six-five, and his shoulders are so broad. It was hard to find something he was comfortable in, but this was wonderful for him. I thought about a small car for myself, but the salesman offered us a deal if we bought two Escalades. We bought one black and one white vehicle, so they are like us."

I chuckled. "You can always make me smile. That is so cute."

She stopped at the end of the street. "Where to?"

"Your place is safe because of the agents, but it might not be private enough. Abby's been fixing up my office at home. Will you feel comfortable there?"

"Of course, and I'll get to play with your dog. We decided on no pets at our place because of guests with allergies, but I love dogs."

I chatted with her about Abby's decision to work for Dr. Erb until we got to my house. Once inside, I pointed to the gathering room. "I was exhausted when the police left last night, but I need to clean that. Jake boarded the window and has ordered replacement glass."

Cowboy barked.

Faith took me by the shoulders and turned me toward the back of the house. "Let's learn from Hope. You go read the diary, and I'll take pictures of your house for insurance and evidence. I even see some fingerprint dust. How about if I make myself at home and fix us something to eat?"

"You're going to spoil me, but go ahead." I opened the crate for Cowboy, and he greeted Faith with a wagging tail before following me to the office.

I sat at the desk and opened Tess's diary. Ready to take notes, I began reading. Soon, I was lost in the day-to-day life of Tess Carranza. It made me smile, when she reviewed books in her private notes. She gave an in-depth analysis of each book she read.

In her musings, she continued to consider new adventures. She hiked at the park on her days off, and she'd never done that before. I kept reading about her simple adventures until the day she met Mason Brown.

Her neat penmanship transformed into a flowing script.

A single man came into the library today. He's handsome with dark hair, and he's in good shape. He was dressed nice, too. When he asked for my help in locating a book on the history and geography around Lutz, I felt something like attraction. I haven't felt that since being left at the altar. Is it time for romance?

Wow. Mason had told me the truth.

A few pages later, Tess found out that Mason was married. She was hurt and embarrassed, but she took his advice and went to a dating website.

My pulse picked up. Who was her date?

I continued to read.

Aha. Bruce Hudson was the mystery man. Tess had written his name in all capital letters. Bruce was fifty-two and a book editor. It sounded like he would have been right up Tess's alley.

I added the information to my notes.

"Are you learning much?" Faith carried a tray with little cheese sandwiches, apple slices, and grapes.

Cowboy moved out of her way.

"Yes, and that looks yummy." I cleared a space on my desk, and we ate lunch while I updated her on what I had discovered.

Faith wiped her hands on a paper napkin. "What would you like me to do?"

"Investigate Bruce Hudson online." I wrote down the name of the dating site. "Use my computer, and I'll move to the loveseat. If you can find a good photo of him, go ahead and print it. I've never met the man, but what if he's using an alias?"

"Some people find true love, and others get scammed. It's always good to keep your eyes wide open, and I think it's a good argument for being friends with a man before dating him." She picked up the tray. "I'll be right back."

I turned on the computer and plugged in my passwords.

Faith returned with fresh drinks. "I figured you like Dr. Pepper since it's in your fridge."

"Of course, and thank you. You really are spoiling me." I took what I needed to the loveseat and motioned for Faith to sit at the desk. "Make yourself comfortable. There's a notebook, and print anything you want."

"I'll start with the dating website."

Cowboy barked and ambled to the back door.

"I'm going to take him outside. Nick killed a fire ant mound for me, but I'm concerned the chemicals might harm my puppy. So, I'm going to leash him and keep him safe."

Outside, Cowboy sniffed around the yard and did his business. When we reached the area near the mound, he barked.

Was it possible he got a whiff of Nick's scent? It'd been a day. I'd been a dog owner for less than six months, and there was still so much to learn. My puppy was always patient with me. "Let's go."

He stared at the mound.

"Come." I clapped my hands.

He followed me inside and drank water while I entered the office.

Faith said, "I have some experience researching strangers. Because we live in the bed-and-breakfast, I like to investigate our guests. I can usually find something, but not so with Bruce Hudson."

"What about the dating site?"

"For his photo, he has a picture of a Sherlock Holmes book. In his bio, he says that reading Sherlock Holmes started his love of reading. He's a book editor, but he doesn't say who he works for, or if he's self-employed. He emphasized his love of books, plays, and water skiing. There's nothing concrete, but maybe that protects him."

"That's a possibility."

My phone vibrated. "This is Hayden Peters."

"You should answer it."

I swiped the phone. "Hello?"

"Hi, Ms. Justice. Hope told me she met with you at the library. I thought you should know that Mr. Ward left for lunch."

"Thanks for letting me know. I'm tied up with something else right now, though."

"No prob. I'll call you tomorrow when the coast is clear."

CHAPTER FIFTY-SEVEN

"Thanks." I put the phone to the side.

Faith said, "What was that about?"

"Tom isn't at the courthouse now, but I want to focus on Tess. I hate being like a dog racing from one smell, or clue in my case, to the next. No offense to Cowboy."

We worked for the next hour, and that's when I hit gold.

July 1. I still can't believe I let it slip out about Paula's baby. I can't sleep and can barely eat. Nick was furious, and Paula will be mad too. She'll probably run. She has prepared for this day. I don't want to lose my best friend, but if she takes off, I'll never see her again. Why did I let Nick provoke me? This must be fixed before Paula returns from vacation. But how?

I gasped.

"What?"

"I know something, but I've been sworn to secrecy by Paula Jones." I dropped the diary and paced. It wasn't helping. "Have you found anything yet on Bruce?"

"No, and I've never come up this blank." She leaned back in the office chair. "Paula's secret. I may know it. We went to a cheese and wine party, and she got tipsy. She mentioned her daughter's birthday, and when I told her I'd never met her daughter, she sobered immediately. I thought that only happened in the movies, but she transformed from a sappy, sad mom to a fierce momma lion intent on protecting her child. She begged me to never mention the daughter, or they'd both be in grave danger."

"Well, yeah." Relief poured through me. I didn't have to betray Paula's secret.

"Do you know where Paula is? Has Nick harmed her? Is that why the police were at her house earlier? Or has she fled?"

"I don't know where Paula is, but to my knowledge, Nick hasn't hurt her." I handed the diary to Faith. "Read that and tell me what you think."

Faith took the diary.

Unable to sit still, I returned to pacing while she read.

At last, Faith said, "This could be a motive for Nick to have murdered Tess."

"I agree. Her death isn't connected to Mason."

"What should we do next?" Faith closed the book.

"You have federal agents staying under your roof. They could maybe help us learn more about Bruce Hudson." I crossed my arms. "Although, why do I care so much? Nick is our suspect."

"You care about people, so it makes sense to me. However, we do need to stay focused on Tess's murder." Faith shook her head. "What we need is a good dose of proof."

The doorbell rang, and I hurried to answer it.

Cowboy ran past me and used his angry bark.

A peek out the window stopped me in my tracks.

Nick's work truck was in the driveway.

Chapter Fifty-Eight

The doorbell rang again, and Cowboy barked.

Faith walked up behind me. "Who is it?"

"Nick."

There was a pounding on the door. "Emma, open up."

The sound of Nick's voice sent my puppy into overdrive.

Faith said, "I'll call Zig. Try to stall."

Stall? I could do a heaping pile of stalling. I walked to the door. "Nick, you're upsetting my dog."

"Tough. You didn't pay me."

It was hard to hear over my puppy. "Wait a minute. My dog's going to attack you if I don't calm him. Stay right there."

"I don't have all day."

Tough right back to you. Instead of replying, I sat on the floor and stroked my dog. "Calm down. It's going to be okay. I'll protect you, even though I understand you want to take care of me. Your instincts are right. Nick's a bad man, and I won't open the door until help arrives." I continued talking in a soothing voice.

Cowboy's breathing returned to normal.

"Let's get a treat." I led him to the crate and tossed a dog biscuit to him. Sophie was trying recipes for pet treats, and my puppy was reaping the rewards.

Faith walked out of my office, carrying the diary. "Zig is on the way, and he's calling Jake and the police. He intends to confront Nick, and hopefully, he'll leave. Like a peaceful encounter."

There wasn't a detailed plan, but at least he was coming here. "It's a good thing that Lutz is so small, but I don't know how much longer we ignore him."

Faith looked at her watch. "Two more minutes before we open the door."

"If you say so, but let me have the diary." I trusted Faith, and if Jake and I moved, there was no need to keep my pantry a secret. I slid open the hidden door and stuck the diary behind boxes of cereal.

"Cool." She shot me a smile.

A car horn tooted.

Faith clapped. "Oh, yeah. That's Zig."

Cowboy barked.

I secured the hidden pantry, gave my puppy another treat, and then we hustled to the front of the house.

The gathering room was neat and clean. "Faith, you didn't need to repair the mess."

"I had time while you read the diary. Aren't you going to open the door for Nick?"

Butterflies did flips in my belly, but I persevered and opened the door.

Nick glowered. "It took you long enough."

The sound of his voice sent Cowboy into another barking frenzy.

I motioned for him to back away. "Let's discuss this on the front porch so we can hear each other."

Nick stepped away. "You need to train your dog."

"He's a puppy who gets along with most people."

"If I was here for monthly treatments, I'd give him treats, and we'd be friends in no time. You should hire me."

Fat chance. "Hmm, it looks like I've got company.

Nick looked over his shoulder.

Zig walked up the steps, and Jake parked across the street. There was a man in the passenger seat, but I couldn't see who it was because of tree shadows.

"Did you decide to call the cavalry?" Nick's nostrils flared.

Jake ran to my yard and leapt up the stairs. His intense expression alarmed me. He pushed his way past Nick. "What's going on?"

I met his gaze. "Nick's here to collect for what I owe him."

Jake removed his sunglasses and tilted his head. "Seems fair enough."

"I need to get a check. Nick, stay out here with the Meiers. I don't need for Cowboy to get upset again."

Nick shoved the bill at me, and I took the crumpled piece of paper. "Be right back."

Jake followed me inside. "Seriously, what's happening? Zig sounded worried when he called me. Wyatt and I were installing a toilet at the mayor's house, and we promised to return."

"Why'd you bring him with you?"

"He's good, but I didn't want to let him finish the project without me. I need to learn how talented he is, and I need to ensure him if he works for me all the time. There's also the possibility something disappears. The mayor will accuse me. Nope. I couldn't leave him alone there." He ran a hand through his hair.

"Sounds like you made a wise decision."

A siren wailed.

"Oh, boy. Nick's going to be furious." I slipped another treat to my whining dog then entered the office and grabbed my checkbook. "I read Tess's diary. On July first, Tess accidentally told Nick he has a child. That could be motive for him to kill her."

"Big time." Jake crossed his arms and rubbed his chin.

"When he arrived here a few minutes ago, he practically broke the door down pounding on it. Faith and I were scared, and she called you guys." I smoothed out the receipt and looked at the total. "Ouch. That's expensive."

"If it'll get him gone, I suggest you write the check."

"Of, course. He deserves to be paid, but that's a lot of money." I filled out the check and stubbed it. "I don't know if you've had time to process this, but now that I've read the diary, I believe Nick murdered Tess."

"I imagined it moved him to the top of the list, but why come after you?"

"The diary. He saw it in the gathering room yesterday. He was acting so squirrely when he was in the house, but the moment he spotted the journal, it was like he fell into a trance. I believe he had to know what Tess had written."

"Makes sense."

Approaching footsteps ended our conversation.

Faith said, "The chief wants you to come outside, and Nick won't budge until he gets paid."

"It's a shame there wasn't enough evidence to book him for Tess's murder." I waved the check in the air. "I'm ready."

When we reached the door, Jake held it open for us.

On the street, Abby signaled her plan to turn Miss Daisy into the driveway.

I waved her off, then texted. **Go to Sophie's. I'll call when it's safe.**

Without rubbernecking, my daughter drove past us.

I said to Matt. "Here's my check for Nick. You can see I'm paying for his services in destroying the fire ant mound."

The police chief took it from me and snapped a picture with his phone. "Nick, here you go. You've been paid, and you should leave unless you'd like to accompany me to the station."

"What for?" He snatched the check.

"Disturbing the peace, for starters." Matt put his hands on his hips.

"Fine."

I glanced across the street at Jake's SUV. It appeared empty.

Nick stomped to his truck and drove off.

Matt said, "I questioned Nick this morning about breaking in last night. Unfortunately, there's not enough evidence to charge him with a crime."

Wyatt joined us.

Jake said, "Where'd you go, man?"

"When I saw the bug guy, I laid down in the seat. Didn't want him to see me."

Faith looked at her student. "Why's that?"

"He's the dude I saw in the restroom at the library. No doubt in my mind. You know. The day Ms. Tess was attacked."

I gasped. "You didn't tell the police yet?"

Matt rolled back his head. "If you don't mind, I need to get an official statement. We'll add it to the report on Tess's attack."

"Yes, sir." Wyatt walked to the side with Matt.

I stared at Matt. Even in casual conversation, he wasn't admitting the cause of death.

Jake said, "Looks like I'll finish the toilet install by myself. I'll see you later, Sunshine."

I kissed his cheek. "Thanks for coming."

"Anything for you, and I'll be back tonight all clean and presentable. I might even bring supper." He jogged to his SUV.

Zig and Faith left, and I texted my daughter that it was safe to return.

I remained on the front porch, because I had to turn the diary over to Matt.

Chapter Fifty-Nine

I handed Matt a glass of iced tea, and he emptied it in no time, gulping it like a man dying of thirst.

"Do you want a refill?"

"No, I promised to take Wyatt to the worksite. What do you need to discuss?"

"It'll be faster if you let me say my piece." I handed him the purple journal.

"This looks like Tess's planner, only it's smaller."

"Yeah. It's her diary. I started reading it last night. In fact, I think Nick broke into my house to get his hands on this." I tapped the purple book. When he didn't explode over me having the diary, I plunged ahead. "I'm sure he saw it when he came to get rid of the fire ants, and he probably knew it belonged to Tess. Her initials are on it." I pointed to the T and the C.

"Let me get this straight. Nick saw the diary and risked breaking in to steal it. He went to all that trouble because of the death of his first wife? He believed Tess had evidence in her diary? It's been a long time, and if Tess had come across more proof, she would've busted down my door to show me. She knows, um, knew, the proper chain of command for solving crimes."

I took a deep breath. "It's more than that. When he was married to Paula, she got pregnant."

The chief's gaze shot from the diary to me. "What?"

"Yeah, but Nick never knew. He was abusive, and Paula left town without telling him she was pregnant. After the baby was born, her parents changed their names and moved to a new location."

240

"Why did Paula return to Lutz?"

"She wanted to give Nick another chance at first. If he had changed, she'd bring the baby home. I don't know how long it took before he became abusive again. So, she moved out but stayed in town so he wouldn't track her down and discover their child. She is terrified of her ex-husband."

"That explains some things. At the request of a neighbor, we performed a wellness check at Paula's house even though we were there the other day for a different reason. Her vehicle is still in the driveway, but she's gone. It makes her look guilty, and I'd like to chat with her. Where is she?" His eyes narrowed.

"I don't know. Honestly." I shrugged. "She was on vacation recently."

"But her car was gone during that time. One of the neighbors said the RAV4 appeared last week. We've canvassed the neighborhood, and I should know more soon."

"I'm not sure what you're accusing me of."

He chuckled. "Multiple things. How about withholding evidence for starters? I'm taking this with me, but you should've turned it over as soon as you found it."

I raised my hands. "In my defense, I know the people in Tess's life better than you or your officers. Plus, who knew it'd have anything connected to her murder?"

"This is a discussion for another day. I've got to go." He left with Tess's diary in his hand, and I entered my house.

After all the commotion, I was left home alone with my puppy. The house had grown eerily quiet.

"Cowboy, you're so good." I opened his door. "I need to record the most recent events."

His bark reminded me to make sure all the doors were locked. After checking, I set the security system for staying at home then went to my office.

What a day, and it wasn't suppertime yet.

My phone buzzed, and I answered, "Hello."

"Emma, I've been calling for over an hour. What's going on?" Paula's voice shook.

I sat on the soft pink loveseat. "Quite a bit, actually. You should call Chief Young. He knows your secret."

Paula gasped. "I can't believe you told him. I trusted you."

"No, it wasn't me. Not exactly. I'm not sure where to start." I petted Cowboy. "The police did a wellness check at your house, and they believe you left town."

"Arg. What did you tell them?" In the background, there was the ding of a bell, like at the checkout counter of a store or hotel.

"The truth. I don't know where you are, but Chief Young has Tess's diary. Were you aware that she accidentally told Nick about your daughter?"

"She emailed me, and I logged onto my email after she died. I can't believe Nick knows after seventeen years of hiding the truth. My parents and child are staying with friends on the East Coast. They're safe."

"What about you?"

"I'm good for now."

"Nick was here less than an hour ago. I don't know where you are, but you don't need to look over your shoulders."

"Maybe not for now, but if he knew where I was, he'd come kill me, just like he murdered Tess. I knew it was him."

"Please, call Chief Young."

"I'll think about it. Sorry I got so mad." Dishes clanked in the background. "I've got to go."

"Be careful, Paula."

"Yep. You, too. As long as Nick is free to roam the streets, we're all in danger."

Chapter Sixty

J ake, Abby, and I finished eating a fully loaded pizza. Abby had done most of the talking, because she'd had a great day working at the vet clinic. "Once I helped with the first patient of the day, a cat, all my nervousness fled. Time flew, and it was just so awesome."

Jake closed the lid on the empty cardboard pizza box. "It's a beautiful thing when you find your passion."

"And I did." Abby practically sang her reply. "I can't wait to go back tomorrow."

"Jake, thanks for dinner." I gathered the plates.

Abby stood. "Wait. While you had me hiding with Sophie, we tried a new recipe for Lebkuchen. It's a cookie from the fifteenth century. When Sophie makes a German recipe, she always gives me a history lesson. You know, I think she's sweet on Chief Young."

I laughed at how fast my daughter changed the topic. "You may be right. They had a date yesterday."

"Score. I knew it." Abby walked to the kitchen and pulled out a sealed container. She removed the top before carrying cookies to the table. "Sophie would serve this on pretty plates, I'm sure, but they'll taste just as good on a napkin."

Jake leaned forward. "And there'll be less to clean up."

We munched on the delicious cookies and chatted about Sophie's love of her German heritage.

When we finished, Abby leashed Cowboy. "Tyler Legend is coming over. We're going to take the dog for a walk."

"Isn't he dating—"

"No. He's single, and we're friends. Don't make anything out of this."

"All right." I'd watched Tyler grow up. Many times he'd come to the pharmacy after bullies had hurt him. I'd helped Tyler and his parents pick out the best first aid supplies. The child had always been respectful and quiet. By all appearances, he'd grown up to be a well-adjusted young man.

"I'll let you know if we're going to be late." Abby hugged me, then Jake. "Bye, Dad."

He gave her a longer hug than usual. "See you later, kiddo. If that kid gets fresh, give me a call."

Abby laughed. "Wow, you fell right into the protective dad mode. Nice."

I watched my two favorite people in the world and grew misty-eyed.

After Abby left, Jake turned to me. "You raised a great girl, there."

"I had lots of help from friends. In the beginning, my family pitched in, but as Abby got older, my siblings returned to their normal lives with their own issues."

"You don't talk about your family much, and I've never met them."

"Why don't we save that conversation for another day? We're not close like you and Celia. Brett's more like a brother to me than my biological brother." I reached for his hand. "Did you finish the mayor's bathroom?"

"Sure did. Wyatt's going to work with me again tomorrow on a different project. Catch me up on your murder investigation."

After reviewing my day with Jake, I rested my hip against the kitchen counter. "It's got to be Nick who killed Tess, but we need to find proof."

Jake leaned toward me. He wore a patriotic T-shirt and shorts, and he smelled clean, not perfumy like men who wore too much aftershave. "I can think of better ways to spend the next hour in an empty house." He kissed me. "But we can also draw up the timeline of Tess's life leading up to Tuesday morning."

"I like both ideas—"

"Timeline it is." Jake moved away. "Where are your notes?"

"The office."

For the next hour, I reviewed my notes with Jake. He took a clean sheet of paper, making notes on it in chronological order.

"On the weekend, we don't know what Tess did." He had days listed and what happened when.

"Wait. I think that's when she had her date." I grabbed the envelope of receipts. "Here's the one for Amalfi's."

"You're sure it was a date?" His eyebrows shot up.

"I think so, because she only paid for half of a dessert."

"That's right. Tiramisu." He added the date to the timeline. "Do you want to go to the restaurant?"

"If the date's not with Nick, and there's no way on earth she would've dated Nick, how will it help?"

"If we can learn the identity of the man, maybe he can tell us if they encountered Nick. What if the date felt like they were being watched? Or they were followed in their car? It seems worth a shot."

"You could be right. Let me change into something nicer."

"You look nice to me."

"Aw, thanks, but I'll be back. Feel free to read my notes. You might pick up on a new clue."

"It's possible." Jake opened my sketchbook and settled into the loveseat.

I ran upstairs to wear something more appropriate than a faded shirt and shorts. By the time I changed and returned to the office, Abby and Tyler were talking to Jake.

"Hey, Mom. Tyler and I are going to watch a movie."

"Here?"

"Yes. We'll be in the gathering room." She raised her eyebrows. "I haven't forgotten your home rules, even though I am a college student."

I wouldn't embarrass her by reminding her of my rules, even though I realized they were strict by today's standards. "We're going for a short walk, but we'll be back."

"Is that code for track down a clue?" Abby sighed and turned her focus to Tyler. "You've probably heard my mom has skills at solving murders."

Tyler said, "Your mom's a superhero."

"Oh, Tyler, I always did like you." I patted his shoulder.

Jake took my hand. "Let's go so they can pick out what movie to stream."

We walked out the door, and the evening heat greeted us with a vengeance. "Ugh. I'm ready for October."

"I don't want to wish my life away. Would you prefer to drive?" Jake paused by the driveway.

"Walking's better for my body and the environment."

Jake smiled. "I knew you'd say that. When I work at the coffee shop, you're one of the only customers who brings a travel mug."

"Are you making fun of me?"

"No, ma'am. I applaud your commitment. In fact, Brett and I have discussed selling travel mugs with our logo. To encourage customers to use them, we'll figure out a reward system or something." We walked around the square and headed in the direction of the restaurant.

"Oh, the hardware store is open. I wonder if Buddy's working." Despite the heat, I walked faster. Buddy Hewitt was the owner, and he was hands-on with his business. He knew customers and enjoyed helping them.

"Why do you need Buddy?"

"You'll see." I reached for the door, but Jake beat me to it.

"Ladies first." He winked at me.

Buddy looked up from the register. "Howdy, folks. I was just about to close, but something told me to hold off. How can I help you?"

I said, "I'm trying to figure out if Tess let her killer into the library, or was the person lying in wait?"

He walked over and turned the door sign to say the store was closed. "Not rightly sure how I can help with that. Unlike you, I'm not an amateur detective."

"Have you made a spare key for any of the library employees?"

He shrugged. "Do you know the new librarian? The young one with all them curls?"

"Yes. Laurel Holley." I nodded. "We've met."

Jake said, "What about Laurel?"

"She was here a couple weeks ago. She brought a key and asked for two copies. It was thicker than normal. Not a typical house or car key. I asked about it. Laurel told me she had lost her key, and Tess sent her to make two copies. One would be for Laurel, and the other would be for emergencies." He sidestepped to his computer. "I want to look up something, if you have a minute."

His words stirred my curiosity. Plus, I was certain I'd asked Laurel about the key situation. Something wasn't right. "Take your time."

Jake looked at some tools. I was familiar with gardening tools, but normal things like wrenches and screwdrivers were not my thing.

"Here we go." Buddy pointed to the computer screen and adjusted it so we could see. "It's like I remembered. Laurel paid cash for the keys. The library has an account, and I offered to put the purchase on it, but Laurel used her personal money. I thought it was peculiar, but I've learned not to question why people do the things they do."

"That's the opposite of me. I question everything when it comes to murder." I made a note to talk to Laurel about the keys. "But you couldn't possibly have suspected the sale could be a clue to murder."

Buddy shook his head. "Never even occurred to me."

Jake said, "We'll get out of your hair, but I'll swing by in the morning to buy some supplies. One specific item I need is a ceiling fan for Emma's front porch."

It shouldn't have surprised me that he'd remembered.

Buddy slowly moved to the door. "How's your LLC application going?"

"Almost there, but it's probably my fault. I need to make the paperwork my top priority and hold off on home repairs."

Guilt stung my conscience. "Helping my investigation is most likely slowing you down, too."

"It's all good." He gave me a warm smile.

Buddy opened the door. "See you in the morning, Jake. Emma, good luck."

I smiled. "Thanks for not telling me to be careful. Bye, Buddy."

Paige met us on the sidewalk. "Hi, y'all. I could've guessed you're the reason Buddy is running late. He's usually very punctual."

"He's also very polite. Do you two have a date?" It made me happy to know Paige and Buddy were hanging out.

"Yes. We're going bowling. I haven't bowled since high school, but he loves it." She pointed at the man. "Before we started dating, I'd probably go home and read a good book."

"You're not going to drop out of our book club, are you?"

"No, but depending on how this date goes, I might drag Buddy along one week."

Jake laughed. "I'm pretty sure he reads articles. Not books."

Buddy stepped out of his shop and locked the door before joining us. "Paige, are you ready?"

"Yes, but I hope you're not embarrassed by my performance."

"You can never embarrass me." He reached for her hand, and they walked away.

Jake looked at me. "Do you still want to stop in Amalfi's?"

"Yes. Let's see if we can learn more about Tess's date." Everyone was suddenly dating. Maybe Sophie and Matt's date would also turn into a relationship.

For now, I needed to focus on proving Nick was the person who murdered Tess.

Chapter Sixty-One

Ethan was bartending at Amalfi's, so we found two empty seats and sat at the bar.

His eyes widened when he spotted us. "Hey there. What can I get you tonight? We've got a nice chardonnay. Plus, there's a new bourbon from Kentucky. We're trying it out to see how customers like it."

We gave Ethan our orders, and when he placed them in front of us, he looked at me. "I assume this isn't a casual encounter. What do you want to know? Have you gone back to suspecting me of committing Tess's murder?"

"No. I believe you're innocent. For one thing, my daughter knows a lot of high school students. If you need a babysitter for a few hours in the mornings, I can give you some recommendations."

"I'll think about it. The second thing is?" He lifted one eyebrow.

I showed him Tess's receipt. "I believe Tess may have been here on a blind date. I don't believe the guy killed her, but he might know something to help me."

Ethan took the receipt and looked at the date. "Yeah, I saw them. Hold on a second." He returned the receipt, and then he walked down the bar and poured beers for two guys.

When Ethan returned, he said, "Those guys got stood up, and a friendship may be forming. I introduced them, and the beer and misery are helping them bond. You may think I only serve drinks, but there's more to this job. Take your situation. The police haven't asked me near as many questions as you have. You're continuing to push for answers to the murder. I can't figure out if they're dumb or if they don't care."

Jake said, "It's possible they're overworked and short of staff."

Ethan wiped the counter with a white rag, then pulled out a bowl of peanuts. "These are fresh. Help yourselves."

"Thanks." I picked up a few. "Do you know anything about Tess's date?"

"He bought drinks while they waited for a table. Seemed nice enough, but I wouldn't have imagined them as a couple."

"Did he pay with a credit card? I really need to know his name."

"I'll look after closing. Tomorrow I'm going to take Mia to story time. Meet me there, and I'll let you know what I find."

That would be perfect, because I wanted to question Laurel about the keys. "Okay." I popped the peanuts into my mouth.

"And if you don't mind, maybe bring me a couple of names of babysitters. They should be able to drive, because I might have them take Mia to the library. My car, of course, because it has the child seat."

"Okay. A responsible teenager who can drive but doesn't need her own vehicle. Must like children, too."

Ethan tapped the counter with his fist. "Sounds good. I'll check on you later. It looks like I've got some thirsty customers down the way."

"Thank you, Ethan."

He waved as he ambled away.

Jake said, "I'm not sure that could've gone any better."

"I agree."

"And that was nice of you to suggest a babysitter."

I shrugged. "Who knows if it'll work out, but he seems decent. I'd hate for him to lose custody of his daughter if there was a simple solution."

"Makes sense to me." He finished his drink.

"I'm sorry this investigation is slowing down progress on making Jake of All Trades an official business."

He took my hand in his. "I could say no to some job opportunities, but everybody seems in desperate need of a handyman. It's hard to turn down people in need."

"You always imagine how you'd feel in other people's shoes. It's one of the reasons I love you. But—"

He chuckled. "How'd I know a but was coming? Go on, Sunshine."

I rubbed my thumb across his knuckles. "But I want to take care of you. If we're going to work, we need to look out for each other. You can't be the only one to give."

He leaned forward and brushed his lips against mine. "You're more giving than you realize, and I understand how important it is for you to find justice for your friend's murder. I wouldn't want you to care less about others."

"I still need to work, and I'd like to look at the farm again, but with a different agent." I shivered. "Tom Ward gives me the creeps, and I'll be happy never to cross paths with him again."

"I'm really proud of you."

"For what?"

"Allowing the FBI to solve Mason's murder."

I laughed. "I'm just an amateur sleuth who has gotten lucky twice. If I can find more evidence to prove you know who killed Tess, I'll be happy to hang up my investigating hat."

"You were more than lucky. You were tenacious. What'd you think about Ethan's comment on our local police?"

The bar was getting crowded and loud.

I leaned close and spoke near Jake's ear. "Something weird is going on there, but I can't decide what. Are you ready to go?"

"Yep. It's been a long day." Dark circles under Jake's eyes confirmed his comment.

On the walk home, we discussed how we imagined our lives would look if we lived at the farm. My plans for growing more flowers would happen sooner because the place had some flowers growing already. Also, I'd need to transplant as much as possible from my current gardens to the farm. I yawned.

Jake kissed me goodnight at the door, and I headed inside.

After I spoke to Abby and Tyler, I grabbed my sketch pad and went to my room.

Cowboy could chaperone the date downstairs.

I fell asleep, adding the new information to my notes, and dreamed about

Tess.

Chapter Sixty-Two

I woke up sad on Tuesday morning after dreaming about Tess. She hadn't been my bestie, but she'd been a good friend. I missed her.

The TV weather lady forecasted on-and-off rain for the day. So, I skipped working in the flowers and drove Abby to work. On the way, she gave me a list of five friends who'd like to babysit Mia.

It was too early for the library to be opened, so I stopped by Anytime Coffee House. Brett fixed my green tea, and I sat at a table working on the questions I wanted to ask Laurel.

"Good morning, Sunshine." The warmth in Jake's voice helped me shake off the sadness of the day.

"Hi, honey. What are you doing?"

He sat beside me. "I was at the hardware store and saw Miss Daisy. So, I decided to find you. I told Wyatt to meet me here."

"It's definitely my lucky morning."

"By the way, I've got a replacement fan for your porch."

"You amaze me. With everything happening, I don't know how you remembered." I pushed my notes to him. "These are my questions for Laurel. Can you think of anything else?"

He read over my list.

Brett appeared with a travel mug and placed it in front of Jake. "I'm trying a new brew, and it's on ice. Let me know what you think."

Jake took a drink through the reusable straw. His eyes widened. "I like it."

"I created a special sauce."

"Thanks, man. Put it on my tab."

"Naw, you're one of my guinea pigs. It's on the house." Brett left us alone.

Jake said, "The questions are good and to the point. I'll be interested to hear her answers."

"Me, too." I looked at my watch. "The library opens in ten minutes."

"I'll walk you to your truck."

Outside, the wind whipped my hair, and thunder rolled in the distance.

Jake looked westward and pointed at the sky. "We're scheduled to build a playhouse and a backyard playscape for a young family, but we'll probably have to do it another day. If that's the case, I'll have time to deal with paperwork for my business."

Black and gray clouds filled the sky. Not a ray of sun filtered through. "Looks bad."

"It might not be terrible, but we're not taking a chance. I need to call Wyatt."

We reached my truck, and I opened my door. "Hop in."

Jake walked around and slid into the passenger seat as fat raindrops hit the windshield. I started the truck but waited until he finished talking to Wyatt. I could give him a ride to his Sequoia or his apartment.

The call ended, and Jake put his travel mug in a cupholder. "I'd like to go to the library with you."

"Really? Why?" I tried to ignore the happiness inside me at his words. I was an independent woman. Although, it was easier to be independent when I wasn't solving murders.

"Safety in numbers. We don't believe Ethan or Laurel killed Tess, but we don't know positively. Plus, what's going on with Tom? Mason used to hang out at the library. What if Tom shows up? I'd hate for you to deal with him by yourself after Sunday's experience."

"Thanks. I'm happy you can go." I pulled out and drove the short distance to the library. "Oh, there's Ethan and Mia."

"I see Faith getting out of her Escalade." Jake waved to her.

"She was here last Tuesday. She attends a group who meets once a week. Coffee and coloring, or something like that. So, we may see some of the same people who were here when Tess's body was discovered."

"This should prove interesting."

I backed into a parking space, stopped the truck, and gathered my belongings, including an umbrella. "Let's try to get inside before it pours down rain."

"Sounds like a good idea."

We dashed through the drizzle and strong wind to the entrance.

I caught a glimpse of my appearance in the window. "Oh, dear. I need to stop by the restroom."

Jake nodded. "I'll wander around."

When I stood in front of the restroom's mirror, I sighed. My red hair was a tangled mess. I dug out my brush and began brushing from the bottom, and worked my way up.

The flushing of a toilet surprised me.

The door opened, and Celia walked out. "Oh, Emma. Hi."

"Hey there. I'm trying to fix this mess."

Celia washed her hands. "If you hold my bag, I can braid your hair."

"What a kind offer." I reached for her purse and sack from the bookstore. "Whatcha got in here?"

She brushed my hair, divided it into three sections, and crossed one section over the other. She continued by alternating sides until she had created a braid. "Paige sent me with coupons from the store. The library has summer reading programs for children, teens, and adults. When they reach specific levels, they win prizes."

"That's very generous of Paige."

"It's a marketing plan of mine. I'm going to keep track of the discounts versus sales. Then I want to compare to the store's sales this time last year. I sure hope it works." Celia pulled a hair band from the pocket of her skirt and secured my hair. "There. What do you think?"

I studied my reflection in the mirror. "Better than ever. Thank you so much, Celia."

"You're welcome. I better give these to Laurel and go back to the store before Paige gets anxious." She took her stuff from me.

"Jake's here with me. A storm's brewing, and he's going to do paperwork today." I held the door for her, and we entered the main area.

Jake smiled at his sister. "Shouldn't you be at work?"

"Funny." She held up the paper bag with coupons and swatted his arm. "I am working."

"If you say so."

I smiled as they continued teasing each other. My brother was younger, and it was probably my fault that we weren't closer. At this stage of our lives, I wasn't sure how to remedy the situation.

"Emma?" Ethan interrupted my daydreaming.

"Hi. I've got some names for you." I walked to the nearest table and found the list. I tore it out of my sketch pad and handed it to Ethan. "You can refer any of the girls to me, if they seem suspicious of how you knew to ask them to babysit."

Ethan read the paper, folded it, and stuffed it in his wallet. He also removed another piece of paper. "Here's the name of Tess's date. Bruce Hudson."

I kept my voice low. "I've seen his name, but there's no information online. Doesn't that seem weird? I don't guess you have a picture of the man?"

"No, but I remember him distinctly. He looked like the actor Bruce Willis. It seemed odd that the two guys look so similar, and they have the same first name."

"Interesting." Was the name an alias? Was he a scammer of some sort?

The sound of happy little voices reached me.

Ethan looked around. "I need to get Mia before they call the cops on me. Thanks again for the list."

"Hey, thank you." I sat at the table and searched social media on my phone for Bruce Hudson. Faith hadn't found anything on the man before, but it was possible I'd get lucky. I'd seen the man around town, and we'd even talked. He'd been with the paramedics the day of Tess's murder.

Jake joined me. "Celia is with Laurel now. When I mentioned you were here to see Laurel, too, my sister said she'll let us know when they finish."

"Good. Can I do anything to help you?" I set my phone down and pointed to the paperwork in front of him.

"No, but I appreciate your offer. Brett and I took a class before opening the coffee house. This probably isn't much different."

"I took a class, too."

"That certainly makes sense. I'll start on the paperwork and ask for your help when I get stuck." Jake met my gaze. "Your hair looks nice like that."

"Thanks. Celia styled it for me." Thunder boomed, and the lights flickered. People squealed, and at least one child cried.

"Uh-oh. I don't believe I signed up for a building full of scared and crying children." Jake stared at the mothers and kids. Despite his words, his face held a tender look.

"You're a great brother to Celia. Have you thought about having your own children?"

"Never allowed my mind to go there." He shrugged.

"I'm thirty-eight and not getting any younger. My younger self never imagined that Abby would be an only child. The years rolled by, and before I knew what happened, I figured my days of having more children were past." I held my breath, anticipating Jake's response.

He angled his body to face me better. "Is there a physical reason you can't have another baby?"

"No, but my biological clock is ticking. If you've got your heart set on having a child of your own, I may not be the woman you need to marry."

Jake took my cold hand in his warm one. "Emma, I proposed because I want to spend the rest of my life with you. If we want to raise children together, but you can't get pregnant, we'll adopt. Children are not a game changer for me. The only thing I need is to be with you. For better or for worse and all that jazz."

My heart swelled with love. "You're all that I need, too. We'll figure out the rest."

Celia sat across from us. "Guys, Nick Jones is here. Isn't he the one who—"

"Shh." Jake motioned for her to quit talking.

Nick walked to our table, and my heart dropped.

Chapter Sixty-Three

"Bet you didn't plan on seeing me today." Nick's fake smile frightened me.

Jake said, "We're here, minding our own business."

"What do you know? I'm here to spray for pests. Emma, any more fire ants show up?"

"No. Are you sure it's safe for my dog to be in the yard?"

Nick pointed to the window. "That rainstorm will help."

We all looked in the direction he pointed. The earlier rain had transitioned to a downpour. Lightning flashed across the sky.

Thunder boomed, and more children screamed.

Poor, Cowboy. Home alone. Was he afraid?

Celia jumped to her feet. "I'm going to help Hope with the kids. Maybe we can distract them."

Jake snapped his fingers. "Do the Jack and the Beanstalk story."

"Good idea. That's always a crowd pleaser."

Nick walked away without another word, and Celia headed in the opposite direction.

I smiled at Jake. "Is there something special about the story?"

"Yeah. She rolls up newspaper and builds a beanstalk and a secret something at the end of the story."

"That should hold their attention." I glanced at my sketch pad. "I've gotten nowhere on Bruce Hudson. It's like he's a ghost online, even though I've seen him in Lutz. I may as well see if Laurel will talk to me. Her answers could be enlightening."

"Good luck."

I left him and headed to Laurel's office.

She was coming out, when I reached her. "Oh, Emma. What are you doing back here?"

"I need you to clarify something for me. It might be best if we speak in your office."

She lifted her chin. "You're not the police, and I don't have to answer your questions."

"That's true. I'm sure Chief Young won't mind joining us." I pulled out my phone, prepared to dial Matt's number.

"Oh, all right." She reentered the office and sat behind the desk.

I closed the door behind me. "According to my notes, you didn't know who possessed a library key besides you and Tess."

She opened her mouth.

"I know you had two keys made when you supposedly lost yours. You even paid cash instead of charging them to the library. Who did you give the keys to?"

Laurel stared at her desk. "I lost mine. When I went to make a replacement, it seemed fair to pay out of my own pocket."

"But you had two made. What happened to the other one?"

"Tess put it in the desk for emergencies." She opened the drawer. "Um, it was right here."

I waited.

Laurel stuck her hand in the drawer and shuffled items around. With deliberate movements, she pulled things out, one by one. "I know this is where she put it."

"Could you have thrown it out with her personal belongings?"

"No, because it wasn't her property." She huffed. "I didn't lose the key this time. Either Tess moved it, or—"

"Or what?"

Her eyes darted around the room. "Or somebody stole it."

"Who is the first person to come to your mind?"

"I don't know. Some people believe I killed Tess to get her job. Yes, I

259

wanted her job. But I was hoping she'd quit or retire."

"She wasn't even fifty."

A tear ran down Laurel's face. "Yeah, but she acted so old."

"She was conservative and always tried to do the right thing." I'd gotten off track. "Wait. It doesn't matter if she acted old or not. How did Nick Jones get into the building today?"

She reached for a tissue. "It's the second Tuesday of the month. That's the regular day for him to treat the building."

"But was he here when you opened?"

Laurel stared at me. "I'm not sure. I opened the building, and I didn't see him. Then he suddenly appeared."

"What about your security system? Say he got a hold of a key, is there any chance he knows the code?"

"I can't imagine how either is possible." She opened the desk drawer and searched again. "I just don't get it. Where is the key?"

"Laurel, do you know where you lost your key?"

Her eyes narrowed. "If I knew that, then the key wouldn't be lost."

"I was trying to ask if it might have been stolen while you were at work."

"It's possible."

My thoughts raced. "Nick is still in the building. You opened less than an hour ago. Please, try to remember. I know you have an early class with coffee and coloring. Did you see Nick when you opened the doors?"

"Why would Nick enter the building early today?" Her face grew pale. "Unless he wants to hurt—"

"No, stay calm. Nick and Tess have a history, and it's ugly. There would be no reason for Nick to harm you. Right?"

She wailed and dropped her head to the desk, cushioning it with her forearms. She cried in earnest. "It's all my fault."

My heart blipped. Was she the killer after all? "What are you talking about?"

She continued to cry, and I handed her more tissues.

I texted Jake. **Call Matt. I think Laurel is about to confess to something big.**

CHAPTER SIXTY-THREE

"Laurel, please calm down. It can't be that bad."

She raised her head. Mascara left trails down her red, splotchy face. "You have no idea."

My phone vibrated, and I glanced at a message from Jake. **Matt is on the way. Tom is in the building.**

I couldn't think about that now.

Laurel snatched my phone and read the message. "I'm not going to prison for a murder I didn't commit."

"Okay."

She slid the phone across the desk, and I caught it.

"I need to call my parents before Chief Young gets here." She tapped on the screen of her phone. "Mommy? I need you. Please come to Lutz and bring the best lawyer you can. I'm afraid the police will arrest me for my boss's murder." She broke down in sobs.

I said, "If you didn't kill Tess, why do you feel guilty?"

She looked at me and pounded her fist on the desk. "I gave the spare key to Nick Jones because I didn't want to get up early just so he could spray the building."

Yelling from the main room drew our attention.

Kids screamed and cried.

Thunder boomed.

And the lights went out.

Jake texted me. **Nick has a gun. Locked front door. Celia and Hope snuck the children outside in the storm.**

I looked at Laurel. "You need to snap out of it right this minute. This is a hostage situation, and your opportunity to redeem yourself."

Nick's looking for you.

The lights came back on.

Laurel's face was pale. "I'm not brave like you are."

I said, "I'll surrender to Nick. You tell the police how to get into the building without Nick's knowledge. I'm dialing Chief Young."

Matt answered before I passed the phone to Laurel. "Emma? I'm on the way to the library. Jake said things are bad."

261

"They went from bad to worse. Nick has taken us hostage. Here's Laurel. She can tell you how to enter the building. And the children's librarian and Celia escaped with some of the kids, but it's storming."

"I'll figure that out."

I passed the phone to Laurel. "You can make a difference. Help the police end this before anyone gets hurt."

She swiped at her tears. "I don't know if I can do it."

"There's no other choice. And maybe stay low. Crawl."

I walked out with my hands in the air.

The lights flickered, followed by a crackle and whistle.

No more electricity, and the unsettling stillness in the room frightened me.

The sight of Nick with a gun terrified me, but when he turned the gun on me, my knees weakened. I lost my balance and sagged against the wall.

"Oh no, you don't." Nick crossed the room. Heading straight for me. "I'm not falling for the damsel in distress. I thought Tess was a pain, but you're worse with all of your questions and accusations. It ends today."

Chapter Sixty-Four

Nick advanced with the gun pointing at me.

I'd just lectured Laurel about being brave. It was time for me to stand strong.

In the lobby behind Nick, I spotted Laurel ushering people past the conference rooms.

We were on the ground floor, and there were windows. Maybe they'd crawl out. I averted my eyes so Nick wouldn't grow suspicious.

"Nick, I never accused you of murdering Tess."

He sneered. "You suspected me every time someone was killed in Lutz."

Jake strode toward us with slow, confident steps. "Last week, Emma and I agreed that you were not on our suspect list. We know we can't always think of you because of your past."

Nick turned the gun on Jake. "Stop."

"Sure, man." Jake didn't move.

Nick's eyes darted back and forth. "No, stand beside your woman."

I said, "This morning, I believed Laurel was responsible for Tess's death. Was it you?"

"It was never in my plan to murder Tess, but she was like a dog with a bone. She wouldn't let up. A couple weeks ago, we argued about my first wife's death. Again." His gaze shifted to Jake. "Hurry up."

Jake had fought in the Marines. No doubt he was assessing the situation.

Tom stood. "This has nothing to do with me. I'm a rich man and willing to pay you to let me go."

Nick's eyes widened. "Fat chance, Rich Man. Stand over there with the others."

"What others?" Tom's smart-aleck tone irritated me.

Nick's gaze passed over the large room.

There was a teen in a chair near the magazines, napping with big ear phones on. An older couple sat at a table, watching us. A mother stood near the children's area with an empty stroller and her hands in the air. A handful of other people remained in the shadowy library.

Ethan must have left earlier or helped the children escape. There was no sign of him or Mia.

"Where is everybody?" Nick roared like an angry lion.

I said, "Maybe they left before the rain turned into a storm."

"Impossible." Spit flew out of Nick's mouth.

Tom took a few steps toward the entrance.

A streak of lightning brightened the room.

Nick noticed Tom's movement and shot the gun. A bullet dinged near Tom's feet. "That's a warning. I'm a crack shot. Don't push your luck."

I shivered.

For once, Tom didn't have a comeback.

Jake held his phone and angled it so we could both read the text.

Ethan's name was at the top of the screen. **I made it out alive with Mia. Bruce Hudson is in the parking lot, wearing all black. Stay safe.**

I met Jake's gaze and whispered, "Don't reply."

He nodded and slid the phone into the pocket of his jeans.

Nick threatened Tom, and I was relieved the exterminator's focus was on somebody besides me.

Tom held his hands up in surrender. "If you make it out alive, you will be arrested. I promise to make it worth your while if you'll let me go. I can recommend a good attorney and pay for his services."

Nick stalked to me and grabbed my arm.

"Let go of me, Nick." I tried to yank out of his grip.

Jake lunged toward Nick.

Nick pistol-whipped him in the head, and Jake stumbled back and fell.

Jake's head smacked the hard floor and bounced.

I screamed and sprang toward my fiancé.

Nick grabbed my hair and yanked me toward him. He snaked one arm around my shoulders, and with his other hand, he held the gun.

Others screamed and dispersed behind furniture and hid in the library's bookstacks.

Nick looked around the dim room and growled. "You're coming with me."

I might have been able to escape, but he could've shot me or Jake. I went with him to Laurel's office. He barricaded the door, huffing.

I sat in the desk chair and rolled as far away as possible. "Nick, this is spiraling out of control. Wouldn't you prefer a peaceful resolution?"

"If I knew they'd let me see my child, I'd turn myself in to the cops." He rubbed his forehead.

"What child?" It hurt to breathe.

"Tess claimed that Paula and I have a secret child. I don't know if it's a boy or girl. I can guess the age, but I have no idea how to find the teen."

Not knowing the best way to respond, I remained quiet.

"My first plan was to ask Paula, but she was on vacation. It was driving me crazy, and I couldn't keep waiting to learn the truth."

"Is that why you came here last week? You had to confront Tess?"

The lights came on, and the normal sounds of air conditioning, computers, and printers hummed to life.

Nick looked around.

The desk phone rang.

I said, "It could be the police."

He glared at me. "Answer it, but don't say anything that will make me want to shoot you."

It was easy to believe he had an itchy trigger finger. I picked up the phone. "Hello. This is Emma Justice."

"Emma, this is Matt. What's happening? People are streaming out of the building, but it's hard to see through the rain."

"I'm in—"

"Stop." Nick pointed the gun in my face. "Don't tell him where we are."

"Emma!" Matt's voice boomed over the line.

"Um, I'm okay. Kinda. I'm here with Nick. Jake's hurt."

"What are Nick's demands?"

I looked at my captor. "Do you have demands?"

"Talk to my child."

"Do you know her name?"

"Her? It's a girl?" He leaned over the desk and held the gun closer to my head. "What do you know, Emma?"

"I'm sorry, Nick. I have a daughter, and assumed your child was a girl too." My hands shook. "Maybe you have a son."

"Nick!" Matt yelled through the phone.

"It'll be easier for you to talk to the police chief directly." I gave him the receiver.

Nick took it and tapped the speakerphone button. "In order for Emma to live through this day, you need to find my child."

"Let's talk through the specifics, Nick. I didn't know you have a child. What details can you give me?"

"The child is around sixteen years old. That's all I've got, man. Paula is the child's mother."

"It's not much to go on. I've been looking for Paula for a few days, and I'm coming up empty."

"Why are you trying to find her?"

"To question her about the attack on Tess. She's not at home. Where do you suggest I look?"

Nick glanced at the clock. It was barely ten in the morning, and it seemed like we'd been in the library for hours.

"That's your job. I'm not a cop. You've got an hour. Call me back then, or Emma will suffer." He slammed the phone back into the cradle. "Are you sure you don't know more about my baby?"

"I didn't know Paula and Tess in those days. If your child is sixteen, I was raising a toddler and barely surviving." I saw movement in the shadows.

Did Nick realize the building was no longer locked? How would he react if the police became visible to him?

Not good, probably. I needed to distract him while law enforcement took

266

their places.

Chapter Sixty-Five

My heart raced. If the police were in the main room, would they shoot at Nick? How could they possibly hit Nick and not me? Where could I dive for protection? There was nothing special about Tess's, or Laurel's, desk. The glass walls weren't bulletproof, but if I hid under the desk, would I be protected?

What had I been thinking when I gave Laurel my cell phone?

How was Jake? He'd tried to protect me and gotten buffaloed for his efforts. Poor guy.

"Do you think they've found her?" Nick's raspy voice revealed his nervousness.

If he wasn't holding me hostage, I would've felt a shred of sympathy. The gun reminded me to stay strong. Still, I didn't want to antagonize the man. "Chief Young doesn't have much information. What if your child lives far away? Maine? Alaska? Will you agree to meeting them through FaceTime or something?"

"Of course. I'm a reasonable guy." He punched the wall, and then cried out in pain. "In fact, I only came here last week to have a conversation with Tess. Nothing more."

"I understand how a situation can quickly spiral out of control."

"That's right. Tess wouldn't tell me anything, even though I begged her. On top of that, she badgered me about Rhonda's death."

"Did you kill your first wife?" If he admitted his guilt, did that mean he planned to murder me too? "Never mind. I don't need to know."

He snickered. "You mean you don't want to find out how I poisoned her a little every day until her body gave up? People in town think you're brave, but it seems like you're a coward."

"I don't want to die. If that's cowardly, then you're right."

"Thought so. You know, it surprised me when Tess died. We were fighting, but I didn't think I hit her that hard."

A vision of the crime scene popped into my mind. "You hit her with a flower pot, and it broke. How did you not know?"

"Killing her served no purpose. I needed her to tell me where my child is, and now I'm worse off than before." He stared at me.

"Nick, were you in Paula's house the other day? Did you answer her phone when I called?"

He huffed. "Yeah. I thought I might find something that would show me where my child is hiding. Answering it allowed me to open the phone and look for other information."

"Hmm." My mind raced with ways to get away from Nick.

The rain was so heavy, we could hear it in the office. Lightning struck, and the lights went out again.

Crash.

I yelped.

Nick glared at me. "We're going to see what happened."

I backed away.

He frowned and with the gun motioned for me to move.

His distraction over the child might be my means of escape. If he remained unfocused, I could clobber him and run. First, I needed to make sure Jake wasn't still lying on the floor.

"Open the door and go to the right." Nick's voice was gruff.

I unlocked it and turned the knob. With slow steps, I walked toward the main area of the library.

Tree limbs scraped against one of the windows. Thunder rolled. I entered the big room and looked in the direction of where we'd left Jake's body.

Nothing. Either he'd gotten away on his own, or somebody helped him.

I didn't see a soul in sight.

Game on.

Nick screamed, "Where is everybody?"

I gritted my teeth, surveying my best means of escape. "I don't know."

"Liar." Nick wrapped an arm around my neck.

"I've been with you. How would I know what happened out here?" I stomped on his foot, and then elbowed his midsection.

"Ow. You little—"

I turned and shoved my hand under his chin.

He doubled over.

I ran with all the speed I could muster.

"Out of the way, Emma." Matt's voice rang through the library.

I dove into the entry area and out of Nick's line of fire.

Jake knelt beside me. "You okay?"

"I think so, but you were hurt."

"Nothing to worry about now. Let's get out of here." He took me by the hand, and we fled the library. Outside, the rain made the race to my truck treacherous.

"Whoa." I slipped, but Jake kept a tight grip on my hand.

Police officers stood near the front door.

FBI agents ran across the parking lot. I did a double-take as a bald man resembling Bruce Willis ran past us.

"Do you have keys?" Jake's steps slowed.

I felt my pockets. "No, where are they?"

A red Honda honked, and the window lowered. "Hop in." Brett unlocked the doors with a click.

We jumped into the car, and he drove away before we could speak. "Man, your sister is frantic. She told me to get my rear end up here and save you. Good thing Matt told the officer to wave me through." Brett glanced back. "Brother, that's some goose egg you got on your noggin."

"Yeah. Nick whacked me with his gun." Jake touched the spot and winced. "Where are you taking us?"

"Away from the gunfire in case the situation gets any more out of hand. Call your sister."

Jake called Celia. "Hey, sis. We're safe in the backseat of Brett's car."

270

I nudged him. "Ask her to call Abby. Laurel has my phone."

"Gotcha." He spoke into the phone. "And please alert Abby that her mother is fine. Okay. Love you too, sis."

Brett slowed the car. "Guys, there's an ambulance sitting at the curb. Let's get you two checked out."

We tried to argue, but Brett refused to listen.

"They're waiting here for victims. That's you guys."

I touched Brett's shoulder. "We'll go, but would you please try to find Laurel and get my phone back? Unless it's not safe. Or unless the police tell you to turn around. The last time I saw Laurel, she was helping people get out of the building. But don't put yourself in harm's way just for my phone."

"Calm down and call me after they examine you."

The rain was lighter, and when we exited the sports car, two EMTs met us. We were each taken to a different ambulance. I wasn't as concerned about myself as I was Jake. In fact, I hadn't been hurt. Terrified, yes. Physical damage? No.

It didn't take long to examine me, and I got a good report. While waiting for Jake, I allowed my mind to drift to Bruce Hudson.

Was it possible he was an FBI agent? Why had he pretended to be a book editor when he dated Tess? Then I'd assumed he was a supervisor for the paramedics. Just who was Bruce Hudson?

Chills zipped up my back.

Had Tess contacted federal law enforcement about Mason Brown and Tom Ward? If so, she must have believed they were breaking federal laws. There wasn't any other logical reason for them to be here. And had one agent pretended to be Tess's perfect match, so they could talk without it seeming suspicious?

Farfetched or genius?

Questions circled in my brain.

Nick murdered Tess. He'd admitted it to me. He also declared he'd poisoned Rhonda. So, what about the other two men? Had they possibly threatened Tess? Or had she been so distracted by their actions that it was easier for Nick to kill her?

Chapter Sixty-Six

After we'd been examined by the paramedics and questioned by one of the cops, Brett drove us to my house. "Guys, I've got to check on the coffee shop, but I'll be back later."

The library and parking lot had been taped off as a crime scene, and my truck was still there. Nick was at the police station being questioned, but it was doubtful he'd tell the truth.

Tom had left some of his belongings at the library, but he was on the loose.

The rain was only a drizzle when we ran to the front door. I unlocked it, and we entered the house. "It's so good to be home."

Cowboy barked.

"Hey, boy. Were you scared? That was a bad storm." I walked to his crate and opened the door.

He licked my face, and I hugged my puppy.

Jake said, "I'm hungry. What about you?"

"Surprisingly, I'm starved. Must be from all the anxiety." I stood, and Cowboy headed for his water bowl.

Jake opened the refrigerator and studied the contents. "Grilled ham and cheese sandwich?"

"Sure, and I have a can of tomato soup. Even though it's July, I feel chilled from the day."

"Soup it is. You should get out of those wet clothes. I'll fix lunch and take care of your dog."

"Cowboy will be your puppy too once we're married."

Jake laughed. "You've been trying to pawn him off on me since the day you found him."

"Abby may take him for herself, and then we'll have to find another pet." I put my phone on the charging station. "I'm glad Brett got my phone from Laurel. She feels bad about giving a key to Nick, and she's aware she may be in trouble with the police."

"She could also lose her job, but that's not our problem."

"I'll be right back." I hurried upstairs and tossed my damp clothes in the bathroom. I put on yoga pants and my three-quarter sleeve baseball jersey. After running a brush through my hair, I returned to the kitchen.

"Soup's on." Jake motioned to the French harvest table. Once we were seated, he took my hand in his. "Seems appropriate to bless the food today. We both survived a killer."

"Go ahead."

He said a short prayer, and we ate until Cowboy whined at the door.

I led the puppy to his crate and gave him a treat. "You're going to need a bath today, but I don't have the strength right now."

Jake said, "I bet you can pay a certain teenager to do that tonight."

"She is saving up for a new vehicle, so you're probably right." I smiled. "Nick confessed that he poisoned his first wife. He also admitted to fighting with Tess. He didn't realize he hit her so hard. I wonder if it was a deadly angle? It's a real shame that he didn't mean to murder Tess."

"Have you told Matt?"

"No. I haven't seen him, but I figure he'll swing by and question me."

Jake shook his head. "Text him in case he thinks about letting Nick go."

"Oh, good idea."

Jake cleared the dishes, and I grabbed my phone.

Matt, Nick admitted that he poisoned his first wife. He also confessed to attacking Tess last week.

I put the phone on the counter and hip bumped Jake. "Scoot over. You prepared lunch, and it's only fair for me to clean."

He moved and dried his hands on a towel. "Did Nick mention anything about Mason?"

"No." I washed and rinsed the soup bowls then placed them in the drainboard.

"So, there's no reason to suspect Nick of killing Mason?" Jake leaned against the kitchen counter and watched me.

"Nothing comes to mind. What do you think?" I continued the mindless task of washing, rinsing, and putting dishes in the drainboard to dry.

"The only thing I can come up with is Mason had some proof that Nick murdered Tess. If Nick didn't kill Mason, who did?"

I let the water out of the sink, and Jake handed the towel to me. "Who killed Mason? Good question, but let's trust the Feds to do their job."

Jake wrapped his arms around me, and I leaned into his strength. He said, "I'm glad you will let the federal agents handle Mason's murder."

Cowboy pushed his nose against my leg.

Jake laughed. "I never imagined competing with the pup for your affection."

I leaned over and petted Cowboy. "There's no comparison."

"You didn't say who's your favorite. Me or the dog." He laughed harder.

"Very funny." I motioned for him to follow me to my office. "Who do you believe murdered Mason?"

"I barely knew him. Tom is the only person we've met who knew Mason before they arrived in town."

I sat at the desk and opened the sketch pad. "It could be one of the victims of the land deals that Tess believed were crooked. That's another good reason for me to stay out of his murder investigation."

Jake sat in the comfy pink chair. "Emma, do you think I want you to investigate Mason's death? Because I don't. If the federal government is involved, it's much bigger than a small-town murder. I was only curious as to your thoughts."

I leaned back. "I think we should go back to the farm and look at it without feeling pressure from Tom."

His eyes lit. "I know just the person who can make that happen."

"It'll be good to quit thinking about Tess's death and Nick. I almost felt sorry for him, but he brought it on himself. Paula suffered from Nick's abuse, and she ran and protected her daughter from his evil ways."

Jake sent a text message then looked at me. "My SUV's on the square. Let's get it and go for a ride. Why don't we take Cowboy to the vet clinic? They have a person who does dog grooming there."

"Are you sure you want my dirty dog to ride in your nice vehicle?"

"It's all good." He looked at his phone. "Hey, we can see the farm in an hour."

"I believe that gives us enough time."

It didn't take the full hour to drop off Cowboy and drive to the farm that would potentially be our future home.

The sight of a red Mercedes stole my breath away. "Oh, no. Did you contact Tom?"

"No way, but that's his car. We'll come back another day." He shifted into Reverse.

"Wait, Jake. He's holding a gun on someone."

Jake stopped the Sequoia. "Call Matt and the FBI. I'll see if I can diffuse the situation."

I grabbed his hand. "No, don't go."

"Have a little faith." He kissed the back of my hand.

"Please stay. Give me two minutes to call the authorities."

Jake gave a curt nod. "Go ahead."

I started by calling Matt and tapped speaker mode, so Tom wouldn't see me talking.

"Emma, I'm kinda busy.

"Matt, we're at Gary Conway's farm. Tom Ward is here, and he's holding a gun to a man's head. It's not Mr. Conway." I leaned forward to get a better look. "Oh, my goodness. It's the man that went on a date with Tess. Bruce Hudson. I think he's an FBI agent."

"Get out of there!" Matt's voice roared over the phone.

"Too late. He's already seen us."

"We're on the way. Try to stall him." The call ended.

"Matt said to stall Tom."

"I heard, but it's going to be a little hard with him advancing on us."

Sure enough, Tom continued to walk our way, holding a gun to Bruce

Hudson's head. "He must be desperate."

Jake opened his door. "Stay back. At least stay behind me if there's no other option."

How could this be happening? Jake and I had come to this farm thinking about our future. We never intended to face off with another gunman.

Chapter Sixty-Seven

T om Ward pointed the gun at us. "Don't try anything stupid. Put your keys on the hood, and move over there."

Blood soaked through Bruce Hudson's shirt, and the man was pale. His eyes opened and closed in slow motion.

Jake placed the fob on the hood of his SUV. "Sure, man. No need for anyone else to get hurt."

I stepped closer to Jake.

Shadows crossed the barn's entrance.

Somebody else was on the property. If I could keep Tom's focus on us, maybe the other person could rescue us without more bloodshed.

"Hey, Tom. Let me help your friend there. He's only going to drag you down." I made a move to approach him.

"Stay back."

Jake said, "Take me instead."

I grabbed Jake's arm. "No. You have a head injury. Take me, Tom."

Tom's back was to the barn, and the big Dutch door was being pushed open.

"A federal agent is worth more than the two of you." He dragged Bruce with him.

Jake said, "Are you responsible for Mason's death?"

"Yep. He grew a conscience. I couldn't risk him turning on me until after I left the States for a non-extradition country. Bruce here knew what I'd done. Just another reason to take him with me. He's got the proof."

"Why does the FBI care if you buy land from people at unfair prices?" I kept my gaze on the man with the gun.

"Unfortunately, some of the heirs live in other states. We mailed paperwork, and the victims returned it by mail. Big mistake. The Post Office and the FBI got involved at that point."

My pulse pounded in my neck. "Money's all you care about. I can't believe you killed Mason."

Jake said, "What about his sick wife?"

"I'm not heartless. I didn't fire him for going to Houston when she was put in the hospital." Tom opened the passenger door and shoved the agent onto the seat.

Bruce slumped over the console and groaned.

"You've ruined a lot of lives, my friend." Jake grimaced.

"Not my fault." Tom held out his hand. "Give me your phones."

We handed them over. Twice in one day, I'd lost control of my cell phone. Twice a man pointed a gun at me.

A car engine sounded.

To distract the gunman, I said, "Tom, look at my recent calls. You can see that I contacted the police."

He glanced at it. "I don't see nine-one-one."

"I'm friends with the police chief. Matt Young." I pointed to the name.

He slammed the door and ran around the front of the Sequoia.

A big old pickup truck roared out of the barn and aimed straight for us.

A woman drove it and skidded to a stop near us. "Get in before he shoots us all."

We dove into the truck's bed, and she accelerated away. The speed knocked us to our backs.

Tom fired his gun.

"Stay down." Jake shielded me with his body.

"Jake, either the ghost of Tess Carranza is rescuing us, or she's alive."

"I noticed. Let's make sure we stay alive so we can question her."

More shots were fired. One pinged the back window of the truck.

Jake held me close with his arms covering my head.

Sirens wailed.

The truck bounced along the bumpy ground, slowed, and turned, fishtailing.

We slid across the bed, bumping into the side.

Police cars zoomed past us.

Tess straightened and drove smoothly for the first time. We were on the highway.

Jake said, "It sounds like the police are headed to the farm."

"Yes. I think we're going to be safe." My heart rate began returning to normal, but I kept my arms locked around Jake.

The truck slowed, took a few turns, and eventually parked.

Jake said, "I think it's safe to sit up."

I pushed myself to a sitting position. "We're home."

"Yep. You know, both times we visited the farm, it's been dangerous. If you don't mind, maybe we should live here. It does feel like home."

"Hello, am I interrupting?" Tess's voice held a note of amusement.

"Tess!" I squealed, and tears flooded my eyes. "You really are alive."

Jake opened the tailgate and hopped out. He reached for my hand and helped me land gracefully.

Tess walked around and hugged both of us. "Boy, do I have a story to tell you."

"I can't believe you're alive." I blinked back tears.

Jake said, "First, is it safe for us to stand on the street?"

"Who knows anymore?" Tess shrugged, and despite the danger, she seemed more carefree than I'd ever seen her.

"I suggest we go inside." Jake walked behind us, keeping watch.

Once we were inside, I said, "Tom stole our phones. Do you have one?"

"Mine was confiscated by the Federal Bureau of Investigation. Can you believe I'm saying that?" She looked around. "I need to use your bathroom, and I'm thirsty."

"You know where the bathroom is. I'll meet you in the kitchen."

Jake said, "Emma, I'll fix drinks if you want to call from the work phone."

"Thanks." I entered the office and called Matt. When he didn't answer, I left a detailed message.

279

I sat on the chair for a minute. Emotions flooded through me. Tess was alive. And not as important, but it still mattered, Jake wanted to live here. Tears filled my eyes and flowed down my face.

"Sunshine, what's going on with you?" Jake put two glasses on the desk and handed a tissue to me.

"Despite the wild rollercoaster ride we've been on, life is good."

"Amen to that."

Tess joined us in the office, carrying a glass of iced tea. "Is this for me?"

"Yes. Do you need food?" Jake grinned. "I can offer you a peanut butter sandwich."

"No, my stomach is on the queasy side, but I've got to tell somebody what happened, or I might just explode." She sat on the pink chair. Her stern demeanor was gone, and there was a sparkle in her eyes.

I moved to the loveseat and sat next to Jake.

Tess took a drink of tea. "Did you keep notes on my, um, attempted murder?"

"Sure did. I ruled out a few people and landed on Nick. I discovered you're right about his first wife. He poisoned Rhonda."

"I knew it all along." She sighed. "It took way too long to prove it."

"I know. You and Nick fought about the child Paula hid from him."

"Right. I was such a fool to spill the secret. He has always been able to trigger my temper. I got mad at him again. Laurel gave him a key to the library, and he let himself a couple weeks ago, expecting the place to be empty. I was upset that he could come and go as he pleased. That's the day the secret slipped out. Last Tuesday, he snuck in and demanded I tell him more about his child. We fought, and he lost his mind. I tried to fend him off, but he knocked me out with one of the planters."

I could picture everything she said. "Why did the police let all of us believe you were dead?"

"That's another story. Emma, do you remember my suspicions about Mason Brown?"

"Yes. He said you wanted to date him. I must admit, that threw me."

She finished her tea and set the glass on a coaster on the nearest table.

"One of my goals this year was to date somebody. He was handsome, but it turns out there's a wife. Mason suggested I try a dating website, and I decided it couldn't hurt."

"That's how you met Bruce Hudson?"

"I'm impressed, and yes. I was looking for romance, and the FBI wanted a way to bring down Mason Brown and Tom Ward. They were buying valuable property for pennies and making huge profits. They crossed state lines with their schemes. Bruce was focused on the heirs' property crimes and anti-competitive practices. Other crimes were committed. I just don't know what."

Jake said, "How did you fit in?"

Tess wore jeans and a T-shirt, and her hair was messy. She looked nothing like her normal self, plus she was assisting the FBI in bringing down a criminal. "I was feeding them information about Mason's actions at the library. They asked me to listen to conversations, and once I wore a wire. Mason studied atlases and books on local history. I also think he liked the library because I kept it quiet, and we have good WiFi."

Jake leaned forward. "So was it a coincidence that you met Bruce on the dating site, and he just happened to be an agent?"

"No. When the FBI learned I signed up for dating, they had a couple of agents reach out to me through the site. They decided it'd be a good way to use me to help their investigation. I happened to pick Bruce. What could look more innocent than dating someone you met online?"

"When did you find out he works for the government?"

"He told me on the first date."

"But in your diary, you said he was a book editor."

Tess blushed. "I was trying to get into character."

"Were you scared?" I was impressed with my friend.

"Early this year, I decided to try new adventures. What's more adventurous than helping the FBI bring down a criminal?"

"Good point." I chuckled. "What else did you do?"

"I continued trying to gather information until Nick attacked me. Bruce was in the parking lot last Tuesday. He asked the police to get me, or my body, out as fast as possible. If there were any last words spoken by me, Bruce hoped it'd be connected to the crime."

I gasped. "Even the EMTs were in on it?"

"Yeah. I'm surprised the ruse survived the rumor mill. I left the library unconscious in an ambulance. I came around, dazed and confused because of a concussion, but they didn't release me. I was in a hospital surrounded by guards. They kept my recovery a secret while they questioned me on the housing thing."

"I still don't understand why they pretended you died." I crossed my legs.

"Mason was getting suspicious about me. He caught me snooping a couple of times, and I'd asked him questions. I was getting on his nerves."

"Do you know he's been murdered? Or at least I think so, but after this situation with you, I could be wrong." I placed a hand on my chest as if I could calm my heart.

Tess nodded. "He really is dead. It's too bad, because he was about to become a witness for the government against Tom Ward."

Jake said, "That's what Tom meant when he said something about Mason growing a conscience."

The doorbell rang, and I stood. "It's weird not to have Cowboy here barking when somebody comes to the door. I'll be back."

When I opened the door, Matt stood there holding two phones. "I believe these belong to you and Jake."

"Yes. Come in. Do you know Tess is alive?" I gripped our cell phones in my hands.

"I do." He followed me through the house. "Why do you think I wasn't trying too hard to solve Tess's so-called murder?"

"Hmm, I'm not sure."

He chuckled. "Relax. I really don't want to know what you were thinking."

We joined Jake and Tess in my office.

Tess leapt to her feet. "Is Bruce okay?"

"He's in surgery, but he's expected to recover."

She sank into the comfortable seat. "Good."

Matt chose to sit in the chair behind the desk. "The Feds have arrested

Tom Ward, so he's in their custody. Tess, how are you holding up, and why were you at the Conway farm?"

"I'm tired, and I want to sleep in my own bed tonight, but I'm fine." She yawned. "Agent Hudson was driving me to town for another round of questions. They are exhausting, but necessary, I guess. There was new evidence, and they wanted to mention names and see if anybody sounded familiar. Bruce was driving the truck that's now sitting in Emma's driveway. He thought it'd be less conspicuous than one of their usual SUVs."

Matt took notes. "Keep going."

"We heard about a hostage situation in town, so we turned around. I had seen a sign at the Conway farm. I talked Bruce into going there. It was raining, and he pulled the truck into the barn."

I said, "How did Tom find you?"

Tess closed her eyes for a moment and rolled her head back. "It's my fault. I encouraged Bruce to contact the real estate agent. I didn't want to risk Mr. Conway coming into the barn with a shotgun and shooting us. So, Bruce did. From what Tom told us, he was in the office when the agent took Bruce's call. Tom drove out and surprised us by shooting Bruce."

"I'm sorry for all you've been through, Tess." Matt folded up his notebook. "Would you like a policewoman to stay at your house with you tonight?"

"I'll ask Paula to let me stay with her."

I shook my head. "She disappeared."

Matt said, "More like she's gone into hiding."

Tess's gaze bounced from me to Matt. "On second thought, I'd like to have an officer stay at the house tonight."

"I'll make that happen. If you'll excuse me for a few minutes." He left the room, and the three of us looked at each other.

Tess said, "I don't know if Paula will ever return. Even if Nick goes to prison for the rest of his life, I believe she'll stay hidden."

Jake stood and paced. "Why live here all these years then?"

"She believed if she was in plain sight, her child would be safe. There was nothing for Nick to be suspicious about."

"Why not come back now?" Jake pinched his lip.

"If Nick somehow escapes from prison or the jury doesn't convict him, the first person he'll go after is Paula."

Jake inhaled deeply. "Makes sense."

The police chief reappeared.

I said, "Matt, I know Tom has been arrested. I guess he'll go to prison for Mason's murder and assaulting an FBI agent, but what about his victims? Can anything be done for them?"

Matt shrugged. "Emma, there's no telling how many victims suffered from Tom and Mason's crimes. It's much bigger than our little town, but I'm sure the government will do their best to find the victims and begin to make them whole."

"I hope they freeze his assets before he can hide his money." I sighed.

Matt laughed. "It sounds like you've done some research."

My face warmed.

Matt looked around the room. "We need to focus on tonight. A federal agent will come for Bruce's truck. Tess, I'll drive you to your house to meet the officer. Jake, your vehicle will be inspected for clues and returned to you as soon as possible. Emma, it's about to rain again. Is your truck at the library?"

I shivered and didn't want to return there today. "Yes."

Jake rubbed my shoulder. "What if they drop me at the library, and I'll come back here with your truck?"

I looked at my watch. "Would you also mind picking up Abby and Cowboy? It's almost time for her to get off work."

"You got it, Sunshine."

Matt clapped his hands. "Let's go, people. Emma, thanks for your help on this case."

"You're welcome." I walked them to the door and locked it when they left. A hot bath would be nice, but I was too wired.

All along, I'd told myself solving Tess's so-called murder was my priority. Was this the time to look for other victims? Ms. Maebell had been saved from the evil ways of Tom and Mason. But how many others were like Ms. Linda Jefferson? And could a flower farmer in Lutz, Texas, do anything to help? There was only one way to know, and that was to try.

Chapter Sixty-Eight

Jake and Abby helped me work my booth at the Lutz Farmers Market on Saturday morning. We'd predicted lots of people would stop by with questions about the fake murder and the real murder. Most of my time was spent explaining what I knew. At least I shared what law enforcement allowed.

I'd even handed out flyers. They said I was looking for victims of Mason and Tom's heirs-property scheme. Abby had helped me create a website as an easy way for people to contact me.

As the hoard of visitors became a trickle, Jake and I got lunch in the food court area. We sat next to each other at a square picnic table.

I said, "I'm going to take flowers to Agent Hudson when we shut down. Bruce is staying at the bed-and-breakfast until they wrap up the case. Tess is on paid leave for the rest of the month, and I think she's watching over Bruce. He's single, and they may start dating for real."

"That's a lot to unpack. Let's start with Tess. Why does she get so much time off? Is she injured?"

"Technically, she had a head injury and was in a coma. Plus, it happened in the library. I think they want to make sure Tess is okay before returning to work."

"Makes sense. Laurel got fired over giving the key to Nick and lying about it. Celia talked about applying for the assistant library director, but she's happy working for Paige." He shrugged. "I don't know what she'll do."

"I hope Paige can afford to keep Celia on the payroll."

Jake finished his iced coffee. "Paige told me she's making more money since Celia came on board. My sister has some innovative ways of attracting customers. She's scheduling reading events and author signings."

"Good for Celia."

"Have you heard from Paula?" Jake crunched an ice cube.

"No. I guess Tess was right when she said Paula wouldn't risk returning to Lutz. I don't know what will happen to her belongings, but she was well prepared when she left town. I bet there's a plan in motion for selling her house and other stuff."

Jake chuckled. "She would've made a good spy."

"No doubt." I took a sip of my green tea. "I'd like to spend time focusing on us. Are you certain you want to live at my place? We can look at other properties."

"Your place is perfect. The location works for you to deliver flowers to your best customers. It's near the farmers' market, and there's room to expand. I looked through your sketchbook at the possibilities of how to grow more flowers. Together, we can easily do it."

"And you think the house is big enough for us, Cowboy, and Abby?" I watched his expression closely in case he said what he thought I wanted to hear.

"I do. You know what? Down the road, if we feel cramped, we can expand or move then." There was no deceit in his eyes.

"You're right. I just want you to be honest with me."

"Always." He took my hand in his. "Are you ready to set a wedding date? Do you want a big wedding, a small one, or do you want to elope?"

"I don't think it's possible to elope. There'll be a lot of hurt feelings if we don't invite most of the town." I held my breath, hoping he wouldn't reject my suggestion.

A slow smile covered his face, and he winked. "It took us a long time to find each other. We should invite our family and friends. Let's celebrate our marriage."

My heart raced with happiness. I leaned over and threw my arms around Jake. "I love you, and I'm glad we're going to have a big celebration."

"Me, too." He kissed me, and butterflies fluttered in my belly.

It was time to plan our wedding. Our town had survived more than its share of murders this year. With a little luck it'd be calm for the next few months, because I wanted to focus on Jake and our nuptials. No more murder investigations for us. Although, if somebody contacted me about knowing a victim, or being a victim, of Tom's, I'd take time to listen.

About the Author

Jackie Layton is the author of cozy mysteries with Spunky Southern Sleuths. Her stories are set in Texas, Georgia, and South Carolina. She lives on the coast of South Carolina, where she enjoys walks on the beach and golf cart rides around the marsh. Reading, gardening, and traveling are some of her favorite hobbies. Jackie always keeps a notebook handy to write down ideas for future stories. Many of her ideas come from people watching and watching *Dateline* and *American Greed*.

AUTHOR WEBSITE:
   https://jackielaytoncozyauthor.com/

SOCIAL MEDIA HANDLES:
   https://www.facebook.com/JackieLaytonAuthor
   https://www.pinterest.com/jackielaytonauthor/
   https://twitter.com/joyfuljel
   https://www.instagram.com/jackielaytonauthor.com

Jackie Layton (@jackielaytonauthor) on Threads
Goodreads: https://bit.ly/49XTfpf
Bookbub: https://bit.ly/37RqGQ8

Also by Jackie Layton

A Low Country Dog Walker Mystery Series:
Bite the Dust
Dog-Gone Dead
Bag of Bones
Caught and Collared
A Killer Unleashed
A Suspicious Breed

A Texas Flower Farmer Cozy Mystery Series:
Weeding Out Lies
Clover Covered Corpse

An Organized Crime Cozy Mystery Series:
Clutter Free
The Con